IN THE HEART
OF THE
WHOLE WORLD

IN THE HEART

OF THE

WHOLE WORLD

JOHN ROLFE GARDINER

ALFRED A. KNOPF NEW YORK 1988

THIS IS A BORZOI BOOK
PUBLISHED BY ALFRED A. KNOPF, INC.

Copyright © 1988 by John Rolfe Gardiner

*All rights reserved under International and Pan-American
Copyright Conventions. Published in the United States by Alfred
A. Knopf, Inc., New York, and simultaneously in Canada by
Random House of Canada Limited, Toronto. Distributed by
Random House, Inc., New York.*

*Grateful acknowledgment is made to Hudson Bay Music Inc.
for permission to reprint an excerpt from the lyrics "Family
Reunion" by H. Gabbard and A. Holt. Used by permission
of Hudson Bay Music Inc. on behalf of Fort Knox Music
Inc./Trio Music Co., Inc.*

Library of Congress Cataloging-in-Publication Data
Gardiner, John Rolfe.
In the heart of the whole world.

I. Title.
PS3557.A711315   1988   813'.54   88-45217
ISBN 0-394-56901-6

Manufactured in the United States of America
FIRST EDITION

TO NICOLA

in mind of her smile and laughter

I

CHALKMAN

Wash me in the water
Where you wash your dirty daughter
And I shall be whiter
Than the whitewash on the wall.

—SONG OF 1914

In June of my twenty-eighth year, in a heat ennobled by devotion, I hurdled the lowered bars of conscience, and landed in the arms of my student Sarah Rengert, and Sarah, who had admired me for months from the distance of her desk, responded with the soft energies of accomplished love. In that season surrounding her high school graduation we hid ourselves in woods and under blankets by the river. Rebounding between stealth and abandon we strung ourselves along a hazy cycle of spasms and fluids, and watched, amazed, as love lubricated our deception of parents, friends, colleagues, and at last, ourselves.

It was the stealth, continuing into the summer, that gave a little lie to our protests of eternal love. Secrecy, which seemed so important to both of us, was a sin against trust. When she conceived my child, no one else in our quiet town on the Potomac had the least hint of our intrigue. Maneuvering under cover of night and trees we had never discussed the possibility of a sunlit, arm-in-arm stroll down main street. When we finally drew back from the sensual surface to consider our future we had already started a family.

It was 1956, the year the seniors dedicated their yearbook to me, Ray Sykes, out of fifty eligible men and women. *"For guidance and compassion, and for caring who we were,"* it said over my photograph. The picture itself was extraordinarily flattering. My straw-blond hair caught the wind and sun. The sharpest edges of my nose and chin were softened to a portrait of gentle authority. And under the photograph were lines chosen by one of Sarah's classmates from *Bartlett's Familiar Quotations.* "A teacher affects eternity; he can never tell where his influence stops."

No one staring at that dedication page could have believed I had gone to purchase prophylactics in the drugstore of a neighboring town for use with a student whose senior portrait lay twenty pages beneath me in the same volume. For all the good they did us, every one of them could as well have been a rubber sieve. In August a doctor confirmed she was pregnant.

Sarah would have the child; there was never a question of that in her mind. But she was refusing to marry me. We were full of the prattle of immature romance: we couldn't stand in the way of each other's freedom and all that. She wouldn't think of letting me lose my job. She couldn't bear to see me shunned in a community that was certain to accuse me of abusing my trust among its young.

Beneath the altruism I began to see her real estimation of me. She had placed me a generation ahead of her. Though I was little more than ten years her senior, I was beyond the distance she cared to reach for a husband. While our hidden trysts were sweet mysteries, I could see it would be awkward for her to parade with me before her friends. And to present me in her parents' living room would mortify her. Eventually I'd have to admit to myself that she was a child and the corollary truth: I was a cradle thief.

My arguments with her may have been too academic. Weren't we children of the same century and planet, I asked. In the time frame of astronomers and archaeologists didn't we stand on the point of the same pin? I knew these questions were flawed, even devious, and still I believed her experience would catch up with mine soon enough.

But Sarah was letting me down gently. If she was going to be wed it would be to her old boyfriend, the one her own age, Richard Pless, the one she'd been going with until I'd stepped in his way. She could whistle him back, and she did. Richard was a perfectly nice young man, slow but earnest in his classwork. No spots on his record; no stars either.

"He thinks he's the father," Sarah told me.

Of course I hadn't been the first. She wasn't quite eighteen, but I should have known from her ease with me that she'd been guilty of lovely teenage crimes. Hadn't I watched her trailing her toes in the water from the back of our rowboat as we drifted in the river; so relaxed as she removed her blouse to take the sun. And later in the underbrush on the shore didn't she take my hand and lick clean the fingers that had pleasured her before we moved into the rhythm of the last union she allowed—a gesture full of premeditated grace.

In the early days we had found meaning for ourselves everywhere. Driving home from an evening in the city—an evening stolen from her parents—we took for our beacon and our warning the red light blinking on the mountain over the government's nuclear bunker. And when we camped for hot love on the same mountain we found solace afterward in the red signal we could see sixty miles to the east, flashing in the tower of the cathedral.

But that September of 1956 Sarah and Richard were enrolled together in the community college, and living in a little apartment over the hardware store, and I was back in my English classroom, pacing as I taught, breaking chalk in my fingers and crumbling it to dust. I was waiting for the ill-considered marriage to fall apart, when I'd step forward and become the father of my child.

I knew Sarah was far brighter than Richard. She hadn't volunteered diligence, only surrendered it on cross-examination or the privacy of her test papers. Never mind that she was for the moment immature in love, reducing romance to selfless, logical choice. She could diagram a dissected frog or complex sentence with equal ease. I believed she'd race ahead to scholarships and higher honors; any world of ideas could have been hers.

But there was Richard trotting along behind, panting to catch up. I never embarrassed him in my classroom though he humbled himself from time to time, stumbling over his oral work. His enthusiasm led him into blind alleys. While he and Sarah both displayed an endearing humility, he came to his without guile.

THE FLAME THAT MELTS THE BUTTER FRIES THE EGG, I had written on the blackboard one morning, asking for a generality that would embrace the statement. I didn't call on Richard; he raised his hand and plunged ahead: "Well, the butter and eggs are in the same pan, I guess, and you can cook them together and then you've got really one thing when you started with two. Or it's just that for breakfast you can get the whole meal into one frying pan . . ." I glanced at Sarah. Her head was down. She was hiding her dismay as Richard went on: "And then there's not so much washing up to do. So maybe a general rule would be you use less water in the morning or something like that. Or wait a minute . . ."

"Sarah," I called, thinking she'd be grateful for the chance to rescue her wandering friend. She feigned confusion, and asked me to repeat the question, then answered softly, "The flame makes the butter get soft and the egg get hard. You could say the same energy can have opposite effects on different substances."

Easy? Then why the vacancy in the eyes of her thirty classmates as they struggled with the same problem and listened with admiration as she translated aphorism into law? Such extrapolation was nothing to her: she simply wanted to please me without damaging Richard, and I stood there as admiring as the children around her.

My own deduction that Richard would eventually fall out of favor with her, from this classroom example and others like it, led me falsely from the start. And I began the next fall to offer my presence in the community as a constant promise to my dislocated family.

Of course I'd been sworn to secrecy by Sarah. "Forever," she said with her child's faith in absolutes. And I promised. It was a negative wedding vow, sealed with a gentle kiss and a long, unblinking correspondence of eyes.

That fall it was almost impossible to contact Sarah. She and Richard were always together, rushing from their two-room walk-up over the store to make their first class at the community college, driving off in Richard's old car, and returning together in the evening to study. I could watch their door from the café across the street where I sometimes had breakfast before strolling across playing fields to the high school.

They never ate out, probably didn't have the money, living as they must have been off their parents' limited resources. I knew she was aware from time to time of my gaze on her, but she gave no return signal, no encouragement. She was protecting her marriage with constant attendance, holding hands on the way to the grocery store, or singing too loud, shameless as they carried their soiled sheets into the laundromat. They looked very much in love. Even this bitter evidence I tried to turn on its head. The other side of constant attendance was assured friction and return of the rightful husband and father.

I spied on the progress of her pregnancy. Looser clothes came in the fifth month, and a duck's waddling gait in the eighth.

Once I saw them stop suddenly on the sidewalk and watched her take Richard's hand to her belly. Whatever he felt was making him smile. I had visions of him disturbing the quiet rest of the fetus, poking at my child in the night.

That September my principal, John Lambert, paid unusual attention to me. Lambert was a tall man, his face ruddy and pitted with acne scars. He looked at you with an up-from-under stare, as if peering over glasses. His look suggested doubt—doubt in you. That was the tricky aspect of a meeting with him.

Lambert was uncommonly good at discipline, always knew when a child was trying to deceive him, but never made accusations unless the evidence was clear. The children trusted him, and he walked among them in the halls without academic pretension, putting himself on their level with jokes about report cards, and sympathy for their problems.

One morning he called me into his office to praise me for my rapport with the students, and for the fine scores my classes made on their achievement tests the previous year. He wanted to take further advantage of my talents, he said, by assigning me to the new Stilson County History course. It would replace the History of Virginia, taught statewide for decades from a text that had gained national notoriety with its chapter on the contentment of slaves before abolition.

"This could be really exciting," Lambert said. I was to be the school's representative on the committee developing standard materials for the course. "You'll be the first one to teach it here." The idea was that by giving students a fix on the history of their own county they'd be studying state history in microcosm, but with a new enthusiasm. Tricky political questions could be handled county by county.

"By the way, what are *your* politics?" Lambert asked. "I'd be interested. Just as a friend. Of course, you don't have to answer."

"I'm not sure I have any," I said.

He smiled, then I did, before we broke into uneasy laughter. "That's all right," he said, quickly sober. "If we don't have any, they can't get us in trouble, can they?"

The prospect of extra work didn't bother me. I imagined my influence in the school growing. Students liked my English class. I was pleased to think it woke them up for forty-five minutes. I was sure I'd be able to make them listen to my brand of local history. Stilson County was my home. I knew who had owned the bulldozers and what part of the past they had buried.

"I'm getting married and getting out of here," my brother Paul had told me when he was fifteen.

"Before supper?" I asked, astonished.

This was back in 1942, a year when we walked out in the woods hunting stray Japanese and Germans. We hid in hedgerows and threw rocks at buzzards, or drove tractors for shorthanded farmers making hay. And played baseball into the summer evenings on the field across the road from our house.

It was before the earth movers had come to make the eastern half of Stilson County into Washington, D.C.'s bedroom, though Paul was all ready to elope and live there. "Somewhere closer in," a phrase his Margaret must have taught him. Margaret Payne, two years older than Paul, was promoting this impossible wedding. A tenant's daughter on a nearby farm, she was full-bodied, alluring, and a thief.

I watched her steal lipstick and gum from the drugstore and try to take an alarm clock from our own house. "I saw that," I told her. "What did you see?" she asked, taking the clock from her handbag and replacing it on our kitchen shelf. My telling Paul didn't help. He said to get lost for a while, and left the house with her.

"You're not bad looking," she said over her shoulder to me. "How old are *you?*"

Things weren't happening to me on schedule, the things a thirteen-year-old counts on, the timely appearance of pubic hair, some definition in the biceps. Paul had had working equipment at twelve, which he proved to me, sitting on the dirt floor of an abandoned garage, without emotion or apparent pleasure, only because I had doubted his word.

In high school I began to catch up, but locker-room finger-pointing and classmates who followed me all the way to the university kept me off balance. My brother's early betrayal still disturbs the peace I've made with his passing.

"Grasshoppers?" he asked one summer afternoon, setting off for another rendezvous with Margaret.

"What do you care what I fish with?" He'd lost his right to the streams and woods I patrolled. Without him I rode hay rakes in the rolling fields, making perfect windrows for farmers who charmed me with compliments. "A little boy like him?" With my small earnings I bought ammunition for the .22 rifle my father had given me and shot at bottles and cans set up in lines that marched as German infantry. Paul grew stupid with love while I killed the enemy alone. The shocking deaths came later.

My father, regional manager for a now-defunct grocery chain, and mother, who was working then as a volunteer instructor at a canning plant, made a comfortable home for us. We lived in an angular Victorian house with a cone-roofed turret at one corner and intricate gingerbread under the eaves of its wraparound porch, the kind of place that needed the company of similar structures in a row to give it any architectural sense.

But the house, which we owned without lien, stood by itself on a little rise—a lost building, a mile from the village of Clayton. As a child I didn't like hearing my mother call it hideous, and as I grew I saw this for the apology it was. Her affection for the place lay in its very eccentricity. When I was young I thought it was the shape of a normal American home, and when it was torn down prematurely I went back over and over again to mourn the rubble.

At seventeen I should have been too old to hold it against my father and mother that they picked the same year to die, he with a heart attack and she during a gall bladder operation. But after my father was gone I actually thought mother had conspired with his spirit to make herself sick. And her death seemed a willed act.

What about Paul and me? We didn't matter. If she couldn't have her husband, she'd order something to go wrong inside her. Something bad enough for a doctor to have to cut and make repairs. And if the doctor foiled her, if he got the job done right, there was one more she could give the evil eye to, the one who'd give her the gas. Thus dared to miscalculate, the anesthetist had done just that.

Too wild, this theory? No, in that state of mind I could have spiraled down through any layer of reality to reach a place where blame would stick to her. These notions were mine alone. Paul wasn't given to analysis and torment. After the shock of the second death had worn off him, he showed little concern for our parents' passing. Almost coldhearted, it seemed to me, in his hurry to leave memories behind, to sell all connection with his childhood.

Paul and I had been left to shift for ourselves. After the funerals we didn't settle well together. I was in my last year of high school, and too fond of my teachers, Paul thought. He was a hod carrier for a construction company and already sick of it.

Our inheritance was the house and five acres. Right away Paul was eager to sell. I argued against it, but he was already fighting with the executor, insistently reading his favorite line of the will: "to be distributed equally between my sons Paul and Ray as their needs shall be deemed to require it."

"And they require it right now!" he shouted into the phone.

He couldn't get all his money at once, but he could force the sale of the house. We had money to continue our lives but our old piece of Stilson County was gone forever, and I held Paul responsible.

Paul got out in a hurry, all the way to Oregon. He'd heard stories that made a romance out of huge trees falling close to tough men. "You come, too," he said. I was a scholar by then, on my way to the university. He wrote as soon as he settled in the West. "Come out to the real world." As far as I could tell he was making a success of it, going from lumberjack to heavy-equipment operator in his first few months.

The university was a breeze for me. I jumped all over the curriculum, from English and history to biology and chemistry. It was my game to make professors congratulate me before I disappeared from their departments. In my senior year I was writing editorials for the paper and had one of the coveted rooms on the Lawn.

Paul's correspondence drew on our fading childhood. "Remember the clock you thought Margaret Payne was stealing? We were going to use it in case we fell asleep in the woods. God, those times were crazy! Get on your horse. Things are lying on the ground out here waiting for you."

With each letter his life seemed less admirable. "I'll teach you to drive the Cat," he said. "There's nothing like it." He told me he'd mashed his hand in one of his big yellow machines, badly enough that he would always have to hold his pencil between his thumb and fourth finger.

After graduation I took a few more courses that qualified me to teach in the public schools. Paul couldn't believe it. "You can't make the earth shake in a school room," he said. By then the rumbling machines he loved had come to eastern Stilson, smashing across the apple and peach orchards where we'd taken fruit, and clearing the forest where I'd hunted Germans and squirrels. They knocked over our old house, and for a time it sat with its insides exposed to the world, picked over by strangers for door-knobs and plumbing fixtures before it was buried behind the hill.

When the machines were finished there was no more hill. The close geography of my childhood was three hundred level acres, land prepared for a new age. And the nearby farms had been planted with seeds that sprouted houses neatly spaced as corn. I couldn't resettle around Clayton. To teach I retreated up the Potomac to the northwest, to the far end of Stilson County.

The news of Paul's death came before I'd taught my first semester. I had a phone call and then his company's telegram, which was very precise, a sort of legal document I think. It laid blame for the accident squarely on Paul. Instead of falling cleanly, a tree had split up the middle and jumped backward at him. I asked that he be cremated.

His ashes were sent to me in a sealed can. For ceremony I drove with the can back to our Clayton homestead and sowed Paul over the newly level plane. Perhaps some of the ashes fell where the house had been, some in our victory garden, some in the woods and hedgerows where he had lain with Margaret Payne. There was no telling, not a boulder or single tree for a landmark. I'd have to say I was lost.

And there was no one left to tell a soul: "He couldn't have done that, not little Ray. He'd be the last one in the world to get a girl pregnant."

In the spring of 1957 I was assigned to the cross-country team. "Take bigger steps faster," I told the boys on the first day of training, the only advice I had for them in this, my first coaching assignment. They laughed with me and took my incompetence with good nature as I sent them off each day for an hour of roadwork. During that hour I sat in the front of the village café with a Coke and a newspaper, watching Sarah's door.

My child had been born in March—Sonia, according to the

published birth announcement. A name I'd never have thought of. I drove thirty miles to a store in Winchester, where no questions would be asked, and bought a stroller, which I left as an anonymous gift in the middle of the night in their hall with a note: to Sonia from friends.

You'd have thought I was afraid Sarah would forget to take the infant into fresh air or be reluctant to show it in public. When she called I was elated but she was in a phone booth and very angry. "Look, Mr. Sykes," she said, "I don't want anything from you. Please keep away from us."

"What are you going to do with it?"

"The baby can't use a stroller yet," she said. "It needs a pram."

Another time I left two dozen diapers in a brown wrapper at their door. Sarah came secretly to my place with the baby to say she had tried to persuade Richard to leave Stilson but that he had no intention of quitting the community college. That's when I learned she had dropped out herself the month before. Richard was doing very well in his practical courses and he meant to make his career and his home where his family had always lived.

"You're the one who has to move," she said. "You could teach anywhere." She wasn't pleading but stating fact. "Eventually, you'll want to go. If you do it right away we'll both be happier." I thought it remarkable that an eighteen-year-old could speak with such cold clarity of duty beyond affection. Staring fondly at her did nothing to blunt her argument.

"It's my home, too," I reminded her.

"But your parents are dead," she said. "You don't have to stay here."

"My child's here," I yelled at her.

"It's not going to be yours," she said firmly.

"You'll have to go back to college."

"I'm reading a wonderful book. It's about a woman who

marries to live in a castle," as if that answered for a life's curriculum.

My child was crying, but Sarah didn't offer to let me hold her. She walked through my downstairs rooms with the baby on her hip, surveying my situation. My bungalow was comfortably furnished, extra cushions on the sofa, a generous bed, things I wanted her to notice. In the kitchen she stopped at the refrigerator and opened the door.

"You should get married."

"I eat out a lot."

She advised me to empty the whole thing, wash it with ammonia and leave the door open for a few days. "In fact, open all your windows." It was all practical chatter, rapid-fire, and she left my house with a chaste touch of my arm and a word about scouring powders and the brand her mother favored.

"She looks like you," I called after her. "Especially the mouth."

When Sarah finally outgrew Richard I'd be standing by in Stilson where I meant to wake up a sleepy high school and perhaps a whole school system. I had plans for River High in those days, along with my plans for Sarah.

With passing seasons the situation that was destined to change did not. Year by year I struggled to establish myself more firmly in the one place I had a foothold. You could say I was being brought back each fall by popular demand. A good many of my students found my classes entertaining, and their continuing achievement overrode the plans of those among the faculty who hoped to see me discredited.

I had become the author of the local-history textbook, *Stilson,* which brought me some notoriety and the jealousy of certain colleagues. The text began with King Charles II's grant and carried on through log cabins and tobacco to tract housing and the westward advance of the real estate market. Warts were on view for those who read closely, and it had been tricky steering the manuscript through committee reviews. Continuity was my thesis. Hadn't we been settled by investors, speculators, and their agents, in the first place? My detractors preferred to see them as "men of great energy and vision." I was proud to think the facts were there for a teacher with enough imagination to turn a student's head.

I wanted students who would stand on their desks and translate Manifest Destiny into their own lives. Who would shout at me that it meant the right to acquire a rectangle of land close to the hum of an interstate, a small lot to be planted 40 percent rye, 60 percent fescue, and trimmed to the length of its neighbor. Something a little angry, a little poetic.

In the summers I stayed right there in Stilson to be near Sarah and my daughter in case the call came for me. I drove back and forth across the county, keeping abreast of changes in the landscape, and was there beside the barren plain, the site of my old family home, when the stakes were driven marking the corners of the future Whole World Mall.

I watched my Sonia progress from infant to toddler to preschooler, and then on a clear, fall morning, in a time of fresh accommodation to my world as it was and might always be, I saw my daughter walking in the street beside her mother. Their backs were straight and their heads high. The child's hair was the same straw blond as my own and halfway down her back. She bent over to work on her own shoelace, and my eyes filled. I'd been absent for the first steps, the first haircut, the first loose bowknot accomplished by her small fingers.

I had to accept that Richard Pless was making his own way.

Sarah was very proud of him. After graduation from the community college he had worked for a year and a half as a carpenter in a local construction company, and then taken on small jobs independently. He had put money down on a good-sized lot in the back of town with large oak trees and a creek behind, and had already begun the foundation of a house of their own. I knew it would be several years before they could complete it. They hadn't the money or time to spend on a large project, but I imagined the day coming when Sarah and Sonia would be largely hidden from view, taken off main street and placed behind a veil of homemaking and scheduled trips to market, and the chaperoned activities of children. I hadn't really dwelt on the notion that Sonia might eventually be heading my way, toward the Stilson County school system, or that once she was in high school things would be different.

I *was* aware of the triangles I could still make of young love in my classroom; myself at the acute point asking sharp questions. I could snap a head to attention by naming it, and observe the wriggle of that student's friend across the room. It was a game of silences and glances, not played meanly but with a teacherly concern. They whispered about me. They found my slight lisp and unkempt hair youthful and affecting. If they wanted to please me with good work I was happy to consider my attractiveness a legitimate pedagogical tool.

Discipline had never been a problem for me. I knew how to roll with a little disruption without getting flustered. I was healthy and tough, and if there was a real challenge I wasn't afraid to meet it. In those days we used to be able to knock the students around a little, take boys by their elbows and shake them or grab their shoulders and get up in their faces.

I had seen dunces in the school who kept A averages simply by doing all the donkey work the teachers asked of them, while bright ones could fail by paying no attention at all. My classes had always been different. The students knew it was impossible to fail with me; also that it was very difficult to get highest marks, and those used to sliding along on the honor roll with no special effort may have resented me.

I never drilled my classes. Nor was I the kind of teacher who tried to amuse with pervasive sarcasm or superior wit. When I saw the energies, sexual and athletic, gathered daily under the flat roof of the sprawling school, I knew that only a fool would try to frustrate those forces. I recognized the improbable glories of their daydreams, a ball thrown from twenty feet passing with regularity through a circle of string, or intimacy with forbidden arms and legs, the daily scenery of their classrooms.

Of course the county was always there with immunization records and grades, guiding them toward careers and citizenship, while I stood by with a different message, watching them pass from Mendel's peas to Euclid's angles to Jefferson's catechism, on their way to recess or a bus. The community saw only the buses, the long yellow vans named with black numerals, that fetched their children in the morning and delivered them in the afternoon with great deference to their safety, red lights flashing, all traffic brought to standstill while tomorrow's mayor and grocer were given safe passage across gravel or macadam.

"Move away," Sarah whispered to me beside the fresh-produce counter one winter evening.

"It's been six years," I said. "We've been all through that. No one's moving."

"I mean from in front of the sweet potatoes," she said. "Rich loves them," and then she told me she was pregnant again. After a swallow and congratulations I retreated toward bread. I'd always considered Richard an interloper in my phantom family, but as I chose an unfamiliar brand of English muffin I thought how old and neurotic that notion had become. I wasn't sure I could ever be a fair parent to a child that wasn't my own.

"Those won't tear," Sarah said. "They're presliced. They taste doughy." She had followed me down the aisle and was guiding her cart between me and the shelves. Sonia was in the cart seat kicking the air. A little too old at six to be pushed around a supermarket, she seemed to me beautiful and alert.

"You're Sonia," I said, trying to sound bright and cheerful.

"My name is Sonia D. Pless," she corrected me. "The *D* is for Dimbrell."

"You should say how do you do," Sarah admonished her. Instead Sonia stared up at me and said, "Our dog Max will chase you if you run."

Looking at my daughter for the first time in months I saw a small white line on her nose, an extension of the natural cleft underneath, which curled up over the end in a little semicircle. It was like a very small scar, hardly noticeable, a tiny genetic accident.

"Rich thought this was a good time to have another," Sarah went on. "Sonia's old enough so we don't have to watch her all the time. She always said when she grew up she was going to be a sister. Of course Rich and I are hoping for a boy."

I stood there listening to more about Richard, his contract to frame five new houses in a development by the river, and his intention to dig a well on their own place that summer. Then more about how happy and settled they were, really making it on their own, even paying money back to their parents. They had moved into a house that would do until Rich built theirs. All of it wonderful news and quite depressing.

"How do you like first grade?" I asked Sonia.

"She's a little bit daydreamy in school," Sarah answered for her. "She has a couple of demons in her class who attack from behind."

"Do I know their names?" I asked.

"Lucas and Matthew," Sonia said suddenly. "They're boys. I kicked Matthew, and he got chicken pox. I had it before so I couldn't get it back."

"All right, honey," Sarah said. "That's enough."

"I didn't know she'd had chicken pox," I said.

"Why should you? She's had a lot of things you didn't know about."

"What else has she had?" I said, waiting to be shocked.

Mother and daughter were both looking at me strangely. "You're asking for six years of medical history?"

I didn't like it, but Sarah's idea that I would drift away from her life seemed plausible then, even to me. We should have known that could never happen, that I was going to be a hovering presence and a danger to Sonia however sheltered her mother kept her. I checked out at a register right beside them and we walked together to the parking lot, passing before the rude group of loiterers known in our town as "The Club."

"Move away," Sarah advised me. "Before you turn into one of them." I looked a second time at the loiterers, the ones who drank and gambled in the woods while they no doubt boasted of impossible romance, the stiffening of their members probably more a sensation of circulation than a danger to the women they watched from the ends of the supermarket aisles.

This early warning from Sarah of the impotent kind of figure I might become in the community set me off on a long period of questing which I still refuse to call promiscuous. In the six years of her marriage I had been miserably inactive. But with that fillip of Sarah's scorn I convinced myself that my heart was open to romantic opportunity.

I began to dress in softer clothes after school hours—velour pullovers, corduroy pants, buckskin shoes. I let my hair grow a little longer and washed it every day. I went looking, and with immediate success, with hardly a trace of my old shyness. Teaching had changed all that, made me a public speaker and private charmer. I was surprised at how manipulative I could be.

Over the next few months I slept with five women. The first was a cousin of Richard Pless. She put me off with a single remark about "Richard's spoiled daughter." Then there was that cousin's friend, a dentist's assistant who used a very potent perfume, and asked intrusive questions about my social calendar. After that, an old classmate of Sarah's recently separated from her husband, and a little too anxious. She asked why I only called on Wednesdays. I left her for one of Sarah's neighbors, a woman with beautiful hands who had an electric organ in her apartment which she played with great feeling, but which was going to be repossessed if someone didn't help her with the payments. The last was a lady who had just been hired by Richard to keep his books.

All of these women I took into my house with an honest heart, open to the chance that each might be the friend for life, and each time I accompanied them back to their own doors with the despair of failed communion and spent seed. It hadn't occurred to me that the purpose of all this neurotic affection might be to come circling back to Sarah.

In the end, strain and infection forced me to a full accounting in a urologist's office. "Well," the bemused doctor said, "you can count them all on the fingers of one hand."

I'd been sleeping all around the Pless heads, and it was Sarah herself who put a stop to the drifting. At our next passing on the sidewalk she told me she'd been hearing not very nice things about me. Some of her friends would prefer that I didn't call anymore. I asked what she could possibly mean, and walked away in despair.

After that I set out to recover my reputation with a return to the solitary ways I'd been known for. At school I was fighting my own complacency, troubled by phrases that had begun to slip from my tongue too easily, as my work became more of a cycle and a litany.

In 1958, the year my Stilson history was published, they began work on the Virginia portion of the circumferential highway around Washington. It severed our county, which was then cut again by the six lanes that ran to the new airport.

The land Paul and I had let go was suddenly famous and unbelievably expensive. The scalped plain where our house had been sat at the junction of the two new roads—Ripton Corner—where they were building the massive shopping complex, the Whole World Mall. The developers called it a neo-Gothic crystal palace. I cursed the place, ashamed of my passive part in its birth, but watched in awe over the next year as four stories of steel and glass went up on thirty acres, and asphalt rolled out over the land around it.

With nothing left there of what I'd known, it was impossible to tell whether the site of our house was somewhere under the new crystal roof or outside in the massive parking area. When it was finished I ignored the ribbon cuttings, the grand openings of the hundreds of stores and restaurants, sulking at the other end of the county in my classroom, telling snickering students to beware. "When your land is utterly changed, you have no past."

When I finally went to see the place out of curiosity it swallowed me up. I was actually lost in it, unable to find my way back through the series of corridors to the doors I'd entered. I moved through long, tiled halls, disoriented and unnerved, then took an escalator to a second level, blinking in the brightness of glass and chrome. The actual vistas, endless rows of shops, and false vistas made of mirrored walls doubled my confusion.

There were others like me, looking around for their bearings. No one seemed hurried. I gave myself up to the natural entertainment of the place, watching the people I drifted with. There were hundreds of children there, cruising or standing on parade, and tricked out for romance. Children from my own high school, too, twenty or more miles from their homes.

I stopped in one of the halls to watch a glassblowing demonstration. A man was making farm animals, horses, pigs, and cows with exaggerated udders. When he blew teats on the enlarged bags he smiled shyly and got a big laugh. Further along the corridor someone was painting shower curtains with scenes from the ceiling of the Sistine Chapel and scenes from *Brigadoon.*

Eventually I found myself looking down over the great atrium and fountain sending a spray four stories high to the vaulted glass ceiling. Below me dozens of young people were circling the water. I was relieved to have found a central landmark.

As I gazed up and down at all the wandering children I was seized by an idea for my students. If they liked the place so much, perhaps they would tell me why. I could send the older ones on field trips to the mall, and have them write reports on what was happening in its myriad stores and diversions.

In the big classroom where I taught Stilson County History, we began to keep maps of the floor plans of the mall's four levels, a record of the shifting leases and walls as the great department stores, shops and restaurants came and went, or changed their shape.

I thought that if I talked about antiquities—milk bottles, nickel sodas, a grove of trees where the mall now stood—it might excite their curiosity, widen their vision. Instead there were grunts and snickering. One morning I yelled at them, "Listen! My childhood is under this! Your history is buried here!" following the outline of the parking acres with my pointer. When I turned to face them I was staring into the glazed eyes of apathy.

In the first years after Sarah graduated, my hands were always on chalk. I rolled chalk sticks in my palms the way some men play with change. I broke and crumbled them as I lectured. I carried chalk home in my pockets. My hands were always white, my lips like a Maalox drinker's. I paid my laundress to replace her washing machine's motor, clogged with white powder. At the end of a school day I was dusty head to thigh—that is, as far as my hands could play.

In 1959, when blackboards became green and chalk yellow, the only change for me was in the color on my hands and clothes. Chalk was my swagger stick, my cigarette, and on rare occasions, my missile. There were days when John Lambert would send me off to the lavatory for a cleanup. In the end chalk had a part in my fall.

I was assigned the largest room in the school so two sections of the senior class could be gathered for one of my Stilson County History lectures. There were eighty children. I was terribly excited by the things on my mind. King Charles II, who had given seven men all of Virginia between the Rappahannock and Potomac rivers. It hadn't been mapped and they didn't know what they owned. My capital letters stretched from one end of the green board to the other: UNMAPPED UNGOVERNED UNPAVED UNPOLICED. I was walking under the words, leaning into the board with my chalk, underlining in a continuous track, back and forth, talking as I went.

A voice came from the middle of the room, and caught me with my back to the students. I could accuse no one. I had seen no lips move but the word had been mean and mocking. "Chalkman," the voice called again. There was scattered laughter. I whirled and hummed the chalk at the back wall. The chalk cracked and scattered. I ordered the boy closest to it to pick up the pieces. He stood and sauntered over with a smirk to begin a lackadaisical cleanup.

I thought that was the end of it, but several weeks later it popped up again. From several directions, "Chalkman," in falsetto, like the cooing of unseen doves in a cornfield. Each time I turned my back to write on the board, it erupted. I confronted the class, and asked if my attackers would like to say something directly to my face. Someone was wailing "Chalkman, Chalkman" without moving his lips. People were laughing.

In the middle of the room a girl sat, palms up and shrugging. "Don't look at me, man," she said.

"All right," I said, "if this class doesn't want to listen to what I have to say, one of you can come up and take my place."

It was the kind of response I despised in other teachers— the assumption of general guilt, class-wide vengeance. But I wasn't thinking clearly. I chose an inarticulate child in the back, Oren Rayford, whose brothers and sisters before him had compiled a sorry school record.

"Tell us about the chapter you read last night. Make a little outline of it on the board as you go."

He faltered, frightened and miserable. His voice was quavering, his lips trembled. His writing on the board was almost illegible. And it started again, "Chalkman, Chalkman, Chalkman," this time coming from the front. I dismissed the class early and retreated to the faculty lounge.

It became a fad among the children and would not die. The name was passed forward, class to class, season by season, as the years went by in the familiar rotation of the school calendar, from Christmas to spring recess and the replenishing summer.

One spring day, standing at my classroom window, I heard voices drifting across the playing fields from the middle school.

The shouting and laughter of grades six through eight, high-pitched and frantic at their recess. Mixed in that distant, happy cacophony was the lilt of the slender seventh grader with the almost invisible birth scar on her nose, my daughter, Sonia. As I watched she performed a little miracle, a perfect cartwheel, and I clapped my hands in surprise. I'd never dreamed she was so gifted.

In a free period I walked to Sonia's school on the pretext of checking into the early records of some problem students and looked into her file.

"That child there," I asked her teacher casually, "isn't she Sarah Pless's daughter? How's she doing?"

"Bright enough," I was told. "Doesn't try."

"She seems so quick on the playground. So alert."

"Actually she's a little sullen in class. But you know at twelve and thirteen a lot of things are happening to their bodies."

I went back to the principal's office for another look in the files. Pless, Sonia D. There were teacher evaluations along with a set of mediocre grades. The perfunctory stuff of instructors forced to comment every quarter on thirty-five personalities.

Sonia is not cooperative in class. Needs extra work in spelling. Sonia could do well in math but tends to be careless. More effort needed in all her work.

I turned to the medical sheet. Check marks in the right places. Shot record filled with appropriate dates. Nothing in the blocks for disorders and medications. My eye settled on Age at Onset: 12.

Outside again, I winced as I watched a careless child bump into her on the playground and race away without apology. With the rest of an hour to kill I walked to the high school parking lot, sat in my car and tuned in Home Town Radio.

WHTR, a tower tied by three guy wires to one of H. T. Rogers's cornfields, and a studio on River Street, was our town's only radio station. HTR in the call letters was for Harold Thomas Rogers, part of the price he asked for letting the Morancy brothers erect their antenna on his high farm. You wouldn't know it, because every few minutes their announcers tell you, "This is WHTR, Home Town Radio." The Morancys got their license in 1957 with promises to the government to keep their signal on the Virginia side of the Potomac and east of the Blue Ridge, roughly within the boundaries of Stilson County, and to turn their sound on at daybreak and off at sunset.

It was just before sunset on a summer evening in 1957— one year after Sarah's graduation—that I first heard Lauranette Keyes. She was only twenty, not working for the station but being interviewed after her family's tragedy. Even then she was calm on the radio.

A rogue funnel of air had moved off the Blue Ridge and skipped randomly across the Stilson Valley, upending everything it touched. At the western end of the county it ripped off two silo roofs and sent them sailing to distant farms. The tornado cut savage swaths through corn and soybeans; uprooted an apple tree and dropped it into a barn; bounced over the interstate and took a giant leap toward our town line, where it picked out a single house.

The funnel lifted drapes, chairs, lamps and tables, two radios, a toaster, and every pot and pan into the air, hovered over a wide bend in the river, raised a spout of water fifty feet high, lost strength and dropped its cargo right there. Radios and the like sank to the bottom while a bedroom suite drifted over the falls, down to the capital city.

It was Home Town Radio's first disaster coverage. They

had a phone hookup from a neighbor's house and I heard Mr. Keyes explain to the WHTR reporter that first the roof had come off with a kind of explosion. He and Mrs. Keyes had been taking a nap and their daughter Lauranette had been listening to her record machine.

"We don't know how we got out of the house," he said. "We were just rolling over and over, and my wife said, 'I think my leg's broken.' And I said, 'Hold on. Where are we?' And she said, 'Outside by the Chevrolet.'"

The announcer wanted to know if Mr. Keyes had any thoughts about what had happened to him. "You know we moved here from the valley this month," he said. "It's just a heck of a way to treat new people. We made our first payment on the place yesterday."

Next they had on Mrs. Keyes, who was crying. There wasn't any insurance, she said, because this was an act of God. She couldn't continue, and they asked if she could put her daughter on the line. Lauranette came to the phone. "I just want to tell everyone we're all right," she said. "Could you call back another time. We've just had a tragedy here." She hung up. The station called back, but the family had escaped to another house, no phone number given.

I was twenty-nine then, suffering through that first year without Sarah. As I bicycled out along the river toward the disaster, the girl who'd hung up on the WHTR reporter seemed more a curiosity than flesh and blood. Halfway to the scene I realized I was in a small parade of bikes and cars.

Dozens of people were milling and more coming. With no house to look at, only the stone foundation, some were searching through the field across the road for the family's things. While I stood there a small boy brought in a hairbrush and dropped it in the odd pile of broken sticks and plastic. People wanted to help so badly. They shook their heads and wondered at the sky. It was getting dark when the WHTR car pulled into a neighboring driveway. As their reporter knocked on the front door I watched three people step out the back. An older man and woman were being led by a quick-moving figure in dungarees and a halter. Vigorous but gentle, she helped them toward the tree line and into the woods.

That was my first glimpse of Lauranette. From that brief sighting and the memory of her voice I built fantasies of an alluring, resourceful woman leading her beleaguered family out of adversity and through the wilderness, though they had only been tripping over croquet wickets as they made for cover, skirting behind the long backyards, looking for a house where they could be free of the morbid interest in their loss and the microphone of Home Town Radio.

It had been such a freak storm and so particular in its human target that WHTR began soliciting for the family. Money was raised, lumber and building materials were collected, carpenters and masons contributed time. Neighbors made meals for the volunteers as a new house was raised on the old foundation. The station, unable to make Mr. and Mrs. Keyes talk about loss or gratitude, finally got to Lauranette.

We heard her tell us, on the radio, how she had taken the Chevrolet to have its windshield repaired, and found in a field, the antique box that held a picture of her great-grandfather in a gold frame. But what we heard most of all was serenity.

For the two weeks of solicitation WHTR put Lauranette on regularly, and by the end of that time she was asking the questions and the interviewer was trying to keep up with her curiosity and humor. "How long do you think the Morancys will go on working for my family without pay?" she asked. "Do you think they'd like to be asked to supper?" Or "Tell me a little about your*self.* Do you enjoy looking into the corners of this sort of thing?"

She had the radio man twisting uncomfortably on her questions, then let him go easily. I heard her say, "Too much generosity can make a community cry for itself. Has anybody found our bedroom suite?" A few weeks later she'd been hired as the afternoon voice of Home Town Radio.

After a month in their rebuilt home the older Keyeses had had enough. Each way they turned reminded them of their beholden place in the community. Each room and appliance, a memorial to someone's kindness. Windows and roof, all presents. They looked at freshly painted walls and their thoughts penetrated to gifts of insulation, sheathing, siding. Their lives, wrapped in the warm kindness of neighbors, were unlivable.

When they moved down to Lexington, leaving the house to Lauranette, she made excuses for them. It was for health reasons, she said on her afternoon show. "But don't worry, I'm not leaving. I like it here." By then she had a following who wanted to hear more from the tornado child. Twenty years old but their little orphan of the air, forgiven for living alone. She would read her mail on the program—proposals, both prim and passionate, from the far ends of the county, but closer to our village she seemed untouchable, a sort of public ward, her cool voice holding us at an admiring distance.

She called her show "Tumbleweed." It was introduced by the Sons of the Pioneers singing a few lines of their hit song, and then Lauranette telling again how she arrived on the radio. "I came on a twister. Now I'm flying your way from H. T. Rogers's cornfield . . . that's where the station keeps its stick . . . to beat you with a thousand watts . . . of Home Town Radio . . . sunup to dusk." Folksy stuff in a silky voice, for daydreams in our county.

From her first day at the station she sounded so certain of who she was and where she was going, dropping benedictions on our daily lives, innocently building herself a franchise, pleasing the sponsors, putting her anecdotal touch on commercials for the hardware store, bank, garage—whomever the Morancys could deal or barter with. She remained half a stranger to me for fourteen years, revealing little more than her voice. When she finally called to have me on her program, it was 1971 and my daughter had entered high school.

But in 1969, the year of a new president from California, I hadn't even worried Sonia through the middle school. After looking through her file I had left the office defiant, certain that unimaginative teachers were her problem. The medical sheet had stunned me, caught me ignorant of my daughter's progress. I sat listening to my car radio, considering Sonia's emergence as woman, when three large boys came toward me from behind the industrial arts wing. I didn't recognize any of them, but they knew me.

"Hey, Chalkman," one of them yelled. "You could be erased." The other two thought this was hilarious. They walked around me, drumming on my roof, and then began to rock the car. I climbed out and told them to get back to their workroom. "We been kicked out," one of them said.

"Yeah," another told me. "Anyway, we don't have to take nothing from no man that's half dust," and they walked off slapping each other's backs, sassy and proud.

I was on my way to Lambert's office when I saw the new teacher, Rose Edgar, coming out of his private entrance, a door that was seldom used. All visitors, including faculty, were expected to come through the outer office and be announced by one of the secretaries.

The door closed behind Miss Edgar. She was just smoothing her skirt when she looked up and saw me. She hesitated, and then came forward, a little too cheery. "I think I came out the wrong way," she said. "Have to hurry. My kids'll be raising the devil."

Her getaway was too slick, but I had other things on my mind. I was going to tell Lambert what I saw happening to his school. Hardening hearts, vile manners, disrespect. Too easy to blame everything on social decay, on the moral unraveling of the decade. The way I saw it the new public address system put us in custody of faceless leaders. Classes were continually interrupted by bureaucratic commands from the office, the principal's deputies telling us about late slips, cafeteria deportment, hall wandering.

I didn't wait to be announced. Lambert raised his hand. "Stop before you say more than you want to." I'd always been grateful that he'd chosen me to write Stilson's history, but now his head was in his papers as he rolled his eyes up at me, as if this was a very awkward time to be interrupted, as if he hadn't just been in some kind of secret session with his newest teacher.

"Believe me, Ray," he said, "I know you're doing a wonderful job. Never mind what some of these people are saying. You've been one of our best. Now go wash up and get back to your kids. Remember, they're only children. These are troublesome times." He got up from his desk. "They don't understand this war thing. It's different now. We never had all these temptations. The drugs." He was up beside my ear, nudging me. "And all the easy sex."

He guided me out through the secretaries into the hall. I went back to my class feeling a little sullied. At the door to my room I stopped to spy for a moment on the rumpus I thought would be under way, as if I didn't know who'd be the hell-raisers and who the goody-two-shoes, who'd be sitting sullen, cheated, aware of time being wasted.

Instead of commotion, I found the class in progress without me. The maps of the four levels of the Whole World had been let down in front of the green board. Helen Macomber, usually a chatterbox with not much useful on her mind, had the room's attention. She was using my wooden pointer to demonstrate a mistake. "This is really weird, way out of date." She tapped a fried-chicken stall, a tempura bar and a shoe boutique, and landed the pointer on a swath of unused space where a department store had recently gone out of business.

Along one wall was a row of a half-dozen changing rooms. Helen drummed the stick on each of the rooms, "Vacant, vacant, vacant." Her friends thought this was terribly funny. She looked up and saw me in the doorway.

"That's good. Go on." I asked her what else had changed at the mall.

"I dunno," she said, suddenly vacant herself. And I pitied her for the uselessness of this school to her life and for the way she felt obliged to disguise the length of her nose, always wearing her glasses halfway down the bridge. A voice from the speaker on the wall told us that fifth period would be sixth period and sixth period would be fifth period.

I climbed on a chair and ripped the wires from the speaker. "Let's keep this to ourselves," I said and the class seemed to be with me again. We were working together, chatting quietly about the fight for hall-locker privacy, all of us in league against authority.

When the room was empty of students I sat alone, pleased with the day's gains. Then, rolling up the maps, I saw written on the green board in huge ornate yellow capitals: CHALKMAN. Underneath it was a yellow stick figure equipped with outsized genitals. I imagined how a young man must have been the artist and how Helen Macomber would have joined in the laughter.

It takes at least four years to send a high school fad into permanent remission. After three years you may feel relatively safe that an idea has been lost or forgotten. I supposed that in the fourth year I'd find out if the name had died for good, or if some senior with memories of his freshman experience would reinfect the student population and carry the custom forward. I should have known from the start that it was going to last, that my early popularity and success as a teacher gave me no immunity from these gleeful attacks by the few on my dignity. And once started, the practice would take on a life of its own, regardless of my response.

I never began with a fixation on chalk. It was simply that chalk had been the first thing at hand in those months when my heart kept time to the two syllables of Sarah's name, beating against the pretense of all normal work and leisure until my lips and fingers were white, then yellow, as I lectured, and children began to wonder at the extravagance of my insistence that the county had been settled by speculators and their agents in the first place.

Walking through the halls of the high school at class change I could see into the lives of two thousand children. Wit and dullness side by side. Some moved like cows on a string path as if the route had been memorized by feet to avoid having to dwell on boredom, while others shifted and darted, teased and cursed, daring themselves to arrive at their next seat late. From time to time I told myself I loved them all, and forgave every one of them, even those who mocked me. I thought it endearing that the great secrets of their lives were so public, that the truths behind their whispers and giggles and sidelong stares were so transparent.

I watched Helen Macomber, really a quite amiable frump, sobbing as she slammed through the door of the girls' room. The weekend before she had given everything to Lawrence, a handsome black boy, and now he wasn't interested anymore. A second girl entered behind her, prim and offended as the door flew back in her face, a girl with problems of her own, no pals of either sex, her classmates put off by the haughty forward thrust of her hips as she stood, arms akimbo, and alone. A boy called her a "high-cunt, low-ass bitch" to her face, and was ordered home from school for the day for his cruel accuracy.

I was coming out of one of the boys' rooms one morning having just read over a urinal,

Roses are red, violets are blue,
I'm a schizo, and so am I.

when our custodian Mr. Weeks stopped me. I was wondering who was so clever. In two years Sonia would arrive in these halls. What language would she find spoken in her restrooms and what quality of poetry? Mr. Weeks told me confidentially, "The girls use four times as much paper."

I knew the language of the girls. When they talked of doing circles with their boyfriends it meant they had driven down to Ripton Corner, taken the ramp onto the Beltway and done a turn around the city for their evening's recreation. But if one said she had taken his picture, the news was whispered, the aperture of love had been snapped. These were the same ones who kept moon dials in their purses—the plastic disks that held the pills, their month's protection, love clocks timed against the mistake.

I was forty-one years old and carefully counting. Still no marriage and no child to call my own. After eighteen years of teaching, I'd become a bit of an institution at River High, my performance graded many times over by older brothers and sisters, even a few aunts and uncles of the current children. Sometimes the sweet aroma of their smoke hung over the urinals, blending with the scent of blue deodorant disks. It troubled me to see students floating past me with silly grins. Though only a few had let their habit get out of hand, I knew that trickier substances were being used.

One morning I found a boy crouched behind the restroom door. As I came toward him he screamed, "Don't squeeze me, I'm an orange!" I bent over to help him up, but curled in a ball, he rolled to a neutral corner of the latrine, pleading with me not to touch him. "My juice would come out," he said.

Should I get down on the floor and be a brother orange, or try to coax him to stand and walk to his next class? I leaned over and patted his shoulder, and he screeched, "See? See what you've done?" He was uncoiling himself and showing me the growing stain on his pants where he was wetting himself. The last I heard of him he was in a state hospital, still an orange losing juice every day.

These new children didn't ascribe to me the potency that earlier classes had. Why should they place in the backseat of one of their cars, or a motel room, or even a legitimate marriage bed, a man with a yellow splotched face lunging forward to ask, "Do you know what watershed you live in?" The question would have been easy for me as a child simply because I knew the creeks I fished in and the river they ran into. One of my new boys answered that there was a storm sewer behind his house that ran under the airport road, and went—he wasn't sure after that.

For a long time I'd been suppressing the fact of Sarah's second child. Still clinging to the notion of a missing wife and daughter, it had been difficult for me to watch Sarah swell through another pregnancy, and to accept the birth of Rita in the winter of 1964. Another girl. To me it only meant Sarah and Richard might try again for a boy, further eroding my genetic right in their family council. Before this a voting majority had still seemed possible, assuming Sarah and Sonia would one day side with me. It would have been those two and I against the pretender. Rita, with her first cry and suckle, changed all that.

When I saw Sarah in the post office and asked about the baby, she said, "We're getting metal awnings for our downstairs windows. Green and white stripes. They'll really dress the place up."

At home I had a file of some of her old themes and test papers, souvenirs of high promise hidden away in a bottom drawer. From time to time I looked back at them, searching for reassurance that I hadn't been wrong about her. They were for times when she talked about metal awnings or the fade in the color of their sedan's hardtop. And I was never disappointed. Instead of receding as mawkish or immature, her old work held up remarkably well.

One of her papers, called "Why It Won't Happen," was written after I'd told her class that the government was cutting a great cave in the mountain at the west end of our county, a place for officials to retreat and run the nation after nuclear attack. It was hard to believe a seventeen-year-old could have written it.

"It won't happen," she wrote, "because we couldn't accept the long, shrill tone that would interrupt our radio station, or the change of ten thousand robin beaks into a molten state, or the radiation of our turkey's wattles.

"There are many reasons it won't happen," she had gone on. "Further cracks in the dome of the Capitol would be unacceptable. After all, the tar on our own roof gets lesions with any extremes of temperature, which means leaks and wet insulation. And not all the million chickens being fattened on the Eastern Shore are meant to be fryers. A lot of them have to be sold as parts, and a fifteen-minute warning wouldn't be enough time for cutting and packaging."

Lesions? Who'd taught her that word? And where had she

learned to treat unconscionable horror with whimsy? And what had brought her to settle on the plight of birds already doomed?

Communion with that mind had been an honorable pursuit. Going back to her themes I'd always been able to convince myself of that, though she'd thought her compositions only commonplace, as if there was no great merit in being transcribing agent for thoughts that moved so naturally through her. There had always been the sparkle of surprise when she saw her A.

II

CHALKMAN'S
DAUGHTER

Our Polly is a sad slut! nor heeds what we have taught her.
I wonder any man alive will ever rear a daughter!

—*THE BEGGAR'S OPERA*

Her daughter, my daughter, entered high school in the fall of 1971. I knew who her homeroom teacher was going to be—Rose Edgar—what classrooms she'd be using, where she'd step foot through the building every minute of her week. I had her schedule written in my notebook right beneath my own.

As Sonia came through the entrance I stood beside the hall locker which she didn't yet know was going to be hers, watching every move and gesture. She was wearing a yellow cotton dress with a white, lacy collar, and black flats with little leather bows on them, as if she had missed out on a public announcement that the uniform for the season would be jeans, boy's dress shirts and sneakers for the girls. She was a little nervous but taking in the territory around her, sizing the place up.

The children were being herded into the auditorium for introductory exercises, and as Sonia passed me she looked without recognition at my face. A few minutes later I stood at the back of the auditorium listening to Lambert tell the freshmen many things to be careful of. Valuables. Lunchroom behavior. When he ticked off his twelve-item code of conduct, I watched Sonia's head loll back on her seat in overt, utter boredom. I left the auditorium completely satisfied with her first day's dress and behavior, wondering what was to become of her.

John Lambert led me to believe I was a special case, someone who had earned extra freedom from school protocol. He came into my first Stilson County History class of that year with something to tell the children.

"You people," he said, "are lucky to have one of the finest instructors at River High. Mr. Sykes has been with us twenty years. It doesn't seem possible does it, Ray?"

"Not quite as long as yourself, John," I said.

"Sorry I haven't had much time. Come on in for a chat whenever you like. Dodge the secretaries if you want. Use my door." With that he was on his way, continuing down the hall with his pleasantries. I couldn't help connecting his offer with the time I'd seen Rose Edgar coming furtively out of his private door. And I wondered if he was buying off suspicions I might have about the two of them.

The year before, in an effort to purge myself of chalk, I'd had assignments and class outlines mimeographed. I meant to avoid the green board as much as possible. I lectured while seated at my desk. It worked for a while. But one morning, excited by a student's response, I turned to the board to demonstrate a point, and saw that it was bare, and my hand empty. My fingers roved mechanically through my desk and found the chalk box hidden away in a bottom drawer. By the end of the period I was a happy, yellow mess, and my best students were hanging around again after the bell.

With Sonia in the building, ordinary students became threatening. I was especially wary of the little falsetto demons that might pop up around my classroom. I had my lunch duty changed from third to first session to be in the cafeteria when Sonia would be there with the freshman class. Her first day I waited to see which line she'd choose and went to stand by the cash register where she'd be checking out.

"The soup's hot," I told her. "You can sit anywhere." It was like telling someone at the seaside "The ocean's open." But I'd come close enough to see that the little line on her nose wasn't a mistake at all but had become the natural cleft under the center flesh, a finer duplicate of this small feature on my own face.

With Sonia I tried too hard too soon. I wasn't the only one who stared at her, but I did watch her. She was lovely, and aware of it. She carried herself without arrogance but with a content knowledge of where each bone and plane of flesh sat in her passive face. The shift of her pale eyes suggested she wasn't trying so much to please as to avoid contact.

When a dish fell and shattered in the cafeteria, she wasn't one of the hundreds who applauded. I took her general serenity, along with what I assumed must be a superior intelligence, to be part of her inheritance from her mother. I was waiting for her to amaze her new teachers. As the semester went along she changed from dresses to jeans and began to make friends, an assortment of boys and girls who respected her long silences and unhurried passage through the halls.

I was becoming a spy in the house of education. Long before Sonia entered my classroom as my own student, she was aware of the attention I paid her. She saw me in the gymnasium as she went through the spiritless chore of obtaining her "satisfactory" in P.E., or standing close to the loading area when she boarded her bus in the afternoon, and taking up my post close to her locker when I had hall duty.

My plan was to strike up a casual conversation so that a friendship would seem to spring from chance. But she shied away from my approaches, wanting no part of a too-easy acquaintance with faculty. She may have sensed there was something unhealthy in my regard. Once, caught watching her at point-blank range, I felt forced to tell her, "Your mother was one of my early students, one of the very best. You won't remember but when you were very small I used to see her pushing you through the supermarket in a shopping cart. When she introduced us, you tried to kick me."

"If you taught my mother, you must have taught my father, too," she said. "They were in the same class."

After that I was more careful. I began to spy like a bureaucrat, watching for new information in her school file. I did notice that two more boys had added themselves to the clique that had accepted Sonia as its soft-spoken leader. They were an even dozen now, half boys, half girls. There was no pairing up as far as I could tell—just a healthy sharing of hands and glances.

No jocks or freaks in the bunch. In a school of two thousand you could always find children who did not join clubs or throw balls or use drugs or show any special passion, but banded together in small societies against the larger commotion. I saw nothing exceptional in the ones who gathered around Sonia unless it was a too casual, over-the-shoulder regard for the adults around them.

By the end of the first semester there was one pregnancy in the freshman class, four throughout the school. An average season, Lambert said. "You have to remember," he told us, "we're dealing with a large group of people here. You shouldn't be frightened by numbers that don't have statistical significance."

The day after semester grades were recorded, I was into Sonia's file, reading back to front. "Sonia is off to a very poor start." Then from the top, three D's and two C's and nothing promising at all in any of her teachers' comments. Nothing about the delayed performance of an underachiever. Rather, they suggested there was little to hope for. She didn't care, according to her teachers. One had seen "diffidence," another "arrogance." They couldn't tell sly from shy.

I went straight to a phone to call Sarah. I thought she should have time to prepare a firm, sensible response to Sonia's report card.

"This could mean a lot of different things," I told her. "She's smarter than some of her teachers. I'm sure they resent her."

"Wait a minute," Sarah said. "You've got no right to be telling me this. You're not her teacher. Her grades aren't your concern."

"But there's something wrong. A bright girl like her."

"What are you talking about? She's never done well in school. She's never been bright."

An unbelievable thing for her to be telling me. "Did you ever read to her?" I asked.

"Stop meddling," Sarah said. "Sonia told me you'd been watching her. What you're doing is dangerous."

"I was only trying to help. So what's new in your life?"

"Rich put a remote-controlled door on the garage. Leave her alone. Stay away from her."

I did turn my back to Sonia as far as I was able. I spent a lot of time on a revised edition of *Stilson,* adding a chapter on the loss of another great swath of agriculture and plans for an outer beltway that would bring a second circle of hot tar and giant rollers to our cornfields. I imagined children driving circles in their cars, bouncing back and forth between the two loops, mindless particles switching orbit in a social experiment gone haywire. And this attitude of Sonia's, her pose of contented ignorance. Maybe Lambert was right, and the children were actually lost, confused.

The more I avoided Sonia the more her name and face appeared in my daily rounds. I could only turn so far before I was facing her again. On a dark winter morning made more melancholy by the counterfeit brilliance of fluorescent light I looked away as I passed her in the hall, even kept walking past my classroom door to avoid her. I did a complete circuit through the linoleum passage and met her coming back the other way. She was being followed by a large older boy in a pink shirt. He had a metal comb stuck in his hair. The bells had rung. They should have been in their rooms by then. Without running Sonia tried to stay ahead of him. They came by me and again I pretended not to notice. Their steps quickened. I turned to watch and heard him call to her.

"Hey, girl. I'm gonna break your back with my thing."

Without losing a step she looked over her shoulder and told him, "If your thing's so big, why don't you suck it?" She turned into a classroom. Defeated, the boy came back by me and asked, "What's your problem?"

Within a few days my shock had turned to pride in a really gutsy performance. I took comfort in the notion that Sonia had only been speaking the cool language of survival. But something else happened that season to set me off on her case again.

Rose Edgar, Sonia's homeroom teacher, was in her third year at River High. Young and unmarried, she had come from a school closer to the city. She had a clear voice that rang beyond her classroom. With credentials in math and geometry, she'd been given three home economics sections. Rose was wry about her switch but uncomplaining. From my room across the way I could hear her talk about protein in beans and how to lay out patterns to save yard goods, making the most of her assignment. I admired her for it, and wanted her admiration in return.

Rose was a proud woman, current in the children's fads. A little short and unfashionable maybe, but with soft, appealing features and an oval face. If the timing had been different I thought she was someone whose heart could have danced with mine. I suspected there was something more than school business that attracted her so often to the principal's office, and when I'd seen her come out Lambert's private door this notion had taken me over. If it was an affair, however unlikely, I was disappointed in her that she'd chosen her boss rather than, well, me. I envied the way she could lay a hand on a student and have it mean only encouragement. I thought I could look to her for modern wisdom and a long, compassionate view.

Then, one afternoon in the school library, I heard her discussing my daughter. A teacher's aide asked her, "Is there something off about Sonia Pless?" and Rose said, "You mean little Miss Moon Dial?" The aide covered her mouth but her eyes were wide. "Yes, that's the one."

The comment should have been challenged. A jealous estimate of a nubile child's normal erotic affect. I suddenly wanted to warn Sonia about her teacher, how she seemed to be calculating Sonia's deportment on a scale of her own prudery. If my daughter knew where these women's minds were she could decide whether to go straitlaced and unpainted or challenge their censure with rouge and cleavage.

I said nothing, but their talk had set me on alert again. Once more I was spying across the lines of duty, poaching views of Sonia from positions in the building where my presence was awkward and obvious. Behind the gymnasium door, looking through the wired glass at a morning P.E. session, I saw her do lazy laps with some other stragglers in her class, pretty but unexceptional in the same maroon tunic as everyone else. I stayed until the instructor waved me off.

Even in her street clothes there seemed nothing flashy or crude about her. When she changed over to jeans and sweaters they were loose, even dowdy. She didn't make herself up or stand hand-on-hip by the doors like some of our girls, advertising their loneliness and availability with long, steady glances. Was it the way Sonia walked that had caught Rose Edgar's attention? Had she detected the sashay of a slut where I saw the normal strut of a proud girl stepping through what must have seemed to her another tedious day?

Again I called Sarah.

"Is it about Sonia?"

"It's about everything."

"Because if it is, I already know and I don't want your help."

"It's about everything," I said.

She was annoyed. I knew the shape of her mouth as she said, "Well?"

I wanted a whole afternoon to talk, not just a few moments stolen over a lunch sandwich. And after some coaxing she agreed to a whole afternoon. "But where?"

"We'll do a couple of circles," I said, "like the kids."

I called in sick the next day, and made a lunch of fried chicken we could eat as I drove. Sarah met me at Ripton Corner in the parking lot of the great mall. Stepping out of her shiny new station wagon named for a constellation toward my old Plymouth called only Valiant, she hesitated for a moment at my window.

"Look," I reassured her, "this has nothing to do with us." I suppose I meant that after fifteen years, she could count on me not to betray a latent infatuation with some emotional gaffe or inept lunge. Really, I felt quite virtuous, not sneaky in the least. We'd be hiding on the great circle only to avoid misunderstanding, and speaking quietly of our daughter's troubled world.

"Clockwise or counterclockwise?" I asked.

Sarah didn't want to make the decision. I chose counterclockwise, a right turn onto the Beltway coming from the outside. I think I liked the outer lanes best because they gave me the sense of being able to spin off at any tangent into the country, rather than rubbing elbows with the warehouses and square clusters of apartments next to the inner circuit.

We'd only been gone a few minutes when she asked where we were. "I have to be home by four. That's when the girls get back from school."

"Doing circles it doesn't matter where you are. You just remember your exit number."

By the time we crossed the southern bridge into Maryland she seemed reconciled to at least one revolution. She was studying the green signage of outlying communities, keeping alert to her position as we swept the suburban perimeter.

"Remember the theme you wrote for me on your mother's way of timing a soft-boiled egg?"

"No." She looked at me suspiciously. "What are you talking about?"

"It was wonderful. You said she didn't need a clock. She put the egg in when the water was still cold. By the time it was boiling it was almost done. She could tell if it was ready by the speed the water evaporated from its surface. It wasn't the system I liked so much as the stuff about your father and runny eggs.

"And the thing you wrote about chickens after a nuclear attack."

"I never wrote anything like that."

"Yes, I still have a bunch of them. They're wonderful."

"You have old papers of mine? You still read them? You know, you've always had the wrong idea," she said. "I'm not one of your geniuses. I don't even like to read. We have a few programs we watch.

"Arboretum," she read overhead. "That's just trees. Isn't there a theme park around here? It isn't right, you kept those things of mine," she decided. "What else did you keep?" The more she thought about it the less she liked the idea. "It's a little sick, isn't it?" She made me feel as if I was still fondling the spoils of a long-ago panty raid. "Is that what's bothering you this time? My old themes?"

"No," I said. "It's your daughter again. Our daughter. I

mean Sonia. Her teachers are saying some ugly things about her." Sarah had turned stony. "All right, Rich's daughter, if that's what you want me to call her."

"That's exactly what I want you to call her. That's what she has been for fifteen years and that's what she is, period!"

I didn't concede, just slid past this for the moment. Why should I have to explain that genetic truth is final truth, that my absence would never diminish that tie, that I'd forever be bound to Sonia in a way I never had been to Sarah?

Passing the Metroliner station we saw a tractor trailer spread across the inner loop of the Beltway and two broken cars, sirens coming and going. "I don't know why we're doing this," Sarah said. "What if we got in an accident?" Riding past tragedy I came back to family likenesses.

"No matter how far Rich's head is buried in the sand, down there somewhere, he must know."

"Don't you understand," she said, "there are people who don't want to know, even if proof was possible. Do you think he's ever been interested in looking at her blood type? Anyway, it happens to fit with his own. Maybe there *is* a little of your face in Sonia's, but there's some of mine, too. And that's the part Rich sees."

"That's the nice thing about family resemblances, I suppose. You can take what you want from them."

"Take what you like," she told me. "I want you to turn around. I want to go back. You're driving too slow."

"We've reached the point of no return," I said.

"What do you mean?"

"Actually," I said, "we were on our way back when we started."

"Your smart talk isn't getting us anywhere." Sarah was angry. But by the time we crossed the northern bridge into Virginia again she was ready to get on with it. "What about Sonia?"

I wanted to make this as easy as possible on Sarah. I asked if she remembered the horrid kind of stuff that used to be written in the restrooms when she went to school.

"I never thought much about it," she said.

"A lot's changed over the years."

"It's gotten worse."

"No, they don't write it on the walls anymore. They come right out and say it."

"Say what?"

I explained that as graffiti had changed from written to vocal, River High had become a dangerous place for an artless child. I told Sarah about the boy who had threatened to break Sonia's back with his thing. "Do you know what Sonia answered?"

"What?"

"She told him if his thing was so big, why didn't he suck it."

"They wouldn't say thing, would they?" Sarah asked.

"It's city talk."

"Well, thing's not a bad word." She was drumming her fingers on the dashboard. I'd expected a little outrage, not contemptuous indifference. If she was bluffing I had more for her.

"Do you know what her teacher calls her?"

"Tell me."

"She calls her little Miss Moon Dial. You know what that means? That means pills."

"So? I told her to get them." Sarah was turning my rearview mirror to her use, doing something to her hair.

I was amazed. "Look," I told her, "Sonia may be a little confused by what's going on. She may need help that she's not getting at school."

"You don't know the half of it, do you?" She was finished with her hair, opening a compact.

"What should I know? The half of what?"

"Her father wants her out of here next summer. He's sick of all this."

"You can't help," she assured me when our circle was done and she transferred to her own car at Ripton Corner.

"You know," I said, trying to keep her there a moment longer, "this was my home. I grew up here."

"You should have held on to the land." She whistled, thinking about it. "It would have been valuable."

High on the mall a dozen window men on hanging platforms were working on the south facade. Some of the steel window casings had been whitened to make the grid of a football field on which cowboys and Indians were fighting over a ball. People in the parking lot were cheering for the Indians. I tried to part the crowd with my horn but had to wait until another cowboy had been scalped. In my mirror I could see Sarah waving for my attention, and pointing in delight at the mural in progress. It had to do with a very important football game.

I was learning something about an infatuation held too long. That despite all I knew to be negative about Sarah, the accretion of disappointing behavior, a little meanness, the loss of bright hope, despite all of this I could still be a bumbler in her presence, tentative and awkward. There was a certain excitement in testing myself with her to see what parts of me—pulse, speech, poise—still refused to accept reality.

Over the years, I had transformed Lauranette Keyes in my imagination many times. In the flesh, it was difficult to spot her. She arrived at work early and left late, using the station's alley parking lot and back door. For me she was still a heroine who had come up from tragedy and onto the airwaves, blown by fate into the job her clever mind and gentle voice deserved. And at that remove she might have remained a media deity forever, except that in the spring of 1971, Sonia's freshman year, she sought me out for an interview. She called me at home and asked me to join her in her studio the following Friday.

Lauranette had heard I was an unusual teacher. She knew I'd written a history of our county which had received attention beyond Virginia—something quite different from the normal textbook. No time lines, heavy dates, trends, or tricky questions for discussion at the ends of chapters.

The book had gone into several printings and been widely reviewed, an unheard-of success for a high school text. It was even available in a few bookstores. Lauranette had bought and read it, and was prepared when I arrived for my interview on "Tumbleweed."

Through the glass of her broadcast booth she looked cheerful and vivacious, the hostess of a lively party, though she sat all alone. She motioned to me to come in and take a seat. After a polite introduction in which she mentioned that students adored me and parents discussed me, she asked why they had let me write it. And once written, why had they approved a text that included corrupt zoning boards and the 1948 River High homecoming queen who had gone on to be prosecuted for chain-letter fraud.

Lauranette praised the book. She said it was full of the joys of a community's self-discovery and held an underlying message of hope for fields of soybeans against advancing macadam. "But who in the world turned you loose?" she asked, lulling me into the candor of a private chat.

Disarmed, I told her how the director of the project kept asking me for "verbiage." A little here, a little there. "The county schools are a system," he'd told me, "like this fountain pen," which he held between us. Ink flow? Flow chart? It hadn't made sense but I'd seen that substance was going to be mine, and procedure his.

Lauranette asked me to explain my theory of county development. A cycle of zone, tax out of existence, rezone and move west.

"Amplify."

It would take too much time. But if she liked we could talk about it at dinner. Lauranette touched my hand gently, reminding me we were live. I had broadcast my request for a date to the whole WHTR service area, and she had signaled her acceptance sweetly and silently.

"Would Sunday night be all right?" she asked afterward. I had to assume the rest of her weekend was booked, that I'd be waiting in line.

Taking Lauranette Keyes to dinner I was wandering at last beyond the friends and relations of Sarah. I had supposed Lauranette was content to observe the odd moil of our community without participating. Like the farmer suddenly addicted to golf, the auto dealer who won his company's golden circle award and then prepared for religious orders and the teenager who did circles around Washington, I'd been just another subject charmed to garrulity in her confessor's box.

I took her to a steak house with unlimited salad privileges. She looked the place over and told me she'd never put a garbanzo bean, a pickled beet or sour bean sprouts on any salad she'd ever eaten. I led her out the door, not annoyed but pleased in my mistake. We set out for a small inn with a French chef and a view of the river.

"Salad bars are a little like tie racks," I apologized. "From a distance the choices seem infinite. Up close there's nothing you want." As we drove I made jokes about my incompetence as a cross-country coach.

"I want you to do something," she said. "I want you to

keep looking at the road, and tell me what color my hair is."

I tried to cheat. She leaned farther back. "Isn't it sort of brownish?"

"Auburn," she told me. "What color are my eyes?"

I refused to guess.

"Green," she said. "Very green. Noticeably green."

Over our dinner of veal and strawberry crepes I told her how I'd seen her first as her parents' savior in halter and jeans, leading them into the woods.

"Actually," she explained, "my mother and father didn't like me being dressed that way with so many curious people around. There was nothing else left to put on. They made me leave through a back door and get out of sight."

"Later, over the radio," I told her, "you were more like a disembodied spirit."

She began to tell me her life story. She had a brother nineteen years older. She'd been a surprise baby, conceived years after her mother had given up hope. "A mixed blessing." Her parents' delight had been tempered by the rigors of beginning all over again. "As a girl I was supposed to be easier. It didn't work out that way. I started out colicky and then walked too soon."

She had climbed like a boy. Out of her crib. By the time she was two and a half they had her in a preschool, grateful for part-time relief. "They never had enough energy for me. I know it was difficult for them. They used to say I should have got myself a younger set of parents. More than once I told them I wished I had.

"I wasn't very girlish. More sassy and athletic. A sort of tomboy with tits."

I looked around to see if anyone else was listening. She held her gaze steady on me. "By the time I got to high school I was almost out of touch with them. They were kind and quaint and a terrible embarrassment." Lauranette said she was the sort of student who was always reading but never the assigned material. A clever failure. She joined the drama club as a freshman and immediately won a part as a fallen lady who had to let a senior boy kiss her.

"I was quite a little sexpot. Nothing outrageous. More appearance than behavior. It was the clothes they couldn't take. Shorts, T-shirts. Halters. A lot of skimpy stuff. Mostly around the house. If I'd gone away to college or something like that it would have been easier for them."

After high school she hadn't just sat around the house painting her nails and changing outfits. She'd spent most of her time reading for three correspondence courses: two in great books, one in art history.

Lauranette was dancing across the space that had kept us strangers, and I encouraged her. Her voice was growing softer as the evening progressed, winding down from the hale good cheer of her radio day. Her volume dropped again, the surrounding tables were cut off, and I became her intimate audience, treated to the slow movement of her fingers around the base of her wineglass, and the impish play of her mood.

"What about you?" she said.

Without mention of Sarah or my child I told her about my teaching schedule, my bachelor's bungalow, my empty hours out of school.

"That's all?" She was looking around the room again, as if she had made a mistake, or it was time for the check.

"I don't have anyone," I said suddenly. "I lost my parents when I was seventeen. My brother's dead, too." I knew how seductive my story could be. The truths of an orphan, the details of a father's arrhythmic heart, a mother's chance encounter with the wrong anesthetist, a brother's fatal bravery in the woods.

"Where exactly are you from?" she asked me softly.

"Ripton Corner."

"That's all commercial," she said. "No one lives there."

"I grew up under the roof of the Whole World Mall."

She was charmed by the idea.

"Really," I said. "They built it on our land."

"It's fabulous, isn't it? I guess I go there a lot," she confessed.

"Well, you've walked all over my childhood then, and all over my brother's grave." She looked at me quizzically, aware by then that I was working not just for sympathy but for love. And, by God, I was, pushing my phantom family out of my mind where they could not interrupt.

I took Lauranette from the dining room to a soft double seat by a great stone fireplace and we sipped liqueurs from very small glasses. I supposed we were waiting for the dying fire to tell us the time to leave. I was studying her face, ready this time in case she made me look away and then tell her how many moles she had. Two tiny ones on her left cheek. Or if there was a dimple. One on the same side.

She was still thinking about my brother's grave, she said, his ashes covered by the mall's quarry tile and asphalt. For a moment her unpainted lips were contorted as her tongue fought to dislodge a bit of vegetable between her teeth.

The lips were full but what you remembered were Lauranette's eyes. Noticeably green, as she'd said. A slight puffiness of flesh above and below made them thin and deep set, giving the impression of a constant tight focus. She seemed intent on what was right in front of her even when she stared into the distance.

Lauranette dealt with the big news quickly. "I don't want to get married anytime soon, to anyone, prince or pauper. What about you? Do you think about marriage?"

"Not much," I lied.

"Really? I thought marriage was always on a bachelor's mind. Whether he's fighting it off or promoting it."

"Not at all," I argued. "It's usually women who keep the

notion afloat. It's not really their fault. It's the respectable thing, it's expected."

"The men around here are so conventional," Lauranette insisted. She was draining her glass, asking for another. "I mean they ask for things in such routine order. For your hand first. In marriage. Then the other parts." She bit her lip and began to reach for things. For the silver ornaments on her belt, for the collar of her blouse, for hair that might be out of place. We each had another drink.

With the evening just on the edge, when it had to move in some direction, she said, "You know this place has rooms upstairs. I hear they're very nice."

"Would you like to see one?"

"I'd like to stay in one," she said, drowsily. Maybe just sleepy, wanting to get home.

"A place like this," I said, "you'd probably have to ask months ahead."

"Inns are never booked on Sundays. I want to stay here tonight. With you." She turned her palms up, waiting for me to do something. In a happy trance I went to make arrangements at the front desk.

They gave us a room with a fireplace, a down comforter that we had to throw off in the middle of the night, and a remarkably soft bed, the kind that rolls two people toward the center. Unnecessary help. When we were exhausted with lovemaking, she clung to me till we were asleep, and her arms, still around me in the morning, were a fresh, warm surprise.

"I'll be late for my class," I whispered. "I have to go. Why don't you get some more sleep?"

"I'm walking out of here with *you*," she said, putting a stern finger on my chest. "Anyway, what about tonight?"

"The same tonight. At my house." Before I could tell her how to get there, she said, "I know where it is."

At school that day the students were restless again with my wandering lecturing. I was addled, anxious to get home and make my house ready for love. I was thinking of Lauranette and something she had done that morning, turning her small breasts to me as she put on her blouse, so proud of who she was and what she had done.

There was another night, and then another. A week, and the habit of it was taking me over. We began to move back and forth between my house and her place, not wanting, I think, to upset the balance that kept our clothes in our own closets and toothbrushes in our own bathrooms. In those first weeks together she told me her "most awful" secret, that she would never be able to have children. I didn't press for the medical detail, but she made clear there had been a very bad episode with stock characters—cad, bogus doctor, and her as the silly young woman.

Lauranette had warned me from the start that she had no use for "forever." And for a time this gave me license for my silence about my own secret. She called me Sykes instead of Ray. She liked to keep that distance between us, though she began to wear my undershirts for her nightgowns.

Sonia was sent away that summer to visit an uncle on a pig farm in Arkansas where she was supposed to help with chores. In that season when otherwise I might have caught glimpses of her I felt cheated, angry with Richard and Sarah for throwing responsibility for Sonia to some man I'd never met.

Lauranette didn't tolerate my moodiness for long. It was clear to her that I was hiding something behind my long silences. "I'd like to be alone for a week," she told me after an uncommunicative dinner together. "Maybe longer. We'll see. I don't want to live with a cipher."

I was stunned. For several weeks, she'd been floating with me on undeclared but abundant love. I was already dependent on her and she was telling me that she'd toss it all away if it was going to be flawed. I went walking on the mountain the next day and came down to her with a long confession.

"I have a daughter," I said. "Her mother was one of my students. She's going to be my student, too, and she doesn't even know I'm her father."

Lauranette was struck dumb, incredulous. She walked out of the dining room and came back again. "You slept with one of your students?"

"Believe me she was a woman. She was extraordinary." I tried to explain that early devotion—Sarah's experience, my tears—losing myself in the story until I heard myself say, "Richard could never be Sonia's father," and saw Lauranette's irritation.

"What about us?" she said slowly. "Do you want to go on together?" She was watching me very carefully.

"Yes."

She wanted the rest of my serious social history, no more explosive news later on. I confessed to the women who had come between Sarah and her, the five who had fallen so quickly through my life. And she was quick to see how each of the five led back to Sarah and my daughter.

"If all goes right," I said, "eventually Sonia will be my student. If her mother doesn't take her out of the school. She might pay extra to send her out of the district."

Lauranette was looking darkly into the past, sorting things out. She said knowing about Sarah and Sonia made my long bachelorhood more understandable. The period of rutting around the Plesses' acquaintances, she thought, had been a juvenile game played with adult equipment—a scatter of affection around a forbidden target. If she saw design where I remembered a random hunt, that was all right because having a definition of my actions seemed to excuse them in her mind. And I counted on Lauranette's full pardon. Which she gave me two weeks later.

But with a warning. "I don't want to hear any more about those women." As for Sarah, the mother of my child, there wasn't much she could say. Lauranette did suggest that I transfer to another school. In any case I should stay away from Sonia before I caused real trouble. How was I sure the girl was my daughter anyway, she wondered. I showed her the inch-square picture of Sonia wedged between hundreds of other freshmen in the latest yearbook, and even in that diminished scale Lauranette accepted the obvious likeness.

Lauranette worked out a lot of reasons for me to get away from River High. "Hang around kids too long and your world shrinks to their size," she told me. She tried to stay off the subject of Sonia, but it was easy to see the angle in her warnings. "Teachers can't help it," she said. "First they're just hall cops. Then they're part of the thought police."

Never mind that. Lauranette and I were solid again, actually living together at my house most of the time. And Sarah, I thought, had receded to an admissible and manageable place in my past.

In the fall, Sonia was back from her pig chores in Arkansas and again walking the halls of River High with the confident gait and alert eye that I'd always taken to be the common equipment of superior students. I had no doubt that when she put her mind to the task she'd be one of the school's prize pupils. To me she seemed sexually provocative only in the clear grace of her face and limbs. The teacher gossip couldn't convince me there was anything abnormal about her.

Sonia didn't flirt, but seemed absolutely direct in her personal affairs. No slinking, no coyness. I saw her kiss a boy on the cheek and send him on his way down the hall the way a mother might send her little child out of the house to play. I could only wonder at the ease with which life seemed to meet her. The scholastic laziness puzzled me.

Sonia was slipping through the school without distinction, almost unnoticed, I thought. But sitting in the faculty lounge one afternoon, with other teachers grading papers and drinking coffee, I saw Rose Edgar open a student's small spiral notepad. She began to read aloud, unaware of what she had. Just something she'd found in a hall, she said.

Frankie. He's every other Wednesday. Sandra has him the Saturday before me and I think she spoils him. He won't say what she does but rolls his eyes and talks about who comes after me—Janice Carter who shouldn't even be in it, a freshman might tell her parents or something.

"What is that?" I called from the coffee urn.

"One of their slam books," someone said. "Tell her parents what? Go on, Rose."

She continued the section on Frank, who, we learned, had calluses on his fingers from his summer work as a mason's helper, and had been advised by Janice, who had it from a magazine's hints column, that he should put vitamin E oil on his hands and keep them in rubber gloves overnight.

"Whose is that?" I asked.

"What does it matter? Some tenth grader. Read it, Rose."

"Peter," Rose went on. "Alternate Fridays."

Alternate, I remember thinking, quite a good word for a sophomore to be using. And then Rose stumbled into "buns up, kneeling."

"I don't agree with the others Peter is strange because he wants us buns up kneeling," is as far as Rose got before she dropped the pad on the table. One of the ladies asked, "What is it? They're sitting on the floor eating rolls?" Rose looked up at me, shaking her head. She picked the book up again and thumbed through it, offering a few more names as she went. After that there was no more reading aloud.

The pad sat on the table all afternoon and other teachers came in to have their private reading. I wanted to look, too, but not while anyone was watching me. By the time I got to it, after the final bells, it was well thumbed and coffee stained. When I saw Sonia's name inside the cover I slumped in my chair.

"Of course it's none of my business," I admitted to Lauranette. But after reproaching me she read through the notepad too, and was surprised as I had been by my daughter's candid audacity. When we finished our perusals the pad went in the drawer with the mother's old papers, the Xerox of Sonia's report card that I'd made before talking with Sarah, and one of Sonia's blue enamel barrettes that she'd dropped in the hall and which I hadn't felt able to return to her.

"It might be for creative writing," Lauranette offered, but we both knew the detail was too odd, too specific, for that. It was the real article.

Unable to convince even herself, Lauranette paced in the kitchen composing headlines: Teen love ring at high school. Round-robin of love exposed in sex diary. Paraphernalia seized.

"What do you mean paraphernalia?" I demanded.

"You know," she said. "Their moon dials. Whatever protection they're using. Douches. I don't know."

It seemed so passionless, even eerie that a dozen children could have organized a schedule of alternating partnerships. But we had the evidence in my daughter's own round hand—the names of a dozen—six boys, six girls, who were taking turns with each other in bed.

"What bed?" I asked Lauranette.

"They don't have to have a bed," she reminded me.

"But where do they go? If they're so organized they must have somewhere to go."

I thought back to the way Sarah and I had taken our romance into the woods and fields, but this wasn't the season for that. It was getting too cold. In Sonia's text, accommodations seemed to be taken for granted.

"Maybe there's a van," Lauranette suggested, and someone drives circles while the others play. From there her imagination drifted down to squalor and she had them in an abandoned house, then a derelict sedan with mildewed seats in a junkyard and finally in one of those old school buses you see parked by the river with plywood over broken windows and a stovepipe coming out of the roof.

She had it all wrong. These children were well turned out, careful of their shoe leather, particular in their habits, more spoiled than deprived. Which made it the more unlikely that anything like this could be happening.

I had watched two decades of children walk past me into the world, and while the prevailing custom may have shifted back and forth from steadies to playing the field, the old truths held, even in this generation that was making an honest effort to put aside jealousy, competition, possession. And never this, a closed circle of intimates taking turns with each other by the calendar.

I went back to the book looking for something I could have missed that would explain it all away. But the things I *had* missed only made it more mysterious. For instance, the news that Derek Stevens had a "short wick," which I explained to Lauranette was not about size but timing. I thought of Derek, baby faced and without beard, already measured for sexual dysfunction two years before he'd have to hire a tux and waltz one of these young ladies around a gymnasium hung with crepe at his senior prom.

I read through Sonia's book again and again, each time

freshly amazed with her casual erotic perception. In the privacy of her own pages she had a straightforward style and colorful idiom that would have been admired by her teachers in any other context. Though I was shocked and saddened by the promiscuity, I felt completely vindicated in my judgment of her aptitude.

"Derek has a short wick but he's long in his gazes, working with his eyes, and I like to take his picture after he looks at me that way. When we're finished and come out into the night he'll take me for a circle just to let me know he's sorry. And happy. He might just be talking to me about how fast light moves, or the fossil of a cockroach he found last summer in the Grand Canyon." And I was sorry and happy myself, balancing ruin against her chance of happiness.

"Destroy it," Lauranette said. "Burn it."

I refused. I wouldn't let anyone else see the notepad but I might want to go back to it myself. I could see Lauranette was wondering what part of my fascination was the simple curiosity of the voyeur and what that of a worried parent. But the longer I kept Sonia's book, the less pornographic it seemed, and the more gracious in its observation.

It wasn't really a slam book at all. There was none of that harsh, catty criticism. This was a soft record of Sonia's erotic awakening. Against the stark fact of her group's experiment she revealed herself as a calm and forgiving spirit, making mature compromises with chronic disappointments of physical love.

Lauranette was always going to have difficulty warming up to Sonia, though after the episode of the notepad she had a new respect for my daughter's daunting candor. I couldn't fault her impatience with my indulgence for Sonia. Living with me, Lauranette was living with a father's loss.

Sonia missed four days of school, and when she returned she appeared furtive. Her friends were aware of the abnormal attention we faculty were paying them. I guessed she knew her book had been found. Instead of becoming meek or contrite, she and her group stiffened.

I didn't want Sonia punished, or even confronted. I only wanted her warned of her new notoriety, and the fact of her missing book might be warning enough. I knew the faculty were watching my daughter for samples of her practice. Rose Edgar approached me a few days later. "I didn't tell Mr. Lambert," she said, "but you know this is very unusual, very different."

"What's different?"

"The circle-club business. I've never heard of a thing like it. Anywhere. Could you imagine anything so wild? Do you think they have gynecologists? It's a little population for Margaret Mead."

Rose was making me her confidante. To throw me off the trail of her and Lambert? I wondered. Was there anything there? The next time I met her in the hall she did what the children sometimes do, feinted left and right and left, as if to block my way past her. Full of mischief and camaraderie, she brought me to a full stop to chat again about "the Moon Dial kids."

I wasn't pleased to hear her on Sonia's case again. In a time of nationwide distribution of marijuana, amphetamines, barbiturates and acid; in an era of strobes and chemically altered images, how was it, Rose wondered, that sex had become the drug of choice for this ring of River High students. "Really," she said, "don't you think the kids look awfully tired and run-down?"

She was genuinely concerned. She had the impression there was one meeting place. I wasn't ready to believe there could be a single room where the children sat around watching each other's couplings. "No." She tapped my arm, playfully scolding me for a perverse idea. "Not that. A lot of rooms. A motel maybe. You know, actually, I was wondering what you think of all this. I understand the kids take some liberties in your history class."

If this was an accusation, it was made gently. "I only teach juniors and seniors," I reminded her. The children in question knew me only by reputation.

"Yeah," she said, "but in this place behavior works its way down from the top." She wondered if I'd ever suggested a refuge to them or if they'd ever mentioned one to me. "I know you're very protective of their privacy."

It wasn't long before Rose came to see me again. It was just after a terrible class when shrill cries of Chalkman had flown from all corners. She came into the room like a soft savior as I was writing an assignment on the board for the next session.

"I picked you from the start for someone different," she said. "We have a lot to do around here, you and I." I was still writing on the board when she came up beside me, took my chalk hand and began to guide it like a primary teacher leading a child in capitals, with a tremor, her fingers moist and warm.

DON'T GIVE UP. FIGHT BACK.

I had a strong urge to give in to her intimate advice, to pillow my humiliation against her sympathetic flesh. But there were feet shuffling through the hallway. And I was uncomfortable with her assumption that a problem existed. I stared blankly into her open face as she slid away from me and out of the room, frightened perhaps by how much she'd offered and by my stony reticence.

That season we learned one of our students was an innocent-faced narcotics agent. A list of his accused was circulated among the faculty. There were widespread dismissals and three prosecutions. Lauranette said I went too far when I stood in front of my history class and announced, "When police patrol the academy, ideas are trampled. Agents poison our playgrounds with their schemes of entrapment."

I'd become a little reckless, not afraid of anyone in that

school, not even the overgrown, whiskered troublemakers who had come toward my car from the industrial-arts wing—three white, two black. I was in the school parking lot having a brown bag lunch. I looked into my bag for something to offer them, and rolled down the window. They'd had a bad deal, branded so early as unsuited for the academic track.

"Hey, Mr. History," one of them said. "You got anything for the head?"

"Stomach," I said, holding a ham and lettuce out the window.

"Get that poison outa my face." One of them slapped my offering to the ground, stinging my hand. "You think we're poor?" He walked over to the scattered sandwich and mashed it on the pavement with his heel.

They were leaving when one of them did something I'd never seen before. It was the boy who had threatened Sonia with his "thing." He appeared to be walking toward me but was actually moving backward as if on a treadmill drawing him away. As I stared, his legs and feet were contradicting each other. And the next moment his head seemed to move toward me in elastic defiance of his shoulders which tended away with his friends. In the next few months I saw others working on these rubbery illusions in the halls. Including my daughter. A decade later the same routines appeared on television.

The next fall Sonia was in my junior English classroom. Sarah had tried to shift her to a Winchester school, but Richard wouldn't allow it. For one thing, he'd told her, Sonia was due to be taught by "old Mr. Sykes." Sarah, softer and less self-assured, even a little trembly, told me as much in a brief sidewalk encounter. "You see?" she said. "That's all you mean to Richard. I'm still trusting you to keep it that way."

I was determined to make the class something special that year. I introduced them to the maps of the Whole World Mall that my history class had brought up to date. And I let them turn the hours they spent there into something useful. They kept a different kind of notebook this time, a journal of their attendance in the mall at Ripton Corner. It was their touchstone, the home base where their circles around the city began and ended.

This was the season I'd hoped to know my daughter. With the full license of a teacher I'd examine her beliefs and know her talents. We'd exchange ideas, even laugh together under the cover of classroom duty. But the day I assigned their mall diaries I passed behind Sonia as she threw her books into her hall locker. "Why can't he stay out of our lives?" she said. Under her breath she called me a motherfucker. Unable to separate the vulgarity from its truth, I walked past without comment.

Each week Sonia and her circle whistled on their way to Friday, content in the knowledge that I never failed anyone. She was quiet, orderly and careful not to show enthusiasm for her work or for anything I said.

One morning I asked her class: "If you knew who cut down the school flagpole and shoved it through the window of Mr. Lambert's office, would it be your duty to tell?"

"Was the American flag on it?" a girl asked back.

"It was at night," I reminded her.

"Then I don't think we should have to tell," she said.

They wanted to take a vote. We had a show of hands. A slim majority thought it would be their duty to report the vandal. Sonia had refused to show her hand. "What about it?" I asked her. She looked startled and angry, as if I'd slapped her face.

"Yes, it would be my duty," she said. "But no, I wouldn't tell anyway." I excused her confusion of allegiance as strength in defiance of my curiosity.

Lauranette was growing more wary of the apologies I made

for Sonia. I could guess what she'd thought up to that point but had been too kind to say—that my daughter was an amiable little slut, passing through school without effort, learning little and caring less, affectionate and fornicating without shame, and destined for a very insignificant life.

It would have been better if she could have come right out and said that. As it was I had to argue against insinuation. "Why isn't loitering against the law in those malls?" she asked. "We were never allowed to stand around in front of stores."

I had a ready answer. "The malls are shopping parks. The halls are greenswards, only paved with tile. You've seen the benches everywhere. You're supposed to sit around. Are you trying to say something about Sonia?"

"You're the one who spies on kids," she said. "When they leave school, let them go home." Lauranette thought my extra interest in the children only made them nervous. But she took me in her arms, and said she understood my misery, that I must feel like a parent who has given a baby up for adoption. She could see me carrying my suffering to the end. I pulled away from her.

The next week I took something else of Sonia's. I was in her homeroom after the buses had gone. I walked in with no special purpose, and found myself going straight to her desk. I stood there for a while thinking of the excitement of the children who sat around her each day and the angle from which her eyes would defy her teacher in front. A moment later I was rummaging through the space under her seat. There were crumpled papers, Kleenex, broken pencils and several textbooks she should have taken home with her. In the mess there was a blue three-by-five notebook. I flipped through its pages, and seeing it was filled with Sonia's script, stuffed it in my pocket.

When I got home Lauranette was spinning with her own

news, very excited about a man she'd met that afternoon, a mall artist who had been working his way up through North Carolina into Virginia. Norentez, he called himself. She'd seen pictures of his work and heard firsthand reports of his unusual talent.

In Durham he had painted the serpentine ceiling of the Black Snake Mall. A miracle of artistic engineering, Lauranette said, because as light played through the glass ceiling there, it looked as if canoeists were moving down his rendering of the Nantahala River. That commission had led to two more extraordinary works, a triptych of an Appalachian deer hunt in Richmond; and in Charlottesville, a map of a public golf course which shimmered when an automatic ventilating system shifted the angle of the window glass.

Now he had set up his scaffolding at the Whole World Mall, where he was expected to be for most of a year, maybe longer, to paint the central ceiling. A great find, Lauranette thought, for the "Tumbleweed" show. The trouble was Norentez had refused to talk on the air. In fact it had taken a great deal of coaxing to make him talk about himself at all. He'd said some very strange things though, and afterward she had taped a program of her own about the man. She wanted me to hear it right away.

"I have some reading I have to do," I said. "Schoolwork," feeling the notepad in my pocket. I was leaving the room but she pushed me back in my chair.

"You're listening to this," she said.

I couldn't see why she was trying to flog an ordinary mall artist into a Michelangelo. She pushed the button of her tape machine as if she were playing the first note of a piano sonata, and I sat back, resigned.

After details of trials and accomplishments, Lauranette had her artist in a huge shopping city she called Locust Blossom Plaza. It was a thinly disguised version of our own Whole World Mall at Ripton Corner, where shiny steel buttresses supported the silver columns that rose four stories and carried the vast network of glass in metal casing above and around thirty acres of floor space.

Why the disguise at all? Simply because Roberto Norentez had insisted, she explained. But where else was there a revolving restaurant of glass atop a great concrete pillar from which you could look east to Washington National Cathedral or west to our government's mountain nuclear retreat depending on what minute of the afternoon you were seated for a cocktail?

Lauranette's taped voice was saying: "Some people find their open spaces in the middle of crowds. They go sporting in shopping centers. Playing sardines in the changing rooms of Sears and Penney's. I'm talking about young people."

I asked her to turn it off. "This doesn't end well."

"We're just getting to the interesting part," she said.

"Not now," I insisted.

"It's not what you think."

"Affirmation of a developer's dream? Commerce made whole by fine art? Children in trouble? Why don't you just tell me?"

She wouldn't. "I want you to hear it. You'll be fascinated."

"Later," I said, pushing past her, up the steps to my bedroom. I took off my shoes and lay back against a pillow to read from the treasure I'd been fondling in my pocket.

I had heard a chemistry teacher call Sonia "hum brain" in front of several of her friends. Neither angry nor defiant, she had looked into his eyes with a kind of sympathy and told him, "You're cute, Dr. Science," and then turned to her pals to ask them, "Isn't he cute?"

The man was dumbfounded, blushing. Even in a classroom there was no way to shame her. She had this disarming way of shifting the field of battle from the intellect to romance—to little contests of charm where the numbers were all in her favor.

Still unafraid of teachers or principal, she rode complacently over their scorn, smiling at her C's. I wanted to believe that her estimation of her teachers had a more humane base—their worthiness of affection. As I began to read her notebook, I was looking for the grade she might have given me. It was another small, spiral-bound kind the children were supposed to keep their assignments in. On the very first page was a note to one of the girls in her circle club.

Carol,

Couldn't get this to you last period. Blue Gums was watching too close. My parents were at it again last night. They're so dishonest. Thank God we're not like that. If we think something, we say it. If we want something, we touch it.

I heard Dad tell my mother she acts like his thing is a cactus. And then they pretend there's nothing wrong. They're going to a marriage counselor, and they call him a chiropractor. Did Michael tell you what we tried Friday night?

I slapped the page. The private life of the Plesses, reflected through Sonia, was suddenly upside down. I'd waited all those years for this kind of news about Richard and Sarah, and now I lay back on my bed, a little surprised at the pity I felt for them. But what I read strengthened my right to be Sonia's guardian. What kind of talk was that for Richard to be using in her earshot? It saddened me that she referred to Rhonda Blay, one of the best in the math department, as Blue Gums. I wondered what Sonia had tried with Michael, another seemingly ordinary child, drifting through school without effort.

Jumping ahead I saw that most of the contents were notes written to Sonia's friends. By using her assignment book she could pass her little letters while appearing to deal in legitimate school information. I flipped back and forth in the notebook until I found my name.

It's so weird with Sykes always watching. Mom says he was always dizzy about malls. Like telling us they're giants who gobble up farmland and kidnap children. And the boy who spent so much time in Quarter Heaven another galaxy claimed him and he never got home. Well, he is clever. Did you know he used to teach my mother. He's ancient!

Guess what? Mom told Rita she's got Dad's nose. She's not picking at it all the time, just feeling to see how big it is. She won't say anything about the circle stuff. Anyway she's not talking to Mom ever again.

I skipped further ahead, put off by the juvenilia but fascinated by every mention of the circle and looking for some meaning behind that incredible go-around of love. Lauranette still thought it was a pitiful descent into wanton sexuality, and that my attempt to treat it as the ultimate sophistication was only further apology for Sonia's erotic path to self-destruction.

As I read on, Sonia's notes became less petulant, less critical of parents and teachers, less given to the whine of us-against-them, and more analytical. The very last entry was a marvel.

Carol,

How did twelve of us get into this? I think when you told me it was okay to take Don's picture the other cameras heard about it and wanted a shot of the same scenery. Maybe it's our way of saying life isn't a photo contest. You know how Mrs. Blay says there's more than one kind of geometry? That's the way I think of it. If you're not Euclid, parallel lines can get together. So when we look at the world the lines bend a little. We can all meet. Good old Blue Gums!

I don't know how long Lauranette had been watching me. "What have you got there?" she asked. I was getting up to put the assignment book in my bureau. Not satisfied with my "Aw, nuthin'," she took it from me to have a look for herself. She took it downstairs and I remained in the bedroom, lying down, waiting for trouble.

Lauranette must have read through the whole thing. It was a half hour before she came bounding up the stairs again and stood in the doorway, shaking her head. "You've got to be stopped," she said. "You're trying to collect her whole life in your sock drawer. What does this make you, keeping all this stuff?" She threw the notepad on the bed. "Do you think anyone would understand? I want you to burn that and all the papers, too. And her mother's stuff with it."

It *was* getting to be a very strange collection, but in it there were remarkable observations, evidence of two flexible minds, mother's and daughter's, making extraordinary connections.

"You're not giving Sonia any room to turn in." How was I ever going to see a different side of her, Lauranette wanted to know. "Assuming there is one. She doesn't have a moment's privacy with all your snooping. Besides, the real story's still down there on the tape. You're going to have to hear it sometime."

"They don't seem concerned with privacy," I said. "That's what I can't understand. How could she leave something like this hanging around where anyone could find it."

Lauranette led me back down to the living room, got me seated beside the tape machine again, and said, "Don't move until this is finished."

The program she'd prepared had too much introductory

material. I had to hear again that her make-believe Locust Blossom Plaza was the largest shopping complex in the world. "Why don't you just call it the Whole World Mall and be done with it?"

"Would you please keep quiet and listen?" So I heard about the best names in fashion, silver, and jewelry. Nationwide catalog companies. All under a great glass canopy of a neo-Gothic crystal palace. Not to mention the restaurants of seven nations scattered through the maze of halls, along with more than a dozen fast-food franchises. Pizza, beer in mugs, root beer in mugs, ice-cream soda in mugs, fish and chips, very thin hamburgers, truly everything.

Lauranette's fascination with the mall, so much different from my own, seemed to excuse every excess. She went on about the magnificent diversity of the place. She put a finger to her lips as we listened to her taped voice turn cautionary. In spite of the inclusiveness, the great variety of merchandise and food, there was a surplus of space, evidence of miscalculation, areas hidden behind sheetrock partitions when a department store or smaller retailer failed. She was suddenly like a student, answering a question on one of my tests.

The recorded Lauranette was explaining how there would always be lost leases, shifting tenancies, and merchants who gambled beyond the margin of common sense while the real woman held me fast to the sofa. What she really wanted me to hear was still to come. All about the fallow footage hidden by bright posters on drywall—space that had become the secret playground of mice and children.

"This won't work on the air," I said, guessing what was ahead.

"Who says it won't? You haven't heard anything yet." Her eyes flashed, and she pressed the stop button, waiting for an argument from me. I raised my hands and surrendered to the rest of her program. These were obviously things she'd been thinking about for a long time, long before she'd met the mall artist.

She pressed start. There was a girl named Sally whose father didn't trust her beyond his driveway. Sally wouldn't compete in school. She was affectionate everywhere. Sally floated free, and sang with her radio: "One, two, three, what are we fighting for?" She did fast circles around the Beltway in older boys' cars. To go even faster, or sometimes slower, they used little capsules, any color of the rainbow. The color was their clue to what would happen to the speed of their hearts.

"Sonia doesn't do drugs," I whispered. Lauranette pressed stop. She wasn't going to let me miss another word of her tape.

"How would you know?"

"Who is this Sally?"

Start. Sally runs a string of six boys, or they run her. She shares the six young men with five of her girlfriends. They can't take each other home. You can see them on parade in the mall. They stand girl's back to boy's front, his arms around her, hands on her belly, an embrace tolerated by mall security. They might stay that way for an hour. A little bit like turtles. Watch them and they don't move, turn your back for a minute and they've disappeared.

Now the artist. "So full of confidence the man thinks he can paint anything." The glass ceiling was going to be the mirror of our community. Norentez has a peaceful vision, a happy crowd shopping and sporting, bright clothes and flowers, long hair, some neat, some tousled.

He starts by painting a fabric shop, delighted by the brilliant and variegated bolts of material, then does a restaurant, a red-and-white pattern of checkered tablecloths against a black-and-white mosaic of floor tiles. There are crowds in tank tops, business suits, shorts and halters, pastel summer dresses, raising forks of chicken pie and pizza, licking popsicles or ice-cream cones, or saluting with mugs of beer.

On across the central ceiling he paints, pleasing people with his skill and with their own lives. Not the crude treatments you might find in a high school auditorium or possibly on the walls of a Greek restaurant. "To appreciate this"—Lauranette's voice on the tape was breathy—"you have to imagine the brightest work of Renoir, then give it a perspective and scale that could make men marvel a hundred feet below the colored surface."

Lauranette watched me chafing at this overblown praise of a mall artist. She stopped her machine again. "Stop fidgeting. Sit still." She said she was asking me for the last time. "If you think I'm kidding about this, you're wrong. You're listening to my work. This is what I do." She glared and I sat chastened for the better part of an hour, held not just by her warning but by her outlandish story.

The reels turn again. Lauranette is asking us to imagine Norentez lying on his back, painting a figure leaning over a balcony with his hand in the spray of a fountain. Water splashing out of bounds appears to threaten the atrium below. The people skirt wider around the fountain, dodging an imagined shower.

From his cherry-picker platform over the mall's central hall the artist maneuvers himself over the area where Sears and Penney's rub elbows with Bloomingdale's and FAO Schwarz. He finds himself staring over a darkness segregated from the bustle and color of the active halls by tall partitions of gypsum board. Squinting into that blighted space, he sees it is actually the aisles and counters of a failed department store. Shifting farther he brings himself over a line of small enclosures that must have been changing rooms.

There was movement in the small chambers. As his eyes adjusted to the faint light he saw a half-dozen couples in naked embrace, each in their own quarters. From his high perch, Norentez heard no murmur or moaning. Silence freed the scene of prurience, left him shameless, filled with admiration. He was watching the moving illustrations of a modern Kama Sutra, the flesh and hair tumbling below him.

Norentez had found joy in the scene. Why stop love? Without leering he observed the easy motions of the young people under his view. If the six pairs were in adjoining rooms they must be aware of each other. It seemed very organized to him, like the children's baseball leagues. If not for the sport, you would have suspected adult supervision. As the artist went back to work across the ceiling he decided that in America, if the greatest wonders of business and affection existed side by side, you should not be too much surprised. When he moved out over the changing rooms again the children were gone. He was happy for them that they had completed their lovemaking and escaped and that he had not disturbed them.

The next day Norentez moved his mechanical platform several times around the great central hall, again moving over the dark changing rooms. For two days they were empty but on the third evening he watched from on high as six couples entered the cubicles and began to undress. Though they could easily see his scaffold moving over them, they must have supposed they were hidden in the darkness. and they were unaware of the small cracks in his platform from which he observed the scene below him.

The children moved without haste into the preliminaries of their gentle acts. There were two sets of blond hair together this time, though before the hair had been easily differentiated in each couple. Either the artist was seeing new people here or the same group of young men and women had changed partners.

Several days later they came to their love chambers again, and Norentez was convinced that he now recognized them all by the angles and curves of their naked bodies, the set of their shoulders and hips, by the personalities projected in the tilt of their necks, the gestures of their arms and wrists, by the hang of their breasts and buttocks. He knew by then that he was dealing with the same twelve people, and they were in the habit of sharing each other.

I was enthralled by Lauranette's wild treatment. She was performing way beyond her customary program style, inspired by the scenes she imagined her artist would be painting. Either that, or she was reaching out in a brand-new way to make me see Sonia in this Sally character.

The tape spun on. From his far perch Norentez still found no shame in the children, only grace in their intimacy. He wanted to bring their secret from the floors of their dark rooms onto the public ceiling, to make it no more or less remarkable than all the other planes of color with which he explained the world beneath him. He'd have to work quickly. If his new subject were reported too early he might be sent away.

Norentez, according to Lauranette's fantasy, wanted to make it all as natural as sunlight and blue sky. He wasn't trying for the ecstasies of gaping mouths or the shock of abnormal play, though the children had amazed him with their versatility. He wanted it seen that these compartments were the changing rooms of a once-grand department store, and that instead of try-ing on clothes, the young people were simply trying on each other. Part of the social commerce of the mall.

The artist worked through a night sketching in six attitudes of love, each enclosed in its own square room. Before the first shopper entered the mall the next morning, he draped sheets from the ceiling, covering the new work, and he slept through that day, not painting again until closing time. If the coupling figures, white and pink, and draped in one another's arms stirred him erotically he painted over the offending surface until his groin was still. He was attempting the impossible, Lauranette said, a chaste still life of flesh at love.

Norentez had struggled with the same problem in each chamber, and watching his progress was like viewing a scrambled television channel showing a blue movie, the painted bodies bending back and forth between distortion and clarity. When the scene became too clear he mussed the defining edges avoiding what he saw in favor of what might be allowed.

In the end he had one room where there had been six, filled with flesh and discarded clothes. In the middle of the night he tore away the sheets covering the work. When the doors of the mall opened in the morning he came down from his scaffold. He bought a farmer's cap that said Hy-Brid Ten and a T-shirt that said Boogie Till You Puke, and disguised in these, he walked around with the first shoppers of the day.

When the mall manager came to ask him "What have you done to my roof?" he found the painter slumped on a bench in the atrium looking up at his work in despair.

"I wrote the truth on your glass," Norentez said, "and then I ruined it. Now it's only mud in your eye."

A woman asked, "Aren't they in body stockings?" Another thought it was lessons in modern dance, "or maybe just a promotion." Somebody told a girlfriend, "God! They look like they're doing it."

"I want that off of there," the manager said. "What is it, anyway?"

Lauranette's voice on the tape trailed off.

"That's it," she said. "This is me, Lauranette. Sitting next to you. Don't just nod. Say something. Do you want to hear it again? What do you think?"

There was something wrong with the end of the tape, something stilted, not her way of talking at all. And I saw through it to Lauranette's sense of corruption beneath what she'd recorded. The artist may have seen the children guileless and free but not Lauranette. She saw danger and brooding in their game.

"How much of this did you make up? How much did he tell

you?" I was sure she'd heard a few things, then ginned up the unbelievable tale from her own wild imagination.

"What does it matter? All my audience wants is a good story."

"I'm your audience. You can't play that on the radio."

"Maybe. Maybe not."

Tomorrow night, I told her, we'll go to Ripton Corner and find out what's really happening on the mall's ceiling.

I was still thinking of Sonia's household, of what was happening there that had turned my daughter into a malcontent. The academic apathy. The incredible social experiment. For all her display of indifference it was clear from the notebook she wanted peace between her parents. For this to happen it seemed that Richard would have to renounce the president of the United States and Sarah would have to stop serving the family three-day casseroles.

Sonia's notebook made me sorry for Richard. As I read on, I, too, hoped for reconciliation, but Sonia's attention in her notes had swerved back to mall activities. In a message to her circle mate Sandra Boettinger, she said she'd like to switch Wednesdays and Fridays with her, and there was the first mention of "R." "R has had this really incredible life," she wrote. "He wants to put us in his work."

When Lauranette had finished the notebook, she said it was about a lost childhood. The way she saw it, Sonia had passed beyond the excitements of a young woman into the weary awareness of idle middle age. In Sarah and Richard's squabbles, Lauranette found at least a spark of hope. They were at least alive with grievances and expectations. But for Sonia she saw an early jading. What would happen when this unbelievable game of hers was over? And who was this "R"? An older man?

I was more frightened than angered by what Lauranette had said. "That sort of thing doesn't rub off on the skin! She isn't finished! She has brilliant opportunities. Anything can happen. Are you writing off our own daughter?"

"Our daughter?"

I moved behind Lauranette, very close, with my arms around her, the way she'd described the public embraces of the children in the mall, and with a gentle squeeze I asked: "We're as good as married, aren't we?"

And just as gently she said, "No." But she turned to me, her eyes pleading communion. Button and zipper, we obliged one another, and as if in one of the changing rooms we'd heard about, we fell to the floor beside our pile of clothes. Without prolonging anything or searching for extras we hurried blindly and rested again a few minutes later in each other's loving gaze. Nothing more was said about marriage.

"It's Friday. Why wait for tomorrow. Let's go tonight." She was all for it. We dressed and got ready for the ride to Ripton Corner. Lauranette was fussing a little too long, I thought, with her hair and face. And I tried on different shirts until I felt a casual neatness.

On the way a string of six helicopters came thumping the air over us, heading toward Washington from the government's bunker under our mountain. I began to curse generals and bureaucrats, the ones who were advertising the notion of survivability. She moved closer to me, but I was thinking about the end of the world.

"No middle ground," she said. "Either we shout like fools or feel sheepish."

"You've got your radio show," I said. "Why don't you say something about it?" When she refused to speak I said, "We're all sheep aren't we, all going down the same lane."

"What do you mean by that?"

"I mean we're right in the middle of a line of cars, all of us heading for the center of suburban pacification. When was the last time you heard of any disturbance at the Whole World Mall? There isn't any. Maybe a little shoplifting. But all very quiet and quietly dealt with."

On the mall issue she was way ahead of me: Malls were the people's choice and meant to be appreciated on those terms.

"They scrape the chewing gum off the floors every night," I said. "The halls are spotless. The air is conditioned. All fashion on parade, high and low."

"Why do you have to be the country's conscience?" she asked.

"The chain hamburgers get thinner and softer and the crepes at Fancy Français get thicker and harder," I went on. "All under the same roof system. Even the food converges to a single shape and consistency. We're so obligingly homogenized. One movie a year, one book, one place to hang out."

"You know the odd truth?" she said. "You can find hundred-percent cotton things there. You just have to go to Penney's or Sears instead of the pretentious places. I know what's really bothering you. You want to know how Sonia got from the little girl you saw bending over to tie that first bowknot on her Mary Janes to this charming sleep-about that you claim as your daughter while you disown her behavior."

"I haven't disowned anything."

"That's not really the point. You think you missed the changes. You think if she'd been in your house you'd have seen what was happening. You'd have been there to prevent it. Let me tell you something about children. They have secrets. They have them long before they reach puberty. Without them they wouldn't exist; you'd be inside their heads, driving them crazy. You think it's just you who doesn't know Sonia. Believe me, nobody knows Sonia. That comes later and incompletely." She'd surprised herself with this sudden passionate speech.

"And let me tell you something else," she said. "I think you're living for a day that's never coming, a day when you and Sonia weep together and tell each other everything. That's fantasy. It won't happen. You're not that cruel."

She'd been thinking a long time about this, gone a step further than I had with the scenario, and it irked me. Not because she'd reached a conclusion, but because it cast me in an impotent light, incapable of a grand final act.

III

IN THE
WHOLE WORLD

That girls at puberty may find
The first Adam in their thought,
Shut the door of the Pope's chapel,
Keep those children out.
There on that scaffolding reclines
Michael Angelo . . .

—*W. B. YEATS*

The glass towers of the Whole World Mall came into sight. We stopped talking and marveled as we always did at the hugeness of the place, the acres of cars. On the great billboard we read:

ROBERTO NORENTEZ

PAINTS OUR SKY

EVERY DAY

10:00 A.M.—7:30 P.M.

The traffic was unusually heavy. There were police at each intersection struggling against the suburban chaos, snappish as the drivers. The idea of a traffic jam so far from the center of a city made people angry.

The mall was teeming. We came in a side-court entrance and zigzagged our way through the crowd, passing a lot of smaller shops. Went all the way up to the fourth level, and even here the passageways leading to the balcony over the great atrium were clogged with people. There was very little movement. We went farther around the perimeter halls, hoping to come down a less crowded spoke toward the center, but there was no easy approach.

A moment later, over the heads of a small group of teen-agers pressing next to me, I was staring directly into the eyes of my daughter! No surprise that she was in the mall, only that among those thousands of people we should have found each other. Her look was neither of kindness nor contempt but a momentary amusement. She smiled and disappeared into the throng behind her, and I forgave her her embarrassment. I heard myself say quite distinctly, "Sonia will shine on. The mall is not unhealthy," trying to convince myself. I kept repeating it like a wise man discovering a soothing mantra.

Pushing through the crowd we gained the balcony, and there at the center on all levels and on the floor of the atrium people were staring up at the ceiling and the artist still on his scaffold, and we gazed up with the rest at the great expanse of glass he had already colored. At first glance I wasn't over-whelmed. From this angle it was nothing like the magical work Lauranette had described. A panorama of our landscape with the huge mall at the center exposed in all its gaudy commotion.

Starting from a dim red light on the western mountain, Nor-entez had painted the rolling countryside. Beyond the mall he'd moved over the plain to the Beltway and eastern skyline and the cathedral tower. Entertaining, I admitted, though a little static. That was before we began to move slowly down to the atrium itself, and saw that everything changed as we went. By the time we reached the lower floor I was wondering at the complexity of the accomplishment, at the way the coloring and activities had shifted as we'd moved, the same glass sections revealing one figure, then another, depending on where we stood.

Norentez was painting at the southern edge, showing a line of soldiers, a perimeter design of rifle and helmet at the border. The land within was planted in undulating rows of ramblers like the fields of corn beyond them. Connecting links of macadam, dotted with bright autos, worked in parallels and crosses. The artist must have known what an extraordinary thing he was doing, and he must have been exhausted.

There was something else Lauranette hadn't mentioned on her tape, a sense that I could walk into the ceiling and it would accept my three dimensions. A man beside me said, "You know those picture cards, it looks like you can see into them? That's the trick he's using." Refusing to be ignored, he got in front of my face and said, "It's temporary, you know. It's got to come down. They say there's girls nekkid in it. Can you see it? The nekkid ones?"

I was scanning the ceiling, looking for the depiction of a changing room, when I suddenly found Sonia's face over me, rapt, as if the artist had caught her in meditation. By standing absolutely still and looking through the corner of my eye I began to see the tangled limbs of more bodies. Trying to isolate individual forms and attitudes was like trying to make all the sisters of the Pleiades twinkle at once. If I went at it head-on and with determination, the light of one or several destroyed perception of the rest. But as I stared upward, Sonia's complete shape came gradually into harmonious relief, her figure straddled over another body. She seemed to be preoccupied with something beyond her partner, some quiet thought that had nothing to do with physical excitement.

Then, as easily as she had arrived, she disappeared, all but her face; the tangle of arms and legs became unsortable again, and I saw that Norentez had created, by some marvelous graded penetration of the glass surface, and by superimposition, a mix of partnerships, none of which could be made to lie still and content. I tried to bring Sonia forward again but she wouldn't come out of the crowd, and a moment later Lauranette was calling, "Over here! Quick!" She was jabbing my chest and telling me she'd just seen Sonia disappear.

"So did I," I said. "Isn't it amazing?" But she didn't mean

the Sonia on the ceiling. She meant the one who, she said, had just vanished behind a wall.

"Which store?"

"No store. There wasn't even a door." Lauranette was pulling me toward a high, temporary wall decorated with the mall's globe insignia, the usual indication of vacant space waiting for a new lease. "All of a sudden she was just gone!"

Reaching the wall, I saw that Sonia must have slipped into the opening between overlapping sections of gypsum board, and we followed. It was darker back there and we stumbled into sawhorses, plaster pails and scraps of lumber before our eyes adjusted. There were more temporary walls, and we began to weave our way in and out of the maze they made. A short time later, we couldn't tell which way we had come from.

Our laughter brought giggles from someplace ahead and we moved on, pleased to be caught in their fun house. I asked Lauranette, "Where are you?" and a boy's voice beyond mimicked, "Where are you?"

"Here I am." Lauranette pinched me from behind and broke into more tinkling laughter. And then a girl's voice did an imitation, "Here I am, heh heh heh heh."

A whole group shrieked with glee. I imagined them scattering like mice. Chastened into silence we worked our way in and out of the freestanding walls until we came to a large, open area lined with a row of doors on one side and a long, glass storefront on the other. There, leaning against the glass as if she'd been waiting for us, was Sonia. She looked us over casually, came up to Lauranette as if she were an old friend, and said, "The rooms you're looking for are over there. Instead of following us around, why don't you use one?"

"The thing is," I said afterward, "there wasn't any meanness in it." It had been quite matter-of-fact, Lauranette agreed, but that was the disquieting thing about Sonia, her canny understanding.

Sonia had turned away from us and walked through the glass door of the empty store behind her. We watched for several minutes, and when she didn't return we decided she must have her own exit in the rear.

We moved along the other wall, opening the doors she had pointed to, looking in all of the six changing rooms. They were bare but for a single pair of socks. They were a girl's, the one-size-fits-all kind. Lauranette picked them up with two fingers. She was holding them out to me when a bright light hit us from above. Looking up, we were able to see all the way to the painted glass. Norentez was perched at the edge of his mechanical scaffold, looking down into our compartment.

"Why do you keep mumbling that?" Lauranette snapped at me.

"Mumbling what?"

"That Sonia will shine on. That the mall is healthy. All that stuff."

We fled from the overhead light with the socks. Later Lauranette said I should put them in the high school lost-and-found and see who claimed them. But I was taking them home. They wound up in the bureau drawer with the other things.

After some confusion we had found our way back to the atrium. I kept looking at that panel on the ceiling where Sonia had come and gone. As we walked toward an exit hall I said, "What's drawn is drawn. We're the ones who are shifting perspective. It's just like history."

"Are you suggesting that Sonia's development has been misinterpreted? Whatever she's going to be, Ray, it's beyond your control." Lauranette was quite upset with me.

"No, I mean his colors aren't moving. We are. If you see her as a floozy, that's just where you're standing. They won't destroy this. They'll be talking about it for a long time to come." The public-address system was asking us to consider sales in stores on the second level and to remember that the Whole World would be closing in half an hour. I hung back, trying to make more happen on the ceiling, trying to make Sonia come forward and lie still.

There was some question that spring about Sonia's passing on to her senior year. At the faculty session where the fates of seven faltering juniors were determined I stood for the promotion of every one of them, perhaps to better shield the special plea I was making for my daughter. I knew that several of the students had never even satisfied freshman standards.

"I'm not sure the parents really care in her case," Lambert told the meeting. "I wonder if we should let Sonia think we're no more concerned than they are. Would we be doing her any favor by telling her that life is so easy?"

"How easy?" Rhonda Blay asked mischievously. Lambert called for order. I could see them turning against Sonia. Not that they really disliked her; she had been so calm in her unconcern with their curriculum, so polite in her absolute disregard of their academic wishes for her, so adept in excusing her delinquency with charm. But they saw a threat to order in her indifference and beauty.

I rose to make my case counting on that ancient secret of the pedagogue—the desire to be rid of the insubordinate, to raise the incorrigible beyond one's reach or responsibility, to promote the dunce.

"I happen to know," I said, "that the parents are very concerned. Still, are we here to judge the parents or the child? Of course Sonia isn't your ordinary student. She hasn't performed well." I was looking straight at Lambert, unflinching. "But what would we gain by holding her back. Wouldn't it just be a punishment, a detention?" I turned. "What about in algebra, Mrs. Blay? Wouldn't we just be turning a potential scholar into a rebellious prisoner?

"I've seen examples of her writing," I went on. The meeting broke into uncontrolled hilarity. Sonia's English aptitude is remarkable, I told them. She could shine in anyone's class, in any subject. After more assurances of Sonia's hidden talents, I sat down pleased with my defense, my heart beating quickly against the probability of failure.

I hadn't been aware that I had an ally in the room. It was Rose Edgar of all people, whom I'd always suspected of being something more than a pet of Lambert. She got up and said, "I back Ray in this a hundred percent," and smiled at me. I wanted to hug her. "But he didn't go far enough. Let's not sit on this child's life at the wrong time. Let her move on with her peers. Let her find herself." She finished and Lambert stood again, nodding at me. "I think maybe you were right about her, Ray." Whatever had been going on under the table, the result was wonderful. Sonia was promoted to the senior class. I wanted her and Sarah to know the great news right away. Rose was standing in front of me winking as if we'd engineered a devilish scam.

School started before Labor Day in 1974. It was something about making up for snow days before they happened, before winter was anywhere near. I thought it was just taxpayers demanding more for the buck from the county in child-custody services, though to be fair we had a school board that had just approved another revision of my local-history text critical of the same board's own cumbersome procedures. I was walking close to the edge of their displeasure.

I had quite a following, I thought, as the author of that irreverent book. And I was proud to be the man who slept, unmarried, with the soft voice of Home Town Radio. As much as anything now I wanted the admiration of the new seniors.

I went strutting through the village with Lauranette at my side, thinking my achievement and tenure could protect me forever. And many people tried to look the other way, to make allowances, to let my habits ride. Perfectly nice people, content in fields or happy in their commute, hardworking parents of children in my care, all trying to be polite, though it must have been awkward for them.

I'd had this vision of bringing home Sonia's papers with the hundreds of others I was obliged to comment on. Poring over hers with special attention, I'd draw her out (back to the true meaning of educate, from the Latin *educere*, to lead forth, and all just an old fogy's cant to her). She hadn't let me lead her anywhere, hadn't given me a single paper with enough substance to correct or praise.

As she began her senior year, Sonia was still refusing to step ahead. I knew that good students might merely memorize while the best ones could memorize and connect. This time I was going to force Sonia to show her classmates she had both these talents. Her circle was going to know who she really was.

In my Stilson history class I let the children seat themselves, then ordered the last row to change places with the first row, the second row to switch with the next to last, and so on, until everyone had moved except those in the very middle. Without appearing to single out Sonia, who had tried for a remote position, I had her only three rows away, in the center.

She looked cheated as I stared out over all the subdued faces and began to present my unwritten syllabus for the course. "Nobody's drifting through this class in a canoe," I said.

"The materials are simple. Sure, you have a textbook and I wrote it. So what? You live in the middle of your subject. All you have to do is look around you. You can travel a long way in Stilson."

I'd practiced for this, hoping to make it a performance Sonia wouldn't forget. All eyes were on me. "Who knows what year this school was integrated? Who knows who built the house you live in?" No takers. "What happened when the federals wanted to put the interstate through the Rogers farm, and the state wanted it on the other side of the county, and the county didn't want it at all?" All of them, struck dumb. "All right then, who knows what the frost-free planting season is here?" My voice had been carrying into the hall, but still no volunteers.

Lambert was suddenly standing in the doorway. I waved him off, and he shook his head, closed the door and went away. I let it roll off my tongue—news of their county they hadn't thought about before. Forty nonstop minutes. I was going strong. There should have been a recording for Lauranette, a match for her story of Norentez. I was taking Sonia and her classmates from the red light over the nuclear bunker in the Blue Ridge to the red light in the Washington Cathedral tower, and making all the stops along the way, including their beloved mall. As the artist had done I was treating them to another version of their landscape.

"There's a hole out there in the mountain," I said. "Don't fall in. You could drop onto two hundred million Social Security numbers. Not a soft landing. Busloads of workers go underground there every day. A twenty-four-hour operation. Who'll be down for the lucky shift? Know what I mean?"

Hands shot up for that one, but I wasn't ready for their news yet. I was in control of the room, entertaining Sonia. Still, this wasn't history, this was future-gloom. I gestured hand-over-hand as if climbing out of the survivalists' cave onto the side of the mountain. Where the Sky Meadows communards had kept fine gardens until private tics and desires had sent them spinning out to settle in the cracks left to them by the society in the valley.

I brought them down the mountain to a sawmill that had been destroyed by a band of Civil War marauders who had shifted sides as convenience dictated. Choosing a side hadn't been easy around here. "If you think you come from a Confederate family," I said, "bring some proof to class." (Some came back later, bristling with notes signed by their parents or grand-parents, though not one had so much as a uniform, insignia, or any remnant of battlefield gear or even an old letter.)

I moved them down the valley to Dairyland, where con-trolled breeding by artificial insemination had produced a prize herd with the most bountiful udders, though the actual prosper-ity of the farm, camouflaged by the great wealth of the owner, might be as artificial as the lovemaking of its livestock.

Moving them all, perhaps transporting Sonia, I led them east, into the county seat and our nineteenth-century courthouse, past the sheriff's barracks and over the Piedmont, where a Saudi with a thousand acres was building a stone castle to assert that wealth has the last laugh on mere imperialism.

And then past the land of an American self-made man who, with pitiless grit and a three-decade real estate parlay, watches his money work at a hundred dollars an hour, sleeping and wak-ing. From his long picture window he sees the sixty thousand citizens he's surpassed in cunning drive back and forth along the east-west corridor that runs between his fences.

I was taking Sonia and her friends down that same east-west highway, between the great bedroom communities to the neo-Gothic crystal palace and the new treasure on its ceiling, then farther east over supersaturated land to the capital city itself, and the light in the cathedral tower. At the end of my journey I felt a new kinship with the artist, who had chosen the same red warn-ing lights to frame his composition.

"Why do I keep harping on these lights?"

"They're as far as we can see," one child said.

"Yes, they're at the extremes of our visible landscape. But what else? Come on!"

Blank faces again. Cow eyes everywhere.

"What are they on, these lights? A church and a nuclear

retreat," I answered for them. "Salvation by faith and salvation by civil defense! And remember. There's a warning light over each of them!" So I ended my first and most impassioned history lecture to Sonia.

Like many of the others around her, her head was down, embarrassed for her teacher. Or maybe plain bored. "Write me just one sentence," I told the class. "A sentence that explains America's second Manifest Destiny."

Some got part of what I was looking for. A few confessed complete bewilderment. Only one paper, Sonia's, made no reference to the question at all. She had written only this: "If you follow us around anymore my mother is reporting you to Mr. Lambert."

She must have spotted me a few more times at the mall after the group hide-and-seek. I'd been going back and back, looking for new revelations in the Norentez ceiling. And I couldn't deny that I'd been watching her group mingle arms and glances. But only in that shifting circle on the ceiling, which I observed from all angles on each of the mall's levels.

On the first parents' night of the year, when Richard came with the other fathers and mothers and sat in Sonia's desk, I gave the standard talk: not here to pour knowledge out of books into heads, the heads make their own connections; this century with the last, the east of the county with the west, the water we drank this morning with the dangerous path of the rain that fell last night.

When it was over Richard came quickly forward. "Remember me?" His handshake was strong and agreeable, affirming a common history.

"Of course, of course."

"How could you forget, right?"

It had been a long time since I'd seen him this closely. But ever the fine-looking young man, Sarah's early hero, with accomplishments now of his own. Earnestly making clear his old respect for me. "You really knew how to teach us. You were really different."

He turned to Derek Stevens's father, standing next to him, and said, "God, this man could teach. He was something else." Mr. Stevens stood amiably nodding and waiting for Richard to amplify, but that was it. Looking at them, all I could think of was the children, Sonia and how many times her moon dial had spun for Derek, member of the circle and not quite measuring up there.

And of course Richard's problems with Sarah; they were on my mind, too, as he got me aside to tell me, "You know we're trying to make Sonia a little less of a social butterfly, a little more interested in the academic stuff. If I remember right, you're probably the one for the job. You were really different," he said again.

But how was I different? That's what he'd never be able to tell me, and he'd never try. There was nothing veiled in his words. They had nothing to do with Sarah and me. There was a safe place and tradition here; he wasn't going to probe the way I'd been different. That wasn't his line as a man.

"How about Sonia? All right so far?"

"The record isn't good. Capable though. But you know I never put much faith in the record. Hiding her light, I think. We're working on her."

He was grateful, shaking my hand again. He made me promise to keep an eye on his daughter.

Lauranette had taken to having one-sided chats with me over her radio show. They were becoming more frequent and undisguised. I was uncomfortably famous. And she went right on with her "teacher-man this" and "teacher-man that." It was her way of making sure I'd tune in, sharing her celebrity. I had to know what the rest of the people were hearing about me. The Morancys had told her several times that it wasn't professional.

The afternoon of the opening lecture I had gone to my car for my bag lunch—peanut butter and bacon on rye, and a soda—tuned in WHTR and sat back to hear what Lauranette had for me. Her timing was perfect. "Hey, teacher-man over at River High washing the gunk off the roof of your mouth with root beer. You should clean up your whole act. Starting with the sock drawer." So, for a few days I accepted jokes about dirty and unmatched socks and socks that needed darning. Never mind, instead of cleaning out the bureau I was looking for more to put into it.

Sonia still wasn't cooperating with my plan to reveal her intelligence. I had no written work from her that could be called excellent or even passable, certainly nothing worthy of the drawer. On a test about county government she gave me a paper with a picture of a donkey on which I wrote B+. Her next assignment came back to me in one line: "I don't like this class." And the time after that, "Why are you afraid to fail me?"

To all of her backsliding and effrontery I gave the same above-average grade. If she was unable to fail, I thought she might be provoked to new tactics. There was plenty in Stilson's history to set Sonia's imagination roaming over a wilder countryside. Her mouth fell open when I explained that in 1750 five new mothers of bastard children were given fifty lashes at the public post.

We talked about a California rock concert, Sonia on the edge of her seat. She almost spoke. It was one of those events where bikers were supposed to police the crowd. For a few frenzied moments something had gone wrong. Before the music stopped a few days later there had been two births and two deaths in the audience.

I asked the students to write something about it and left the room. They left their papers stacked neatly on my desk, and among them was the jewel I'd been waiting for! Three wonderful pages! A nicely reasoned if fanciful essay by Sonia called "ZPG in California." The title proof enough of the wit that had poured from her for ten minutes while her peers had struggled to compose a paragraph or two. So much like her mother, who might have made the same clever leap from the evidence to zero population growth.

I made certain the whole class read Sonia's composition and put it on the distinguished-work shelf in the library. I submitted it for publication in the school quarterly. I was meddling with her reputation, and she wasn't pleased. A single paper couldn't make up for a career of lazy impudence, but it did wake some of her other teachers to the disguise she wore over her mind—the blank gaze, the indolent posture that could turn any desk into a chaise longue.

I made Lauranette sit still for a reading, too, to prove once and for all what I'd been talking about. Listen to this. "The strange grace of the motorcycle gang who came with muscles and chains to protect or punish as the music moved them." Or her observation that "half of America had been charmed and half disgusted by the sight of the fresh mothers opening their blouses to their new babies and the world, their chests heaving to the rhythms of nature and the Rolling Stones." So Lauranette, too, admitted wonder at Sonia's articulation and wide vision.

I knew the boredom of the school calendar, the repeating cycle, the pathetic side of the twenty-year academic veteran. The unspoken pity and contempt I'd always felt for the marms and masters stuck at the same level, after all those fall terms and summer vacations, still going back to school, threatening failure to children while never graduating themselves, I now reserved for myself. But when my time came to leave, there was no board of inquiry, no band of parents circling hands around me, no colleagues speaking up for me. Before it was finished the school doors were closed against me. Children and parents held me in contempt. My livelihood was gone, my world cut down to a domestic life with Lauranette. I supposed I had lost all contact with Sonia.

I had been writing REAL ESTATE on the green board in my Stilson County History room, on a little high, pleased for the moment with the way clear thought became articulate sound, sending a little army of logic into battle when the old noise came from somewhere behind me, a diminutive falsetto singing "Chalkman." I didn't turn at first though I was stunned, thrown off balance. I thought of a single, horrid mouth shaped for ignorance and disrespect. Then it came in little piping tones from all over the room, the old cooing of hidden doves, "Chalkman . . . Chalkman . . . Chalkman," and I knew Sonia must be singing, too. Not only singing but listening to my humiliation.

There was a dry-cell battery the size of a lipstick in my jacket pocket. Lauranette had put it there as a reminder to buy new ones for my radio. It wasn't much larger than a piece of chalk, and I whirled and flung it toward the center of my torment. I flung it with an accuracy I never intended and watched unbelieving as it struck Delphine Johnson, one of my quieter students. She was a docile girl whom I knew wouldn't have been part of the mocking chorus, and I had broken one of her front teeth. Delphine must have been in terrible pain. She was screaming, while the class watched in revulsion. I rushed to her, led her out of the room and down the hall to the infirmary, where she sobbed and told her story.

"He threw it at me."

I went to Lambert and offered my resignation. He wouldn't accept it right away. He thought something might be done for me. There'd be a lot of paperwork, reports to file. No sense rushing it. Why didn't I take the rest of the week off.

"It's over," I said. "You're well rid of me."

"I don't want to be rid of you, Ray," he told me. We talked about a possible lawsuit by Delphine's parents, who would probably name me and the school system as defendants. He'd better unload me fast, I said, put some distance between me and the school.

No, he didn't want to be hasty. It seemed he really did like me after all.

Preparing for school the next morning I noticed my cadged treasures were missing from my drawer. "Where are they?"

"That's *your* black baggage," Lauranette shot back.

She looked in the drawer for herself, thought about it for a while and then, amazing to me, blamed Sonia.

"She's never been here," I reminded her.

"Actually, she has." This was the guilty look of a thorough deception. Lauranette began talking very quickly, anticipating my questions. "You know, she's been coming to the station after school. She seems to like talking to me, asking about my work. Do I get scared at the microphone? Do I memorize everything I'm going to say? Things like that."

Lauranette had never told me anything of the kind before. Well, if she had, she said, I'd have been up the wall with curiosity, coming to the station myself to see what was going on. Anyway, when Sonia had asked one day if she could come and visit Lauranette at home, she'd been told no. But she had come, all the same, while I was away at Ripton Corner. Lauranette had barely managed to get her out of the house before I'd returned.

And how in the world had she got into our bedroom.

"I didn't watch her the whole time. She wandered around the house while I made a snack. She was curious. And let me tell you something else about your little daughter. She has an incredible nerve. The whole time I was working in the kitchen she was talking to me from the other rooms, saying things like 'Where do you get your hair done?' and 'My mother has a sweater like this.'"

"And now you're saying she's a thief?"

"If taking back what was hers is stealing."

Sonia hadn't even known what she was looking for, though maybe Lauranette's broadcast had led her into my bureau. Finding her things there must have transformed me in her eyes from just a nosy teacher into something truly sinister.

I'd never considered how Lauranette's silky voice over WHTR might have affected Sonia. Of course, Lauranette had been a kind of heroine to us all, blown, as I say, up from nothing onto the public air. Sarah, I later learned, stayed tuned to "Tumbleweed" through the afternoons in her kitchen, and Sonia kept a tiny portable radio hidden in her school locker to listen in herself when she could steal time for it.

It may have been the radio woman's connection with me that intrigued Sarah, but for Sonia it was more likely the woman's mythology. Everyone had heard about the tornado, the lost house, and how the furniture had been lifted into the air, dropped into the river, and floated down to Washington, where it had been found miraculously several years later by Lauranette herself in a used-furniture shop, and, in the meantime, how she had become Stilson County's little orphan of the air.

I had known that Sonia and some of her friends occasionally went over to the station after school to sit in the lobby, where they could look through the window into the sound studio and watch the disc jockey who came on after Lauranette's show. They made record requests in reverse writing on the studio glass. The disc jockey was the kind who'd give a hint of sympathy for a complexion problem and who played songs proving he was hip to the psychedelics. Yet all along, Sonia's real interest in the station had been Lauranette, who was anything but a soul sister.

On that same morning I'd discovered my rifled drawer, I

was interrupted just before noon in my history lecture. A woman was sent from the office to monitor my class and I was told to report to Lambert. He met me halfway, at the watercooler. His hand was on my shoulder as he ushered me the rest of the way, taking me into his inner office and shutting the door behind him.

Ray, it's with a heavy heart. This is the way it ends, I was thinking. "Ray, I like to think I've always had your respect. You know you've always had mine. Please, relax." He pushed me down into a chair. "You won't believe what I've just been through. I've had a wild man in here, a former student of yours. I might as well tell you right off, he's charged you with an un-natural interest in his daughter. I defended you, what else? You've been a fixture around here for years.

"It's about the Pless child. You know her well? Of course you do. You gave a wonderful defense of her in the faculty meet-ing last spring." The whole time he spoke he was looking at the collection of things on his desk—Sonia's barrette, her socks, her essay on the rock concert, Sarah's old papers. I was relieved the diary wasn't there. "Please, Ray, tell me you don't know any-thing about this stuff. It's just the girl's crazy imagination, isn't it?"

"Where did you get those things?"

"Richard Pless brought them in. He said his daughter found them in your house. In your bedroom to be exact."

"I guess she did."

"Will I have to ask for your resignation?"

"I've already given it to you."

"Well. Done and done, Ray. Now let's talk." I couldn't imagine what there might be left to say. "If our professional rela-tionship is over, maybe we could speak as friends. I worry about you. After all you've done for us. You've given the school an extra dimension."

"The fourth? The fifth?"

"Don't be defensive, please. I think you know what I'm

talking about. The creative ways you've handled the curriculum. You've given us some headaches. At the same time, we've all admired you." He was uncomfortable with the things on his desk. Actually, he wanted this over quickly, but with a warm handshake, some gesture of no hard feelings. I offered my hand and backed out of his office. As I turned into the hall I heard him tell a secretary, "Get a bag, and put this stuff in the safe."

The night of my resignation Lauranette went a little crazy. We were on the sofa with a bottle of whiskey and two tumblers when she got up and walked to the open window. Into the black night she shouted, "The Morancys are little people with little hands and little feet." She began to yell at passing motorists that their goddamned, treacherous little children had turned the best teacher of them all into a monster. It was as if she was trying to share my recklessness.

We drank some more and got into shouting at all the world, at each other, and at all the world again. In the middle of our commotion she screamed out, "He's father of the little criminal! He's Sonia Pless's father!" Before I pulled her back from the window, and covered her mouth with my hand, we saw lights come on in houses across the road.

The phone rang. I practiced being sober. Lauranette pulled my hand away from the receiver. It was too late, she said. It couldn't be anyone we wanted to talk to. It rang for a long time, stopped, and then started again and kept on. I thought it had to be someone who knew we were home, maybe a neighbor.

The snubs were everywhere. The supermarket manager ignored me, checkout people asked for my I.D., our mechanic, whose son had gone through my classes with highest praise, said he was too busy for our car, a librarian claimed my card was out of date, and got huffy when I told her "Library cards are forever."

I was quick to learn the self-deceiving habits of unemployment, the running of little errands that amounted to loitering in front of magazine racks, a trip to a hardware store for a screwdriver missing from a toolbox, though there was no screw to be turned, the reading of a newspaper as a whole morning's activity, a compulsion to stay neat, as if new opportunity were more likely to float down on the well groomed, a weekly trip to the barber, though every two months had been sufficient in the past.

"Just a trim." But the cumulative effect was a businessman's clip with hardly a forelock to blow around in the wind. Lauranette fussed that I should get hold of myself, and let the stuff grow back to the careless length she'd always admired. As for the snubs, she thought I was out looking for them and was therefore bound to find them. She had a benign explanation for each imagined slight.

After a month I realized I no longer wanted to be seen, though I was still anticipating a call from some admiring and highly placed person who would want me for a special assignment. I had to stay prepared, keep fit. My health, which had always endured unnoticed, became a daily concern.

I'd never had annual physicals, but if they were important, why not have one every six months to be doubly safe. And why not begin right now. I was nervous in the doctor's office. I'd been keeping track of pulse, a mole on my back, and a softening of my fingernails. The doctor sent me home in perfect health with the advice to look up "valetudinarian" in the dictionary.

If I went for walks they were over fields and fences, not into town. I drove back and forth across the county, using the car the way celebrities use sunglasses. I spent more time at the Whole World, where the crowds hid me. Eventually, I became a daily browser in the mall, arriving early and staying till the late afternoon.

I was one of the many using the place as a park—grand-mothers delivered and picked up, morning and night, by their commuting families, children who hung out in Quarter Heaven, young mothers with their infants in strollers, who sat by the fountain every day, resting between shopping and meals, and the uncomfortably idle like me, who window-shopped and gazed at the great work nearing completion on the ceiling. When the regulars began to smile in recognition I had to find something new. I tried doing circles on the Beltway, but discovered that without company or Lauranette's program, only available on the Virginia portion of the trip around Washington, it was terribly boring.

I stole a box of .22 caliber bullets from a hardware store, and shot them into the night sky over the mountain, wishing them onto the roof of the survivalists' bunker, as if the tiny slugs could have traveled the seven miles to target. I rode an open canoe over the Little Falls of the Potomac, daring them to take me down. I capsized but was washed onto the rocks. Not seeing the way I scampered to safety, Lauranette called it suicidal.

The canoe lodged in the rapids and buckled as the water filled it, but I still had the gun to play with. It was the little Remington pump that had belonged to my father; given to him for shooting rattlesnakes when he was sent west as a boy to recover from scarlet fever. The same one I'd used as a boy. A negligible thing for hurting man or game, my silly little equalizer in a countryside of impressive private arsenals. I'd made it a companion that rode with me under the car seat. Concealed, it was like an illegal toy.

I took it to a range in the hills where men tested the scopes of deer rifles and worked on pistol skills. An expert shooting next to me was interested in the little gun's age, but behind me someone else said his boy had one just like it for blue jays and chipmunks. "A rattlesnake gun," I told them, but when it was seen that I could not touch one of the black circles or any part of their little white target sheets I was dismissed.

Had I done anything so terrible? I kept suspecting I had. Was it so awful to have lost my temper and thrown something at an innocent student? Or just horrid luck that the battery hit a tooth. It was capped, I'd paid for it, the parents hadn't sued. Beyond that I'd had a perfectly sane, if private, reason for keeping the drawer full of Pless things. Still, I lurched over the back roads in the car working on Sonia's case as I drove, taking both sides.

She's treacherous. Faithless. No. Where is the treachery in treating me for what I was—a peeping old intriguer who stalked her through the school? And where were the faithless in a circle admitting no final allegiance? How could she be false to one if she was sworn to affection and tolerance of all? She has no moral core, no political conscience. Don't make me laugh. Why should it trouble her if we all got ourselves fired so close together—the president and a bunch of his friends and me?

After one of these debates with myself, I returned to the house and there was Sonia visiting again with Lauranette! She was lounging on the sofa, a leg dangling over one end, a soft drink in her hand, apparently quite at home. Lauranette, across the living room in an easy chair, looked uncomfortable. I wasn't interrupting anything congenial. Sonia righted herself on the sofa.

"Do her parents know she's here?"

"Her parents are at the chiropractor this evening. Sonia came by for a chat, she says. She's been telling me everything."

"Everything?"

"About the painter, Roberto. That's Norentez. He's twenty-eight. Which is only ten years older than eighteen. Which she'll be this summer. She's going to visit him in New York if he gets to do a mall there. Everything."

Lauranette, in her sly way, was reminding me that the age difference between Sonia and Norentez had its parallel with me and Sarah. High school girls and twenty-eight-year-old men; suggesting that sexual attraction to grown men must run in the family. While this appeared to excuse the men, it annoyed me that Lauranette would demean Sarah and Sonia that way. There was implicit criticism of Sarah's whole dislocated life. And of Sonia, walking in her footsteps, inviting new dislocations.

Lauranette escaped to the kitchen, and Sonia, suddenly freed from decorum, looked straight at me. "Hi, Chalkman," she said, her voice absolutely steady.

"How's school?"

"Same ol', same ol', if you want to know. Words. Numbers. Like that. There was a petition to bring you back. It had some names on it. My father said don't worry, they won't let you, even if we have to tell people the real reason."

For another few minutes, until Lauranette came back, I accepted Sonia's insolence. I was excited, afraid I might say something foolish or offensive that would make her leave. I did ask her how she knew Mr. Norentez so well.

"I watch Roberto a lot. He watches me a lot." She looked up at the ceiling and grinned as if she'd said something very clever. I could only think, she's here, under my roof, in my house.

When Sonia was gone I learned more about her visit from Lauranette. My daughter was very depressed about her family. The fighting between Sarah and Richard was worse. Her sister Rita was stealing things at school. Sonia felt like the only normal one in the bunch. She'd chosen Lauranette as confidante, not because of my connection with her, she said, but in spite of it, and Lauranette didn't like it. She'd been almost rude, but it didn't seem to faze Sonia, who had gone so far as to say she couldn't understand how Lauranette would have me for an old man. "You know, considering the way he is, all covered with the dust and everything."

And more. The circle was finished. Sonia had become leader of a group called Clean Sisters that had renounced sensuality for the time being, and had begun to meet regularly on the weekends in the mall where they paraded their indifference to men. Her old consorts had died a thousand deaths since then, becoming petulant and offensive with name-calling. Lesbie and the like.

After the painter had penetrated their circle from the ceiling, Sonia's head had been turned. Now, according to Lauranette, she had put herself in storage for him. He had spotted her for a mall regular long before he caught the circle at play in the changing rooms. And her face had already appeared in three places in the great glass ceiling, though it might take you days to find them if you didn't know where or how to look.

Eventually they had seen Norentez watching them from his scaffold, and the group had scattered in fright. All but Sonia, who had not even hurried to dress herself. She knew she had already been a face model for the painter even though no words had passed between them. Their eyes had crossed between his perch above her and the fountain court where she lounged on a bench, watching as he stained her features in the glass.

Later, in the changing room, her partner having fled without her, she'd refused to incriminate herself by rushing. In fact, after slowly getting into her underthings, she had changed her mind and removed them again. "Do you think I was wrong?" she'd asked Lauranette, who was already astounded by the story. Sonia had stayed in the booth for maybe another hour, allowing Norentez to work again over her, only leaving when he signaled an end to his day by sliding off through the air on his rolling platform.

According to Sonia she had kept coming back in the early evenings. She would slip away from the crowds, and steal into her booth, where she'd undress and wait for the painter. There were no signals between them, just a silent understanding that she pleased him as a model.

The sessions in the mall had continued, and Sonia had pursued Norentez one evening into the parking lot. She had been charmed. "Looking at me all that time," she told Lauranette, "and all he said was didn't I get cold in that part of the mall where it wasn't heated."

Then, of all things, Sonia had tried to explain to Lauranette the man's spiritual nature, the way he denied credit for what he'd done, calling himself only "a translator." He had left her there, and it was only by sitting at the central fountain, evening after evening, watching for his glance as he worked, that she had lured him down again for a more satisfying conversation. She had learned his age, that he had no wife or lady friend, that he would probably be going next to a mall somewhere in New York State, that she was free to come and see what he would do there.

"Would she really follow him to New York?"

Lauranette thought she might.

I imagined Sonia submitting to his inspection again, Sonia in a bus station, throwing herself on the kindness of anyone who'd take her to the next mall. Sonia without money, angling for a way to hide from the crowd and change into nothing, to be his model again. I wanted to think of the artist as a guardian for her. But who could know his intentions?

How could she have been the single model for Norentez's love box rather than one of many? How could she undress for him over and over again? She was either fantasizing a pure romance for herself, I thought, or just lying for Lauranette's attention. It was only thanks to a photographic phenomenon that I found she was actually telling the truth.

I had taken a camera to the mall once before, hoping to record all parts of the ceiling. It was a week before I finished, and another few days before snaps were developed. Most of the pictures of the changing-room section were so blurred, the colors so washed and confused, that I considered them worthless. But hearing Sonia's story from Lauranette led me back to them for another look. Among them I found one that, when held in a certain light, could be made to show the faint silhouette of a female figure.

I bought a more expensive camera with a tripod, went back to the upper level of the mall and took another roll of pictures, some with flash, some with the natural light. Only two of these twenty-four had untangled the mixed bodies but these two were perfect color images, both of my daughter, one of them with her sitting, arms behind her, leaning back on her palms, the other showing her lying on her side, chin propped on her hand.

Why two images from the same camera position? Why only two successful prints from twenty-four negatives, and why so clear when with my eyes I'd only been able to catch fleeting forms. The flash shots hadn't worked at all. Some backlighting had been necessary, but that wasn't the only answer.

Without revealing the subject of my work I dared calling one of the River High physics teachers for an explanation. She could only guess that if the lens of the camera had been absolutely still, fixed on the tripod, it could be made to do something the human eye could not. It might have recorded the frequencies of color at only one depth in the glass. The two successful images must have been achieved from two angles, no matter how slight the difference. I had probably bumped the tripod slightly without noticing. This, combined with the ever-changing angle of sunlight behind the glass, could be bringing the images in and out of the camera's detection.

I used another dozen rolls of film that week, all on that same area of ceiling, but shot each roll at a different time of day, and each time from a slightly different position. When I was finished, out of those hundreds of negatives, I found twelve clear color portraits: Sonia's body, Sonia's face, repeated in six poses, each of them freshly observed, soft edged and luminous. Where I'd imagined a collection of other bodies, it had only been Sonia superimposed on herself. Sonia in her own embraces. When I tucked the portraits away in a drawer, I was careful this time to lock it.

Sonia tried to make her house calls when I wasn't there. Aware of this, I kept the coast clear for her visits which, as the weeks passed, were becoming more frequent. I begged Lauranette to cooperate. She was my best hope of a link to Sonia. "I'm not sure I like this," she said. "It's dangerous." Nevertheless, when Sonia first started coming Lauranette must have been a little flattered by her trust, even fascinated by some of the confessions she was hearing. There was nothing Sonia wouldn't share with her. A few times I was able to overhear her conversation without arousing her suspicion.

But Lauranette was taking little pity on Sonia, even though she found the underside of my daughter different from the lovely, proud surfaces seen at school and in the mall. Once, almost in tears, Sonia told her, "If you knew what goes on in my house. My parents are hardly speaking. My mother dresses up to walk out on my old man. And then she just sits in the kitchen, daring him to say something about it. I think they're both afraid she might do it."

Later, I watched her at my desk, where Lauranette had let her sit. She opened one of her school books, then hung her head and let the book fall from her hands. I went to her and said, "There's nothing so difficult in there, nothing you couldn't learn in a minute."

She looked at me with the coldest eyes in the world and said: "What are you talking about? I already memorized this stuff. I'm just tired."

Maybe. But she was close to failing. She told Lauranette she was saving for a bus ticket, and Norentez was almost finished at the Whole World.

———

Instead of accosting the artist against his will at the mall, I followed his car out of the parking area on a cold March evening. It was a clunker he drove, billowing smoke through a failing exhaust system. It didn't fit with the stories of his success.

I trailed him off the main highway onto a secondary road and then down back lanes through woods, heading upriver. He sped up, turned left, right and left, and seeing that I was indeed following him, and that his car was not swift enough to escape, he stopped. Driving alongside I called out, "Mr. Norentez, could I speak with you?"

"Government?" he asked through his window.

"An admirer."

Noncommittal, he drove on, but slower. In a few miles we turned out of the woods into a field, bumping over a cattle grate. Passing a decrepit farmhouse, we continued down a long hill to a shed where he parked. He got out and signaled for me to follow. It was very dark and I saw almost nothing until we were inside and he lit a kerosene lamp.

It was the crudest sort of cinderblock building, at one time used for slaughtering pigs. There were two scalding troughs at one end and no windows. An oak cutting table was built into one wall. On this he had made his bed of blankets and a single pillow. Rusty scrapers hung on nails over blackened rendering vats. The concrete floor slanted from the four walls toward a drain in the center. He apologized for the floor, saying he had scrubbed it many times. The dark stains could not be cleaned.

Norentez's wrists were so small and delicate that even his brush strokes must have been exercise. He observed me casually with no daunting intensity in his eyes. They didn't blink, and neither did they bore in in the way of an off-duty painter insisting on a special vision. Black hair fell across his forehead in a single oily lock. He was too thin-faced to be handsome. His cheeks, slightly sunken, were still capable of small dimples, or maybe they were just secondary creases in the larger hollows of his face—a concavity suggesting malnutrition. I was both worried and pleased to think that Sonia had found him attractive.

After starting a fire in a small wood stove he went out the door with the advice that I must not mind waiting. A few minutes later the shed was warm and he was back again with a bucket of water, which came from an old quarry just across the meadow. Young people, who didn't know he lived there, sometimes came to swim and make mischief, he said.

"You live here?" I couldn't believe it. "You're famous."

"Not famous at home. Only famous at work."

"But you have money."

"They give me money. I send it to my father."

"Of course. That's none of my business. I was only wondering where you come from. How you do what you do. I want to show you some pictures I've taken."

"You're not government?" he asked again.

I brought out the photos of his work. "How did you get these?" he demanded. "Has anyone else seen her?"

"Where did you study? Where did you learn how to paint like that?"

"You can't study it," he told me. "It's not painting. You know it from the beginning or you don't know it." He sighed.

"I'm Mexican," Norentez said. "I had to come to America many times. The last time they didn't catch me. Not just illegal alien. They thought I was a drug person. They look into my eyes and the pupils are too large. You understand? That was a long time ago. Maybe I'm safe now.

"I went to New York. They let me sweep where small children went to school before real school. This small." He put his hand down to knee level. "Some of them didn't use the toilet. I cleaned that, too."

His confession was making me uncomfortable. I was shaking my head. "The lady teacher was very fine, very kind to me. She wanted me to use finger paints with the children. To learn letters and numbers. I showed her what I can do on a piece of glass, and sell in Mexico. She was very surprised. She let me paint her. All of her. You understand? So she wanted me to stay at night, too. And a month later she didn't want me. I had to leave."

I was walking around the room, examining his few possessions, trying to distract him from his demeaning history. "How do your colors work?"

"You mix them carefully and they work." He wouldn't be put off his story. I learned how he'd done chalk drawings on sidewalks on his way down to New Orleans. I could imagine how the federal authorities had squeezed him down the map, no more able to resist than a bright color forced from a tube. On the way he had sought the city centers, which were dying and afraid of him.

Norentez described a lower street in Knoxville where he'd been working on a sidewalk self-portrait. "I was drawing what I look like as I'm drawing on the pavement. People standing around could see me drawing and the picture of me drawing. And in that picture was the smaller picture of me drawing on the same sidewalk. And finally too small to draw but your mind understands, smaller and smaller. They saw it, they got it. The people were throwing coins. Then a stream of piss came under a fence washing my work away. Do you understand? I was disappearing."

That was all behind him now, he said. In New Orleans he had painted the glass roof of a public market. Grapes, melons, red shrimp on ice, a striped awning. "I colored their glass without stopping the light," he said, "like a church. They loved me. Now they want it everywhere, and I do what I like."

Norentez's journey north had become a spree of painting in a half-dozen malls, a victory campaign through the states that had rejected him. Now he worked from a mechanical scaffold that could raise him four stories and send him, cantilever, to any section of the Whole World ceiling. It was this special equipment, he said, that had made the work possible.

All this confusion of boasting and humility. "This girl in the picture," I said. "I know she's always at the mall. How many times have you painted her?"

He cocked his head, studied me for a moment, and said what no one else ever had. "She is your daughter, yes? I can see she is your daughter."

"No, I don't have children. I was her teacher."

"Teach her? Yes, she needs it, I think."

"But are you encouraging her?"

"I don't know this girl's name. I don't want to know. Do you understand? But she tells me anyway. Sonia. I didn't want to speak to her. I didn't want her to think anything of me. She came to the shopping place. She showed herself. I painted her."

"Where are you going next? Is there someone there to help you? Do you have a bank? You know the girl is too young to travel with you?"

"You stop about the girl," he said sharply. "If you're not government, why do you ask government questions?"

I was a discharged schoolteacher, I told him, still following the careers of my old pupils. Uncomfortable with my visit, he gently disinvited me for the rice and beans heating up on his crude stove. As I left, he said, "Your girl has a lot of close friends, doesn't she? Why would I be interested in that way." He was looking squarely into my face when he said again, "You are her father."

It was a nervous time for me. I hadn't relaxed into unemployment, hadn't accepted that it would take effort to learn a useful idleness. How long could we live on my modest savings and Lauranette's small salary? More than money I needed the children in front of me. I was drinking a little too much, dealing my disquiet into blurred nights, even berating Lauranette and her program. She was too polite to a county engineer who came on the show to explain the giant interceptor sewer's need for new hookups.

Sonia was still hanging around a lot, accepting Lauranette's tentative receptions, preferring the silence she found in our house to the unpleasantness in her own. She brought Lauranette little gifts—a scarf, an unusual stone, a bouquet of wildflowers. It was an unrequited crush.

When I was around, Sonia spoke very quietly, and I accepted the continued snubbing without complaint, hoping the visits would continue. She was hiding them from Sarah and Richard, who probably thought she was with her regular crowd at the mall. In fact, when she wasn't in school or with us, she *was* at the mall, looking for a way to put herself in sight of Norentez, who was working on the final section of his ceiling. It wasn't easy to make herself seen. The crowds were heavy and the merchants were pleased. People who had come only to watch the painter were jamming the restaurants, spilling over into the stores, charmed by the crystalline depth in the scenes of their community overhead.

The place was becoming a shrine even before the painter was finished. Too many people had learned of his cinderblock hideaway. Norentez had been forced to move into a suburban medium-rise apartment where, Sonia said, he was miserable and waiting to escape to New York.

The crowds were getting in her way too. Now that her painter was getting famous, she confided to Lauranette, "He might let some little chippie fool him." This, from the girl who had run the circle, amused Lauranette. I thought she might be softening to Sonia's esteem, though she still wondered what my daughter was really up to—what Sonia might be using her for.

That spring I learned a shocking thing about my daughter and her mother. Sonia hadn't just defied me in school. She had cheated, admitted it openly to all but me, and then pretended she'd been angered by my discovery and wide praise of her success. The quick essay she'd done on the rock concert had been plagiarized, word for word, headline and all, from a music magazine she'd found in the reception room at WHTR. She confessed it to Lauranette. She hadn't even known what ZPG meant. And I'd spread the thing through the school, increasing the chance of her shame, when she'd just been playing a joke on me.

"And what if I was cheating? My mother used to do the same thing. She told me. She used to cheat on Sykes all the time," Sonia told Lauranette, who passed it on to me as gently as she could. There wasn't any gentle way to tell me that. It made me a twenty-year pathetic fool! From the banks of the river where Sarah had conceived our love child, to the mountain where we had pledged faith, I drove my anger back and forth across the county.

More than once I nearly ran the car off the road in distraction, remembering Sarah's old themes, now little deceits, that had kept me hopeful for so long. I'd been bragging all those years on the brilliance of a cheat. Roofs "suffering lesions" and all that. How could I have thought a child capable of such an overblown conceit? She'd copied this and other things from God knows where.

Even after her drift into adult mediocrity I'd held these pure—our meetings beside the river. Now I had to go back and reconstruct them. The nerviness of it all. The little criminal. Coming back and back, testing her immunity from prosecution by getting as close to her victim as nature would allow. And still, she must have loved me in her way. Hadn't she proved it; pouting at my least slight and gladdened by my tiniest gesture.

By the time I returned to our driveway I had almost forgiven both of them. Neither mother nor daughter had needed to cheat. They'd each said their share of wise and clever things, privately and in the classroom. If they'd only live up to their own gifts.

One afternoon, coming out of the supermarket, my arms full of things for fixing Lauranette a special supper, I nearly bumped into two men leaning against the wall. One politely pulled a grocery bag away from me. "I'll help with that," he said. "It won't cost you."

"Not him," the other said. "It's the one who broke the little girl's tooth, the chalkman."

"Shut up," the man with my bag said. "I'm Walter," he told me. He'd lost his job at the tire-cord factory over at Front Royal.

"Ray Sykes," I said. "Sure, I've seen you," befriending him as an out-of-work brother.

After that I stopped to talk there regularly. I thought there were things I could help these people with. Parking-lot adult education was the way I thought of it. Walter and his buddies began to call me Teacher. Their tough-boy way of deferring to my ex-profession made me tough along with them.

I learned that every fine day Walter and his pals took a blanket and cards to the woods for poker. If the old club would accept a new member, I'd show them some tricks—how they could gamble for fun with no one getting hurt. A thing or two about odds. It was good to hear them talking about what the town should keep—the old constable who smiled on loitering— and what it should discard—the new mayor who wanted to clean up the parking lots and police the new meters. They talked a lot about athletic and romantic opportunity, too, like aging high school children. When they weren't around, I missed the banter.

One afternoon they let me join them in the woods. There were nine of them, five playing and the rest watching the hands. I felt young among them. It was a loose, careless game with outrageous table talk. They didn't seem to mind, drifting as they were in good-natured, boozy rivalry.

"Is he all right?" I asked Walter, pointing to a player who held his cards with one hand and had the other in his pocket, moving against the outline of his stiffening member. "That's just Bones," I was told quietly. "You can tell how good he's holding by the size of his lump."

"You something special?" Bones asked. I sat down, they dealt me in, and I began right away to win. I was showing them some memory devices for keeping track of the deck. When it was over, I was carrying fifteen dollars away from the game—money I used to take Lauranette out for drinks that night.

We went to the Turning Night, the revolving restaurant over the mall. For the view. From a window seat we saw most of the shopping center's roof below us as we turned. It was floodlit and remarkable as an expanse of shifting, sparkling color, though only shadows were visible through the glass from the outside.

It was a clear evening. A hidden motor turned us slowly from the mountain to the cathedral and back again as we sipped tall rum drinks with paper umbrellas in them. One revolution per drink. The second time we faced the mountain I was a little euphoric with our dominion over the city and suburbia. Headlights, streetlights, window lights and the beacons from two airports played across the landscape below.

"Turning in place is good for the ego," I said. "It makes us the center of the world."

"Where were you this afternoon?" Lauranette asked me.

"Playing cards. At my club."

She glared happily at me, as if staring down an amusing lie. "Don't look, but the Morancys are sitting over there behind you. They have small hands and tiny feet." She sent herself into an attack of giggles, and the Morancys looked our way. The wives were there, too, the whole party quite sober. "They gave me another lecture."

Lauranette had wanted to have the Danish couple who wrote *Love's Dictionary* on "Tumbleweed." The publisher had sent her a complimentary copy, which she'd passed on to the Morancys with a memo that said, "This could be fun." The brothers turned thumbs down. No sex talkers were going to jeopardize their license. "I'm supposed to clean up my act," Lauranette said, "and stop gambling with their air."

Below us we watched the outline of Norentez's scaffold move under the glass roof. He was working very late. "Come on, drink up." I wanted to go for a quick slice of pizza and then down to the main floor, where I could watch the artist.

"You were hoping to see her here, weren't you?" Lauranette asked.

"Sonia?"

"Yes. Try to leave her alone. She won't be paying us visits much longer," and Lauranette said again what she'd told me long before. "Ray, she's never going to know. No one wants to know. Whatever Richard and Sarah mean to you, you wouldn't destroy them completely for her."

"You yelled it out the window. You're the dangerous one."

"You're free," she went on, "and young enough." Seductively Lauranette was telling me once more that she didn't mind my being out of work. "You've escaped. They were only holding you back." In the fullness of time, she said, I'd find the something, or the nothing, that would suit me. "You don't have to rush."

Our new plan was to use the money we'd got for selling her place when we moved, full-time, into mine. Although the balance left after the mortgage was settled was far less than we'd hoped. And we still counted on her measly wage from the radio station. No more money, really, for me to be blowing on my photography of the mall ceiling.

"Come on," she said gaily. "Let's see what trick Norentez has Sonia playing now." As much as she wanted me to move away from Sonia's life, she did not expect me to completely forget my own daughter. It was as if she hoped the Sonia on the ceiling could be a substitute for Sonia in the classroom.

"You said she wouldn't be here tonight."

"By now he probably does her from memory."

We made our way out of the Turning Night and down through the levels of the mall, browsing as we went. "Why do you even pretend anymore?" she asked. "The fact is, you like all this." She led me into a glittering shop of American fashions with Italian names, all made in China. The bright garments hung in multiple tiers all around us. Reckless, suddenly in love with her tolerance, I bought her a jacket that seemed too large for her by half, but which she and the saleslady said was a perfect fit according to the rules of the coming season. It was chalk white with a pleated front and double collar, the body full of cozy stuffing. Lauranette wore it out of the store.

"You're softer since you got fired," she said. "So tell me. Where does this club of yours meet? Are women allowed?"

"In the woods. I don't think any women have applied."

"Will you put my name in for it?"

Another level down we stopped for our pizza slices. When we sat down to eat I pulled from my pocket a mimeographed sheet I'd lifted from the counter where I paid for the coat.

"Crime Solver R 37," I read aloud. "This information received on the crime-solvers' phone. A check-writing team is coming to set up here. May be setting up under name of Harold Strawmyer. They like to hit shopping malls, writing about fifteen thousand to twenty thousand dollars."

"What if they like pizza?" Lauranette said. "Keep your voice down."

"Real name of ringleader, Walter Delfo Ramey. W-M, forty-three. Six foot, one inch; one hundred and sixty-five pounds; hair, black; eyes, gray. Note, is a smooth talker. Dresses young. Dresses casually. May be carrying handgun."

Lauranette had slipped down in her seat. "If they know all that," she said, "why don't they just pick him up?"

"They work with children. Claim to be in movie production and casting. Florida, North Carolina, South Carolina, Virginia, and Georgia. Maryland Adult Probation knows these people."

Could be anyone, I told Lauranette, and left the sheet there on the table with our paper plates.

Riding moving stairs down to ground level, we saw electric letters flashing around the top of the information center. THE CEILING IS FINISHED. MEET THE ARTIST. Looking up from the central fountain we saw a half-dozen people standing high on the mechanical scaffold. They were busy with cameras and lights. Norentez was nowhere in sight. As the scaffold moved back and forth, up and down, giving the cameramen any angle they called for, flashbulbs were illuminating the artist's landscape like heat lightning.

There was a cry from the great atrium. A small knot of people was moving quickly toward the west exit. We thought there might have been a robbery or a heart attack. Instead of chasing after tragedy, we went toward the east doors, and came out in time to see Norentez's car zigzagging slowly away from us toward the highway ramp. A woman was running along beside him as he wove between cars and people. Her shoulders fell in dejection when she saw the car wasn't going to stop for her. She took a fistful of hair next to her scalp and lifted her face toward the stars in theatrical despair.

"Is that Sonia?" Lauranette couldn't believe it. The closer we got, the more it looked like her, and when she saw us coming toward her, she circled away, back toward the building. I broke into a run, Lauranette following. Inside, we moved up through the mall's levels, searching thoroughly. Sonia was gone, nowhere to be seen.

We wandered for a while, aimlessly. For all the times I'd been in the mall, for all the charts we'd made, I could still get lost there. Turning down an unfamiliar passage, we saw Sonia at the far end, seated on a bench. There was a man standing over her, stroking her shoulder, talking—a stranger in a gray cardigan and pegged chinos making over her misery. I started toward them. "No," Lauranette said. "Let's just watch and see what happens."

A moment later the man pulled her up from the bench and led her away. They turned together down another hallway, and that was the last we saw of her that night. We looked everywhere again, all levels, even snuck behind the temporary partitions into the unleased areas to search the changing rooms. But there were no changing rooms. Their walls were gone, and in the semi-darkness we could see that the children's old love chambers were now part of the floor plan of yet another haberdasher.

We stayed until the mall closed, watching the photographers who were still there, working close to the ceiling, section by section, taking pictures from all angles. At the information center no one could tell us who they were. But at Mall Security we learned they'd been hired to complete the job I'd started, to find out what Norentez had actually done to their ceiling.

Why was I so interested, the security officer wanted to know. "Just curious shoppers," was all I could think to say.

"Well, we know a lot about you," he said. "You're out of work. You hang out here a lot and you don't buy much." He pulled an album from his desk and leafed through it to two pictures of me, front and side head shots, then snapped the book shut. Not before I'd seen my fingerprints too, probably lifted from a glass counter in one of the stores.

"Closing time," he told us casually. Lauranette reached for the album. He wouldn't let her see it. "We haven't accused him of anything," he said.

Indignant, frightened, too, we sat on a bench in a promenade on the upper level until they had to tell us to get out. "Your hair was longer in those pictures," Lauranette said. "You've been under surveillance for a while. I've been your accessory." On our way down we looked for hidden cameras, stopping once to make funny faces in case they were focused on us.

Outside we walked past a station wagon of River High children having a car party. With a beer can raised, one boy called out, "Chalkman!" and the girl wrapped in his other arm rolled her window down and called softly, "Hey, Chalkman. Get us dusted." Getting no response from me, the girl turned back to her friends and said, "God, I hope I can get that feeling I had last night." Trying to hear more, I was pulled away by Lauranette.

On the way home she said, "Crime Solver R 38. Ray Lewis Sykes, forty-six, white male. Is a native of northern Virginia. Likes to operate in high schools and malls in that area. Carries fountain pen and notebook and will use them. Lectures without warning . . ."

Then, because I was not taking it like a good sport, she slipped closer to me. "If you were twenty-five again would you start teaching the same way? Would you teach at all?"

"The lectures I used to give on hypocrisy in government—committees on false crusades, things like that. I wouldn't give those talks anymore. They should know what's possible before they hear what's going wrong." I talked for quite a while about John Dewey.

"For God's sake, Ray! I'm not asking about your philosophy of teaching. I'm asking about you!"

There wasn't time for more of this. A half-block from home we saw that our house lights were on. Parked in front was Richard's pickup. R. Pless, Carpenter, stenciled on the door. Under that, Custom Construction & Retrofitting. And under that, You Should See What We Saw. In the house Richard and Sarah were waiting for us like a team of television cops.

"All right, where is she?" Richard said.

"You just walk in here, uninvited?" Lauranette asked.

"That's what Sonia does, isn't it?"

"If you want to know . . ."

"Wait a minute." Richard turned to me. "You go outside with Sarah. I want to ask this woman some things, alone."

I followed Sarah out the door. She wasn't dressed for police work. She was wearing a bright spring dress, almost off the shoulders, and flats. Rushing the season. Her face had a spectral beauty under the mercury vapor lamp at the bottom of our drive. Alert and furtive.

I touched her shoulder and withdrew my hand, surprised that after all the lost years I was too strained with her to show a chaste affection. Out of Richard's sight Sarah had lost her hard edge. "He thinks you're capable of anything," she said. "He thinks you could have been sleeping with your students."

"Not for nineteen years," I said slowly. "Did you ever cheat?"

"On Richard? No, it hasn't been like that."

"In school. On your tests and papers."

She looked alarmed for a moment. As if an admission might disqualify her from something. "You wanted me to do so well," she said quietly. "The fancier I wrote, the more you liked me."

I hadn't meant to shame her. "Forget that. Actually it was the intimate things. They still confuse me. The unusual things." She looked quizzically at me. "The wonderful, outrageous things."

She was remembering and she reddened as if I'd dredged up an old crime, long put aside—one with no standing in adult experience or conventional marriage. "Those things weren't nice, were they?"

This time, she touched me. Put her fingers on my belt and then withdrew them. "What are you and that radio bitch doing?" she said.

"I thought you liked Lauranette's program. Sonia told her you listen every day."

"I guess I listen for clues." Quite cryptic. "Richard says if you're hiding Sonia you could go to jail. Richard and I haven't been getting along so well."

I nodded.

"I guess you knew that. I'm supposed to ask when you saw Sonia last."

"Tonight. We caught a glimpse of her twice at the shopping center. She ran both times."

"You're not hiding her?"

"Me? You know she doesn't even want to come near me. It's Lauranette. Anyway, no one has to hide Sonia. She's a master of disappearances."

"Playing sardines with her friends again?"

"I don't think they ever packed themselves together like that."

"Are you and the radio woman getting married?"

"Lauranette says we'll be common-law before long. I don't really know the rules, but I don't think they apply in Virginia."

Sarah touched my belt again, then walked ahead of me into the house.

Inside, Richard and Lauranette were glaring at one another across the living room. She had answered his questions truthfully but not satisfactorily. Richard was sarcastic and threatening. He swore he'd have her job at the radio station the same way he'd had mine at the high school. If she didn't cooperate. His sleeves were rolled up, showing us honest carpenter muscle about to pry truth from under rotten boards.

"What did he tell you?" he asked Sarah.

"They saw Sonia tonight at the mall. She wouldn't talk to them. There was an older man."

"Has she been staying away from home?" I asked. Richard looked puzzled for a moment by my honesty, and then he rolled down his sleeves and told Lauranette, "Sonia isn't what you think. She isn't what she pretends." He pointed a finger at me and asked, "What are you up to, anyway?" but his eyes were filling, and he turned aside, shamed by his emotion. "She just needs a firm hand."

"It's not discipline she needs," Sarah said.

Richard raised his arm. "Whatever she needs from us," he said, "she can't get it if she's not at home." He looked around the room, as if he'd finally said something very wise. Turning his back on me, he asked Lauranette, "Please send her home. If you see her again." His pain was clear. "She's really a very wonderful child," he said.

From our doorway we watched them go across the yard. Before they got to the truck Richard turned on Sarah. The cool air, all the places in the neighborhood where Sonia could be lurking, must have altered his view of the evening. He was trying to whisper, but couldn't, and we heard him say, "If she stays out tonight, she can stay out for good."

We left our doors open, front and back, lights on, and a note for Sonia on a lamp table in the living room. "Go straight home," Lauranette wrote. "Your parents are sick with worry."

Lauranette had wanted to lock the house and leave her message taped to the front door, but I wouldn't hear of that. As it turned out, Sonia did come. While we were sleeping she left a note of her own.

Lauranette, I have not run away. I got home this afternoon but had to go out again. Sonia. P.S. I'll be listening. If you want to talk to me on the radio, my name can be Lisa.

The Plesses, too, had gotten a message from Sonia. Sarah read it to me over the phone.

Mom you are not a bitch, Dad you are not an ass. Sorry. I'll be gone for a while. This isn't about you. And it's not what you're thinking. Dad, it is NOT gallivanting. And I am not in the family situation. So please relax.

"Is the woman there? Can I see you?" Sarah asked. I could hardly tell where Sonia's letter stopped and Sarah's impulsive questions began. "There are some things I can't say on the phone. We could do one of your circles like the last time."

"Maybe someday," I told her.

She asked if she should call the police.

"If Sonia doesn't come home, you don't have any choice," I said.

When Lauranette got back I confessed everything, repeated the whole conversation with Sarah. Lauranette only made fun of my suspicion, the idea that Sarah might be cruising for me. "Of course you have to talk to her," she said. "Sonia could be walking off the end of the world." So if Sarah wanted to drive with me around the Beltway, I had no choice but to go ahead.

"Behind Richard's back?"

"What's the matter with you? The poor woman is miserable with worry for her daughter!"

She wasn't poor, I argued. She was the wily mother of my wily daughter. And I knew both of them were on the loose. Lauranette simply couldn't see the danger here—that Sarah was going to test me for this old affection, or that I could be drawn, for a moment, into the past.

MALL CEILING IS NOT STAINED GLASS ran that week's headline in the county paper. But neither was it painted glass exactly. Experts were puzzled by the elusive artist's technique. They had no name for what he had done. His colors had not been fired into the glass, nor had they simply been applied as an outer layer. They couldn't say how his pigments had penetrated the surface to different depths.

Light didn't pass directly through the glass, but was diffused under the surface, revealing interior color and design. The crew we had seen on the scaffold had been hired by the mall to record and analyze every pane in the Whole World ceiling.

The artist's hidden news was being revealed little by little, and he wasn't there to defend himself. As far as we knew, he'd gone to the Empire State Mall outside Albany. And when the sheriff's men came to us looking for Sonia, that's the trail I put them on.

They had her circle notebook with them, the one Sonia had found in my bedroom bureau. Richard had given it to them, though it must have hurt him terribly to make his daughter's whole story public. He was willing to go that far to see me ruined. I was accused of encouraging the circle's promiscuity. The deputies made no secret of their contempt. I was filthy. I ought to have my privates cut and cooked.

"We saw her with an older man in the mall," I told them, "but Sonia was only interested in the painter. Wherever he works she'll probably follow." This was my answer to all their questions about my habits, my relations with the children, my unemployment. They left telling me to find a lawyer, and promised to be back if the girl didn't "surface." I was ordered to be available at all times for questioning. My house would be under surveillance. I knew that, without evidence, they were only trying to scare me or trick me into betraying myself.

After reading the love diary, they weren't sure what to make of Sonia, but they were insinuating that I might have joined in the children's activities. It wasn't my imagination this time. The word was spreading. I wasn't given time to defend myself. There was telephone harassment.

"Ray Sykes?"

"Yes."

"The Chalkman?"

Callers accused me of perversion. We didn't want our phone disconnected. Even the cranks had their uses, keeping me informed of where I stood in the community. There were a few supporters, too, former students and parents.

Sonia came home four days later. The sheriff's car left our street. And Sarah called to say how sorry she was for involving us in a problem that was really theirs alone. "Sonia's promising to finish school," she said. "Rich is getting her a car." Sarah went on without much to say, and I guessed she was about to ask again for a circle with me.

"Go with her," Lauranette whispered. "You owe it to her." She left the room, making it easier for me to arrange a rendezvous.

"Why are you shouting?" Sarah asked.

"Was I?"

"Listen, is she right there next to you?"

"Lauranette's gone into the next room."

"Can't you speak a little softer."

"We don't have any secrets."

"I still need to talk to you."

"You are."

"I'm what?"

"You *are* talking to me." Lauranette appeared in the doorway shaking her finger, warning me to be polite.

"In the car," Sarah said. "A circle. Like the kids. Could we?"

"I guess we could, but how would you explain it to Richard?"

"How about the day after tomorrow?"

When I got off the phone, Lauranette was already heading for the station, leaving me to twist on my imagination. All along, she'd warned me away from the Plesses. Now, I guessed, she was trying to force me to see what Sarah and I had left of the past—very little by Lauranette's estimation and all outward appearances. She supposed that after eighteen years as a Stilson matron, Sarah could offer me nothing more than a concrete circle, a merry-go-round for children, a slow trip to nowhere.

On the radio that afternoon I heard Lauranette talking to a man who ran a camp in West Virginia where teenagers learned survival techniques. No hunting or fishing. Mostly nuts and berries and edible grasses, much easier food sources, and healthier. No violence to nature. The idea wasn't to be lost but to get found. As soon as possible. Badges were given to those who got back to civilization first.

"We're not trying to kill them. We want them to know how friendly the wilderness can be."

"Turn them loose in the mall," Lauranette advised him. "Without money. And see how many of them can find their way home." She gave her camp man the brush-off and said she'd finish the show with music.

Lauranette played five records in a row, one of them twice, with no intermittent chatter, and I guessed she was on the phone with another caller. She admitted as much when she came home for supper. "I don't know how much I should tell you," she said. A glass of wine later, a whole lot of news came spilling out. The caller had been the artist.

Norentez had reached her from a phone booth in upper New York State. He was quite upset about Sonia. "The young lady tramp," he called her. At the mall manager's office she'd lied that she was Norentez's professional model, that he'd be needing her when he got to work on their glass. She was calling herself Lisa and gave them a phone number where she could be reached. It turned out to be one of the numbers in the bank of phones in the mall itself, where she hung out for two whole days. When they called her to come to the office it wasn't Norentez but her father she found there waiting to take her home.

Norentez, when he did arrive, confessed his acquaintance with Sonia. By then they had learned that she was not twenty-four as she claimed, but eighteen. And they had called south to check on Norentez.

I could imagine the conversation.

"Thank you for calling Whole World."

"This is Empire Plaza. This Mexican who painted for you. Did he try anything dirty?"

"Who do you think you're talking to?"

"No bare ladies?"

"You can't really see it. One little scene. It's modern, you know."

"Better look again. There's a child here says she's all over your glass, buck naked."

By the time Norentez showed up in New York, the Whole World had several hundred color slides on file, and he was no longer welcome. They'd put the immigration officials on his case. The artist barely had time to go to ground. They'd found his car abandoned just off the interstate, south of Albany. He was burrowing his way back to Mexico.

"But what was he doing calling you?"

"Two good reasons. He wanted to deny any serious involvement with Sonia. And to tell us she's in danger and doesn't even know it. It's the men she's cruising with in the Whole World Mall. The older ones."

"He came to you for that?"

"Sure. He knows you and I live together. We're the ones he's told his stories to before. And remember, he thought you might be Sonia's real father. Even if he didn't quite trust you, he'd want you to trust him."

While he traveled away from us, Norentez's fame was turning to notoriety. That week a city paper had the report on the Whole World glass. There was more there under the surface than people knew. The same fields under wheat in one season would be seen as plowed ground, cracked and viscid, in another. Forests would turn brighter for fall when sunlight hit the glass at a lower angle. The squares and circles of pavement in his suburbia would lose their sheen and regain it as the seasons changed. The river would run dark and foamy by turns.

The style was described as "not of stark line and blocks of color but shadings and shifting values that delight the eye by suggestion." There was no simple way to explain the scope of his accomplishment. "A single color slide of any pane in the work cannot be a complete record of what that pane contains," the report said.

"Scenes like the fellatio under the trees on the mountainside and the analinctio in the reeds by the river can only be seen at the sharpest angles and under intense illumination not afforded by artificial lighting. However, with the backlighting of overhead sun, they emerge in clearer focus. In the context of the whole, magnificent work these scenes seem unimportant, no more relevant or out of place than they might be in the real world we inhabit."

Lauranette wasted little time finding analinctio in *Love's Dictionary*. The happy and uncensorious Danish authors called it "a kiss on the bottom, perfectly natural if both partners are willing."

The day I went to the mall to meet Sarah for our circle, I went early, leaving time to examine the ceiling again. I half-expected to find dark bodies coupling under the trees and in the reeds. But I only saw Norentez's beautiful, peopled landscape, muted somewhat by the overcast day. I came out with the shame of a man who has looked for his own picture in a skin magazine and been shown, instead, Creation.

When Sarah waved to me from far across the parking acres, I had little doubt that old times were on her mind, and wondered what tactics she'd use to take us back. She greeted me with a gentle hand in mine, and looked directly into my eyes, a little wistfully, maybe with doubts about what she was taking on for the afternoon.

"You're a little gray there," she said, touching the hair at my temple. I pulled back. After that there was no more touching. Her hands were occupied with getting us to the Beltway and around it. She'd insisted on doing the driving.

"I remember you like the outer loop," she said brightly.

I knew Sarah's age precisely, of course—thirty-six on the coming July 5—and was pleased that she made no special effort this day to fight it. Nothing used against wrinkles. No creams or powder. Just a little lipstick, considerably less than she'd used as a child. In a modest blouse and full skirt she wasn't flaunting her figure either. I let my guard down and spoke more easily with her than I had for years.

For a while, we listened to "Tumbleweed." I had control of the dial. We heard Lauranette introduce a couple with a flea circus. "Silly of her to waste time on that," Sarah thought, "on something that doesn't even exist." I happened to know they did exist; I described pictures I'd seen of fleas attached to tiny paraphernalia—trapezes and coaches. Sarah still didn't believe it, but by then the station was fading out of range and we were on our own.

Sarah wanted my opinion of what was happening to the mall artist. As if capture and deportation were reasonable. And not just because he wasn't a U.S. citizen.

"When the philosophers write about love they can have it

both ways," I said. "They can call the world a hymeneal feast and get away with it. But let Norentez paint a mouth and a phallus, or a tongue at the wrong entrance, and we call him a pervert and chase him back over the border."

"Hymeneal feast," she said. "Does that mean what I think it means?"

"No, it doesn't. That's the point."

She wasn't sure what I was getting at, but we were on a warm topic, and I supposed the long silence that followed meant she was pleased to dwell on it.

Toward the end of the circle I asked about Sonia. "Is she going to graduate?"

"Rita's getting straight A's. I guess I told you," Sarah said.

When we got to our exit ramp Sarah was in the wrong lane. "Let's do another." It had taken us two hours to make the circuit. Another trip around would put us into the heaviest afternoon traffic.

"I ought to get back," I said, reaching for the wheel. She held me off.

"Remember? You're unemployed, you don't have children."

"What about your children? What about Richard?"

"They know how to take care of themselves. And don't worry about Richard. He's moved into his parents' house for a couple of days. Our marriage counselor says it's supposed to make more room for our anger. That, and show us the parts of each other we really depend on. Well there aren't any parts like that anymore."

She must have sensed she was telling me too much. She made no fuss when I turned "Tumbleweed" on again. Lauranette had gotten rid of the couple with the flea circus. She was playing Billie Holiday records and making small talk about a crafts fair she was supposed to tout. "I mean," she said, "they'll even have a woman there turning honeysuckle vine into wastepaper baskets. Very useful magic."

She let Billie sing again, and then said something that seemed completely wrong, even startling. "It's all right. Relax. You're safe." I knew she was talking to me. "Sorry," she said, waking up to her larger audience. I think Sarah sensed a useful danger in what was happening. For the moment, she made no effort to change the station.

Lauranette began to talk about the recreational uses of travel on the interstates—what one of her phone-in listeners had called "nondestinational voyaging"—just before she cut him off. "It's a kind of narcotic," she said. "You have to stay alert in pleasure driving, but where's the fun if your knuckles are white?" When we got to the southern bridge her voice was fading, wishing all couples doing circles on the Beltway safe passage through Maryland.

Once out of the station's range, Sarah seemed compelled to fill the void. She pointed out a row of warehouses, the exit to the arboretum, which she had finally visited; the sports plaza, and the B&O overpass, as if the landmarks we were passing could make this a worthwhile sightseeing tour. She told me again she was sorry I'd lost my job; she hadn't wanted that. And she'd told Mr. Lambert several times she'd never thought I was dangerous to the children.

Contemplative, speaking softly, settling unpleasant accounts. There were six lanes to play in and she used all of them. I believe she knew that in my silence I was looking past her words, suspicious of a turmoil of seduction behind them, and that's why she just kept talking and driving. But all of it was so transparently nostalgic, so clearly leading toward some awkward move or declaration.

"The truth of it is our marriage counselor is a phony."

"He only wants to help," I suggested in hopeful ignorance.

"He's got a boyfriend and three children who despise him, and a wife in her *own* closet."

I was delighted, laughing. "Well, why does Richard keep going to him?"

"He prepares Richard's arguments for him. The ones he uses against me."

"What does the counselor tell you?"

"He says I've been living in a dream house too long."

"And what do you tell him?"

"I tell him, 'Yes, and now we're paying you the rent on it.'"

When we reached the northern bridge for the second time, I was relieved to be able to hunt for Lauranette again. I found her between a man hawking furniture and another reading nonstop news.

"Do we have to listen to her now?" Sarah stuck out her lower lip in a pout, and when I refused to change stations or turn the radio off she said, "Don't worry, you won't need her to protect you."

I tuned out the static to let Lauranette's clear voice wash away all temptation. She played an old-time country number whose refrain in four-part harmony carried the voices into premature regret.

....Come one, come all, to the family reunion,
It might be the last time we meet.

Lauranette said she'd been thinking about reunions. "It's not a bad thing," she suggested, "for a person to go back into his past now and then. Maybe just to see if he's moving in the right direction."

I was listening for the hint of a tongue in her cheek. But there was no guile. She was coming to the end of her program. She played "Harbor Lights" and then "Sentimental Journey," records so old you could hear the needle searching its way through the tortured grooves. The last one she dedicated to "a friend taking his own look at the past this evening."

When the music stopped, her traffic report seemed tailored for us. "For people coming west off the Beltway, there's bad congestion at the Whole World interchange. Take the river road instead. And don't hurry. Remember, when the Lord made time, he made plenty of it."

Almost immediately Sarah was making the turn onto the river road, alert for another traffic bulletin.

"Listen," Lauranette told everyone, "it's going to be slow all the way home." Then she was gone.

"I don't know where this one goes," Sarah said, pointing to a gravel lane on our right. "Let's try it."

We were wandering toward the river and I made no complaint. We turned into deep woods, then veered off again on something that was more path than road. The only exit took us between two farm fields, then to another rutted path under trees. Sarah kept on through tall weeds until the bottom of the car began to scrape. She cut the engine and looked across the seat at me, waiting for encouragement.

I looked back at her, disapproving, though I hadn't told her to stop, or turn the car around. At that moment I was thinking of Sonia, and what I could do to set her life on a happy course. Sarah wasn't wasting time, her hand playing on my leg. I pushed it away. There was silence except for the softest moan, and I caught myself drifting backward into her youth. I sat up straight, as if demanding an explanation with my posture. There was that diminutive moaning again, the faint sound of sexual pleading.

"What did you want to talk about?" I said. Sarah was talking only with her hands. I held them still, kissed her forehead, and then reached forward to turn the ignition key. She gave up and started the car herself.

Her demeanor changed abruptly. Hanging over this whole

afternoon had been the sense of a school reunion at which the gulf of intervening years had shrunk to nothing. I had been her off-duty secret again, and she, the fast student who dared to consort. Having reverted to the old role, Sarah was dismissing me again.

There was the old edge of disapproval. "Are you going to make something of yourself now?" I knew exactly what she meant: I would have been an all right choice in the old days but I'd had the despised profession.

Undefeated, Sarah drove me back. She was smug, in fact, maybe thinking that on a bad day she might try me again. She didn't talk about her TV programs, or her lawn furniture, or the assessed value of her home. Instead she amused me with another description of her marriage counselor and the cloves of garlic he sucked on during their sessions to keep his blood thin and mind sharp.

She told me about the last book she'd read. About a wild girl, raised in the jungle by animals. A trip to the library, a book, the story of an untamed child, all in preparation for my approval. A day's worth of cramming for an old teacher. She said she'd wanted to make me happy. "For old times' sake."

At the mall, after Sarah dropped me off, I sat at the wheel of my car, unable to erase what had happened. Or what hadn't happened.

Lauranette was waiting at home, but in the Whole World parking lot there was no relief from reverie. I had come closer than Sarah knew to returning all the way into our past. Now, in the sea of cars around me, there seemed to be a heart on every other bumper. A man calling in to "Tumbleweed" once had asserted this symbol has to do with anatomy all right, but nothing to do with the shape of the heart. He'd explained, just before

Lauranette thanked him and said goodbye, that it was actually, and sometimes subconsciously, the sign for the human female's rear cleavage in presentation. No one called in to dispute him.

A car that said I ♡ The Whole World pulled out of the space in front of me, and across the drive lane I saw the shiny little Japanese car that Richard had bought Sonia in return for her promise to finish school respectably and to stay away from the mall. He'd bought low-numbered vanity plates for her too—37-373—her lucky numbers according to Sarah.

The car was parked at a careless angle. I sat watching and waiting and lost track of time. It had been dark for more than an hour when I saw a man's head rise in her back window and then duck down again. I was thinking she must have been in there with him all that time, breaking all her pledges, when I turned and saw her coming quickly across the lot. She got in the car, slammed the door and was already pulling away before I could get started. The man in the backseat hadn't shown himself. She didn't know he was in there!

I rushed to catch up, missed the light that let her onto the highway, and, against the red, with cars braking and honking around me, pulled out far behind her, blinking my headlights. She never slowed down. By the time I had passed the several cars separating us we had gone through two more traffic lights and she was picking up speed, maybe aware a car was following her.

I flashed my brights again, hoping she might stop to see if there was trouble. Instead it only seemed to startle her into greater speed. Unable to lose me, she made several turns, bringing her onto a secondary road, heading upriver. And a mile later, when she headed through woods on a dirt surface, I realized I'd been this way before. She was racing toward the old farm where Norentez had stayed. Perhaps she'd heard the artist was again using the slaughter shed as a retreat. Or, in her race to escape me, she was simply making familiar turns that were leading her farther into a wilderness from which there'd be no escape. As she drove on into the unlit country she was becoming reckless, slamming the undercarriage of her new car against the rough road, and when she turned across the cattle grate into the farm itself, she nearly turned over. I was right behind, flashing my lights.

She kept going past the shed, right across the meadow, almost to the edge of the quarry. When she finally stopped, I called out my window, "Get out! Get back here!" Sonia opened her door, heard my voice, and came marching back at me, shielding her eyes from my headlights.

"You creep! Are you sick or what? Why did you scare me like that?"

"There's someone in your backseat," I said.

"What do you mean?"

"Get in."

"I'm not getting in your car!"

"Get in before you get hurt," I ordered.

She was going back to her car. I drove toward her and she jumped out of the way. "Get back!" I yelled. She was screaming at me, but yielding as I moved against her rear bumper and began to push her car toward the quarry's edge. She'd left it in gear and it moved forward in a lurching motion.

It was only a few yards from falling in when a back door flew open and the man came running out. He was waving a pistol as he came past us and fled toward the tree line above. I couldn't see his face. He seemed to be moving as fast as he could, but awkwardly, like a woman in high heels.

Sonia must have been too frightened to thank me. After we checked her backseat and looked in her trunk to reassure her, she drove slowly home, allowing me to follow all the way. I waited till she was safe inside, and watched the light come on in Sarah's room.

Stopping at a pay phone I called the county police and told the officer on duty what had happened. I told him he'd have to call Sonia: she was the target. The wrong thing to say. He didn't trust my excitement, didn't want my advice, and lost interest completely when I refused to give my name. In the middle of my fuzzy description of the man in the backseat, he said, "Was anybody hurt? If someone wants to file a report send them in here." He got rid of me the same way I'd heard Lauranette unload callers on "Tumbleweed." "Hey, listen." I listened, but he'd hung up.

I drove west to the mountain, and up the ridge road and parked where I could look back toward the city and watch the display of twinkling lights across the valley. Through the clear night the faint light in the cathedral tower flashed its warning. As I fell asleep it became a red flower whose petals were falling one by one as I plucked them, holy, unholy, holy, unholy, without resolution.

I woke after midnight with a stiff neck, and came down the mountain wondering what doors might be locked against me. Front, back, bedroom? But everything was wide open, all lights burning and Lauranette waiting in the kitchen with the kettle at a low hum for a welcoming toddy.

"Sarah called," she said brightly, fixing me the drink. "Sonia had them worried to death again. But she's home now, and won't talk to them. Actually Sarah wanted to talk to you. She thinks you may have seen Sonia tonight."

"Is that all she had to say?"

"The other can wait. Now what about Sonia?"

She was incredulous as I gave her an account of the chase and rescue. "She could have been killed," I said. "It wasn't money the guy was after. She didn't have any."

It could have been the car, Lauranette thought. He might have been stealing it.

But I knew from things I could not define—that the man's interest had been in Sonia herself.

Lauranette was behind me, her arms around me, her fingers slipping between the buttons of my shirt. I was trying to shake her loose. "Now," she said, "right now is okay," coaxing calmly, and I wavered between irritation and excitement.

"I thought you'd be home after one circle," she said. "But you were like kids on a merry-go-round."

She was still holding on, rubbing softly, sending signals all over me, electric counter-measures against more talk about my circling with Sarah.

"Admit it," I said. "You pushed us all the way into that ride. What did Sarah say about it?"

"She said you went twice around the city and once into the bushes, and then you behaved like a perfect gentleman. She thanked me for letting her take you for an afternoon. No shame. No spite. Just matter-of-fact. Does she do drug trips, or what?"

"She's never been anywhere she couldn't get on Richard's American Express."

"She's nervy as her daughter, more dangerous than I thought."

"I told you she was."

"The point is, she's Sonia's mother. That's the only fascination she could have for you. Anyway, I promise not to send you off with her again."

We drifted away from the unfinished business of my temptation with Sarah as Lauranette pulled me down onto our stained living room carpet. "I'm your wife," she said, the words raspy in her throat, caught there in endearing uncertainty.

On my way down the mountain I had anticipated trouble, apologies, and a full explanation demanded. Lauranette's rush to heal was premature balm, assuring me of a warm home and passionate companion.

I moved up on my knees to help her along in loving gratitude, but she pushed me down onto the rug again, wanting only to attend to me with her own offering. She was pulling me gently this way and that as she ranged over me.

"Don't move," she said. "I don't want you to move at all." Taking responsibility for everything. I imagined myself safely home.

Afterward, following me into the bedroom, she said, "I want you to promise me this. You won't push yourself into Sonia's life anymore. I mean it this time. You know I don't expect you to just forget her. But now you're going to have to watch her from a distance."

Reluctantly, I promised, knowing it was an empty pledge.

The next day I slipped away, and cruised all the way down to the mall, where I sat in the atrium searching the ceiling for more parts of Sonia. As if her hidden glory could be seen there by someone with the perception to find it. I may in fact have found another view of her that afternoon—her standing figure foreshortened by Norentez, her hands raised to him in supplication, but the shifting light outside erased the image as quickly as it had been exposed, and I wondered how much of his art had been created by me.

Sonia's high school teachers would get an eyeful here. They'd be looking for all the wrong things, for flesh and heat instead of the cool bravery in her presentation of herself to the artist, her recognition of the illusive man's talent, the powers in his pinched, homely head. They'd never believe that Sonia's part in this was any more than self-display.

My heart was not completely at home that season. Though Lauranette and I were living peacefully together, I had made a boundary of the center line of our bed, and most nights kept to my side of it, the side by the clock radio and its earphones. I pretended to need a lot of news, time, and weather. Lauranette forgave this as just a phase, the moodiness of unemployment.

Actually, with the radio almost off, I used the headset as earmuffs against the obligation to talk. When Lauranette went to sleep I thought of new ways to approach my daughter and save her from the school and the society that still misjudged and degraded her.

Sometimes Sarah was part of this impossible plan for a reunion of the family, and for undoing the wrong done to Sonia. In my waking dreams I accepted apologies from the community, and even heard Sarah ask me back. Well, that would be difficult, I'd have to tell her. So many lives would be upset, though perhaps Rita could live with Richard. He deserved that much, didn't he? In any case, we could all remain civil with one another, exchange visits and presents in season, that sort of thing. And what about your radio woman? Well, she may be getting fed up with me.

This fancy would play itself out, longer and longer, until I slid down, drowsy in the bed, the headphones slipping away from my dreams of another time by the river with Sarah. Guilt-ridden dreams. Generously, Lauranette was making allowances for my distance, but there was a limit to her tolerance.

If they were dishonest nights in that month before Sonia's graduation, my days, too, were devious. Slipping away after Lauranette left for the station each day, I'd drive to the supermarket lot, pick up Walter and friends, and chauffeur them to the game in the woods. I was there to teach, to show them how to win.

"No one has to be a loser here," I told them, coaxing them back toward jobs. They threw cards quickly; I pondered decisions, calculated odds. They jabbered, I offered them poker as a science. They asked each other mischievous questions, tantamount to cheating. "You're only cheating yourselves."

As long as they could call me Teacher I supposed their losses seemed less painful. The money in the game came from Social Security and unemployment checks—a common fund, the pool on which they all floated. Enough for beer and cream-filled ladyfingers every day.

They became quieter, I talked more. "Imagine," I said one afternoon, "three jacks in a full house with two kings," turning over the five lucky face cards, two of which had come my way on the draw.

"House full of men," Bones said. "Does that make you a queen?" Out of hearing of the others, Walter said, "You're robbing us. You don't take chances. You don't bring the money back."

I was suddenly ashamed, and wanted to make it up to them. I shaved less, let myself go scraggly, played carelessly, brought twenty-five new dollars into the game and promptly lost it. Bones said I played as if I had wings, "like a goose with palsy."

Instead of leaving, I tried harder with subtle, false efforts at winning. I arrived and their laughter died. I pushed my way further into the game, unwilling to break with the common men of Stilson. They began to take their money back with open contempt.

I was half-drunk with them one afternoon, sharing their lot, I thought, as victims of injustice and the little cruelties of the local police force. One of them said, "Your deal, Teacher, and count good this time."

I looked all around and there, a short distance behind me, was Sarah's face just disappearing behind a tree. Others had seen her, too. When we stood up she knew she'd been discovered, and she walked into the open, away toward the road. Instead of following her I stayed with my club.

"Let her go on," Walter said. "It's the mother of that dumbo split-tail over at the high school, the one with the easy legs."

"Who told you that?" I asked him sharply. "What do you know about it?"

"I got a niece in her class. Everyone knows she runs the sex club over there."

"I'll tell you something," I said, getting up in Walter's face. "I taught her and she happens to be a remarkable student. Too bright for them. They don't know how to teach her. What's more, she's president of Clean Sisters."

"She can come and clean my house anytime."

"It's not your house that's dirty!" I jabbed Walter's shoulder, and two of them came at me. Bones had my arms pinned to my sides when another tackled me, and I went down like a sack. I was aware of a rock coming up to meet my head, and that was all until I woke with a pool of blood and Lauranette beside me.

At the hospital they stitched a wound that ran from my eye to the line where my part had been before they shaved my head. Worse, the doctors said my skull had cracked. I'd have to stay in the hospital a few days, and after that Lauranette was going to have to make sure I woke up in the mornings.

Seeing me bleeding and still, the club men would have been frightened. They hadn't called for help, they'd just disappeared, leaving my poker stake, a few dollars, next to me on the ground. In the second week of my recovery, my face still swollen, I went back to show them they could talk to me, that I'd never use the law against them.

The club wasn't meeting in the woods anymore. I returned a number of times, but I don't think they ever went back to the same spot. When I walked up to Walter in the parking lot and asked who'd been winning, he had nothing to say.

———

The afternoon of my accident in the woods Lauranette had received an invitation to Sonia's graduation. The card with raised black letters said

THE ADMINISTRATION AND FACULTY OF
RIVER HIGH SCHOOL
AND THE SENIOR CLASS OF 1975
INVITE YOU TO GRADUATION EXERCISES

June 6 at 2:30 P.M.   AUDITORIUM

Enclosed in the envelope with it was Sonia's formal calling card with raised letters of its own. Sonia Dimbrell Pless in a delicate script.

All of it confirming Sonia's passing, which had been in doubt for months. Whatever her class standing, I wanted to see my daughter walk in her own haughty review before the graduation assembly and take her scroll from Lambert. All the girls would be overdressed and carrying flowers, more like bridesmaids than scholars, proclaiming open minds and virginal attitudes. Richard, if not Sarah, would see that Sonia fit comfortably in that parade. Whatever hypocrisy was disguised by the ceremony, I wanted to be there, to sit through all of it, once again to see every well-informed smile and smirk of my daughter's intelligent face as she watched the awards presented, heard the valedictorian and Lambert's last farewell.

"You're not invited," Lauranette reminded me.

"You're invited," I said. "You can bring a friend."

"I'm not going, and you're not either."

"I don't need an invitation to my own school," I told her.

"You'll need a police escort."

I walked out of the house and we didn't speak again until that night, when she begged of heaven that I be alive in the woods. With her support I was able to stand and walk to the car, surprised that she, like Sarah, had known where the game was played. When I didn't come home it was the first place she looked. I don't remember saying anything when she found me, only hearing her scream and plead with me to move.

At the hospital they wanted to know who'd done this to me. It was clearly a beating. "I was walking in the woods," I told them, "minding my own business when someone knocked me to the ground. I never saw him."

"Whoever you're protecting," the doctor said, "came this close to blinding you, and this close to murder." He was trying to demonstrate a very short distance with his thumb and forefinger in front of my half-open eye.

After three days in the hospital, I was surprised when Sarah came in to visit, just as surprised as I'd been to see her in the woods. She was uncomfortably honest, saying my head looked like a rag doll's with a zipper to hold in the stuffing—the crosshatch of stitches over my scar. Sarah took my recovery for granted, didn't really want to talk about me at all. She thought Sonia might be in new trouble at school, and asked if I'd heard anything about it. Richard thought Sonia might have come to see me in the hospital. "He doesn't trust anyone," she said.

Home again, I wore dark glasses that couldn't begin to disguise the swelling and discoloration. I tried combinations of scarves, hats, and glasses, even a ski mask, but the effects were always the same—a freak ashamed, or a bank robber. I told Lauranette I was afraid I'd horrify or frighten the children, or make them uncomfortable.

She put a soft finger on my wound and said, "Don't you remember what we decided. You're not going."

Several days later the school reversed itself, and Sonia

wasn't graduating after all. Sarah called to ask if I had any ideas. "I know it wouldn't be easy for you, but couldn't you speak to someone. Richard thinks she'll never get a job, she'll just be a tramp."

I did call Lambert, pretending it was about the way the school system would dispose of my *Stilson* history texts, which had been tossed out of the curriculum for the next year. "And what about the Pless girl? What's going on?"

"I'm surprised you'd ask about her. After everything. Don't you know they're still investigating you. I don't know how much time our people have spent answering questions. I'd like to pretend I didn't get this call, Ray."

"Tell them whatever you have to. Don't lie for my sake."

"Ray, please get some help."

"I want to know why you're not letting her graduate."

There was a long silence. I wasn't going to help him by saying another word until he answered my question. He could either do that or hang up on me.

"Look," he finally said. "If it's any of your business, and it isn't, she called me something that doesn't need to be repeated."

I called Sarah with this much even though I knew she'd run straight back to Lambert with it. And she did. For her he had a different story. An unacceptable academic performance, he told her, and an unfortunate clerical error during the recording of grades. A single session of summer school couldn't fix it. "She'd have to make up a whole year," he'd told Sarah.

I didn't really share Richard and Sarah's anger. I didn't need my child's accreditation from such a flawed system. Sonia herself said the school's diplomas came in thousand-sheet rolls. Still, it was that beautiful time of the year when warm days bring joy, and you can see the students think life is forever and love abundant, even for dunces. And I wasn't there to help her with her failure, through the laughing halls.

"You can't go around calling your principal any old vulgar name," Lauranette challenged me. "What did she call him, by the way?"

I heard later from Sarah that Sonia had gone to Lambert's office to defend one of her Clean Sisters. It was about an article in the school paper—an article censored by him. The whole thing had blown up in Lambert's face. Something Sonia said sent him over the line. After all she had done and not done in her four years there, this late and final punishment was ludicrous.

Sonia stayed in class to the end, but while everyone else watched the chosen ones step forward at the awards assembly, she was in the principal's office, rifling his cabinets. She had filled the backseat of her car with manila folders containing his evaluations of every teacher in the school.

After sharing the folders with her friends, she mailed them out to the teachers themselves. Mine she brought to our house in person. Standing in our doorway, she said, "These are yours," holding the papers out to me. "You might want to know what they really thought about you. God!" she went on. "Nothing's the way you think it is!"

"Miss Edgar has diabetes and keeps a hypodermic needle at school. And Mrs. Blay graduated first in her class at her teacher's college and she can carry a hidden pistol because her first husband is so dangerous. But not at school. I know a thousand new things."

"I read this," Sonia said, as I took my file from her. "And I heard what happened to you." That was all. Because Lauranette asked her to leave.

"Oh, sure," Sonia said, quite amiably. There was no way her heroine could insult her.

When she was gone Lauranette and I pored over my file together. It wasn't the normal collection of perfunctory evaluations the principal was required to keep on his faculty, and which we were made to read and sign twice a year. This was his private dossier on me. It had been kept in chronological order and went all the way back to Lambert's first season as head of the school. He'd come to River High from the other county high school where he'd been an assistant principal.

His wily circumspection as an administrator began early. The first entries in my file began in November 1954. Monitored several of Ray Sykes's classes this fall. Risky fellowship with students? Informal, casual approach to subject matter will make it difficult for him to keep order. Doesn't keep short-term marks. I suggested one grade per week per student. Needs watching.

In 1955, a paragraph on other teachers' complaints. Noises coming regularly from my classroom. Frequent outbursts, foot stomping, desk thumping, and my voice too loud, not calling for order, but part of the disruption. "Out of control like his students?"

I remembered the season well. Maybe my finest. The English class full of children eager to hear me speak, most of them even willing to write, Sarah among them, standing out in wit and cheer, demurely irreverent in lip and limb, and I, denying my seniority and authority in every way I knew how, reaching backward to make myself her contemporary. It was before she'd taken up with Richard, before she'd slowed down and lowered her head for him.

Then the sad fall of 1956, the season of my most forlorn yearning, me at my chalk-grinding worst, when Lambert had made several entries in my file. More fussing about grades because he'd found no marks below B in my books. He'd asked me to "get some ranking going."

A note from a mother: "I understand that Mr. Sykes is sometimes flirtatious." On the back was noted: Answered 2/10/56 J.L. Other letters, too, were scattered through the file with indications that Lambert had replied to all of them. "More complaints about Sykes this week. Warned not to tamper with public-address system. Wrong to choose him for the history course?"

"This is incredible," Lauranette said. "You don't owe this man any apologies."

But these were just a bureaucrat's notes, collected for self-protection. "He was probably afraid of what I could do to him. Rose Edgar and I had the goods on him. He couldn't have fought the two of us. He didn't have the words. We could have made him look like a fool."

"These are words," Lauranette said, tapping the file. I started reading again. No matter our differences, I'd always imagined that each semester began on firm ground with Lambert, in honor of time served together.

"Talked to Ray Sykes today about his assignment of off-campus projects. Has to stop this. Is it a question of competence, or just occasional poor judgment? He has a lot of ideas, but are the kids listening? His classes don't test as well as they used to. Has to pull up his socks and get the material covered."

It wasn't until Sonia entered high school that my folder really began to thicken, and Lambert's little memos to himself took an ominous turn. "Rose Edgar says he's lost his class again. Ranting lectures. Coherent? Doesn't know when the children are making fun of him. She's keeping her eye on situation."

"11/2/72 R. Sykes came to my office this morning with a long bleat about procedures. Too many bells. Too much public address. Cover for problem he doesn't want to talk about? Disruption of his classes, disrespect, whistling, cooing of his name, farting noises. He denied discipline problem and asked about the Pless child again. Asked me to put her in gifted-and-talented program. Out of the question. His unusual attention to this student has been noticed by other teachers and the child herself. Rose Edgar working with me on this."

Further on: "Rose doubts there is anything abnormal in his focus on the Pless girl. She says, not the first time he's taken cause of underdog. Compassionate but excessive. A man without children of his own adopting the unfortunate." What had Sonia made of all this?

It wasn't Miss Edgar anymore, but Rose. The perfidy grew. "Rose thinks the answer is a change of school scenery. Maybe some introductory math. He could do that. Get his mind off the social studies, the politics. Hard to kick an old-timer around. Give him some more rope, see what happens. Rose would like to teach the local-history course herself for a couple of years. She'd be good at it."

Where was my support? What gossamer had I been hanging from all those years? And Sonia had read this, too—their embarrassing tolerance for a foolish pedagogue! Why had I been kept around? Was it only from his sense of continuity and order, that he'd rather hear me rant at students than attack him? And all that time Rose had wanted my job. No doubt she'd get it now. And I'd thought she was so fond of me, perhaps ready to mix chalk and love. Rose, on another team after all. I searched back for some sign of early betrayal. I could only think of something she'd told me after a long-ago faculty meeting when I'd made fun of what we called "Lambert's Rules of Order."

"You're surprised at anybody's big words, no matter where they come from," she'd said. "You forget everybody's brain is a miracle capable of little miracles." Such a leveling, humanitarian sentiment; I remember an impulse to reach out and hold her hand while she spoke.

There had been more. She was standing very close, leaning forward, a lovely confessor, her eyelashes fanning her quiet argument. I thought she might be offering herself as my reward for listening to this. "You've taught so long, Ray, you can't stop thinking about intelligence because you're always judging it." My refusal to rank my students, she thought, was only camouflage for my constant attention to their wit or lack of it.

"It's like your Sonia and her sex clubs," she said. "Thinking about it, thinking about it, all the time. The Clean Sisters nonsense. Even that's thinking about it, you know?"

The last entry in my file had been a few words on me from Rose to Lambert: "I feel sorry for R.S. in a way. Such a dreamer. All he ever had was the audience in his classroom, and now he's losing that. He's lost his little empire."

"I want you to do something for me," I told Lauranette. "I want you to make Sonia feel more comfortable here. If she comes back again I want you to make her a sandwich. Turn the television on. Give her refuge. Maybe tell her she doesn't have to worry about me."

Lauranette's hands were raised and she was shaking her head. "Something very wrong is going on! She could accuse you of something. She's capable of that, you know. It wouldn't take much. Suppose you had an impulse to hug her. Or just gave her a father's affectionate squeeze? Do you have any idea what would happen? What if she just made it up. No, I don't want her coming here anymore."

"But she doesn't have anywhere else to go. She won't stay home now that school's finished. She's not cautious." My voice was cracking. I was afraid for Sonia. The man stroking her shoulder in the mall, the man hiding in her car, the man described in the crime-solver's report. For me they all converged into one face. Something too old and dangerous for Sonia, and closing in on her. And Norentez's warning seemed more like a wise man's truth.

"I'm telling you," Lauranette said. "She and her friends

gave you nothing but insolence. They drove you out of your job."

"They weren't the ones," I insisted.

"They were! You sacrificed plenty for that little . . . that little . . ."

"Say it. Say it this time. That little bitch."

"That's not the word I had in mind."

"Worse?"

"Yes. And now she brings us this."

"If she read it carefully, she knows I care about her." Lauranette was still shaking her head. "I'm not going to be her second mother," she said. "How about twice-baked potatoes tonight?"

"That's nice," I said, engrossed again in Lambert's notes.

"Get your own supper, all right?"

"Oh, just potatoes or something." I looked up to see Lauranette leaving the house.

Lauranette had warned me not to go back into the school. What could be gained from it? By then I hadn't even wanted Sonia to graduate. But I had gone, scars and all, looking every bit the monster, my heels clicking down the linoleum of the central passage, my old checked sport jacket at last free of chalk dust. The dull cinderblock walls reflected the false daylight of the fluorescent bulbs overhead in the long windowless corridor. A giant detention center, and I was going in to pass subversive information to one of the inmates.

A morning bell had rung and students swarmed out of their rooms. They parted around my determined path through the middle of them and closed again behind me. I was forcing them to look up and see what had happened to me, even as I asked them not to be scared. "It's all right. It's only Mr. Sykes," I told them left and right. Some looked away in shame or horror or disgust. Others stared after me, snickering at a freak.

I was marching to Lambert's office, not really wanting to see him. I was there for a last look at Sonia as a schoolgirl, a chance to show her I forgave whatever she'd done or thought, to tell her I had faith in her. I knew how to look for her, where to be standing, and at what moment so that, once again, chance could be the culprit in our meeting.

She was managing her little celebrity so well—the girl who had run the first circle, the one who was not going to graduate, whose amused view of the school that had rejected her was cast so gently over them all in long, thoughtful glances, the one who wouldn't let them define her with grades.

"Think of it this way," I wanted to tell her. "If we never graduate, we'll always be here. Our spirits sitting in their rooms forever, waiting for release into the real world we've already demonstrated for them. Defrocked teacher and shamed scholar, stripped of our credentials." It was a speech I didn't get a chance to make.

I knew Sonia's habit of waiting till the last moment between bells, hoping to walk through the hall alone, unconcerned about being late. And I was close to the door when she came swinging out of her class. But there were two boys in attendance, one of them pleading for more time with her. She suffered them as if they were troublesome pets sniffing around; tolerated but not overindulged.

When she saw me she hesitated a moment. "Ooooh, look at his face!" she said to her thrilled companions. The distance in her sympathy cut the chance of an exchange with her. She was already looking away when she said, "Visitors have to sign in."

A moment later I was in Lambert's outer office getting the brush-off. He wouldn't open his door. I began to hum the school fight song—"River High Flow Onward." The secretaries were whispering into their phones. I stood up and began to call Lambert's name. Maybe I was shouting. Unknown to me, Lambert had called the police. I was marched out of the building between two uniformed men. And the next time I saw Sonia she was handing me my private file. Two days later she had left home with no messages for anyone.

IV

A MISSING PERSON

I learn by going where I have to go.

—*THEODORE ROETHKE*

I was ready for the chase this time. With as many clues as anyone. Good information, a father's knowledge of her little traits, manners, attitudes.

Her car with its vanity plates would have been an easy nationwide target but Sonia had left it in the family driveway. This time the sheriff's men who came to see me were strangely polite in their questioning. You'd have thought they were dealing with a ruined man. One of them asked repeatedly and very softly about my scars and discolored face.

The night someone might have killed her, they hadn't been interested. Why were they bothered now?

"This is a missing person case," I was told with a new and special gravity. And did I have any idea why she might have left the area?

"Area?" They took a statement from me about the man who'd been in her car, and everything that had happened that night. No one asked if I'd seen her since then. But Lambert called wanting to know if I'd received anything odd in the mail, some school business.

"If you do, don't look at it," he advised. "Some personal things were taken from my office and mailed around to a few of you. We've got a good idea who's responsible. These things should be returned immediately to the school."

"Don't you remember what you said? I'm not allowed on the grounds."

"Could you have your lady-friend bring it over, Ray? This is important."

"School business isn't important to me."

"Ray, I tried to stop it. I'm trying to apologize. Maybe we shouldn't have called the police. I know there wasn't any need to get rough, but you were scaring children. What did you expect, looking like that? And you'd been asked."

"How would I know it's what you want if I don't have a look at it?" I could play along with him.

"Did you realize you were yelling, Ray? That the kids could hear from their classrooms? When you wouldn't let the phys ed guys take you out, what choice did I have?"

"Why shouldn't I see what's in these papers you're talking about? What's so secret about your school?"

"Ray, listen to me. I don't know what it is with you and the Pless child, that's your business now. But if you've got any respect for the school that supported you for more than twenty years, I hope you'll do what I've asked."

"Support? I don't know if I'd call it that. Anyway, it's a closed file. Trust me."

"You've already looked through it. I can tell. Was it mailed to you?"

"Hand carried. Right to my door."

"She could be arrested. You know that, don't you?"

"You'd have to find her first."

"She's a thief, Ray. You put your faith in the wrong one. Let's talk about this sensibly." But he was doing all the talking, probably a little nervous, wondering how much I knew and trying to remember just what he'd said about me in his notes.

"Can you admit this much," he asked, "that she couldn't make the grade? Not much concentration there. We knew it from the beginning, didn't we? The tests."

That was his big mistake. The pedagogue's worst and most damaging conceit. Predictions based on faulty numbers. Numbers which, in the end, stood for nothing. "No," I said. "She was too complicated for your system. We didn't measure her. We didn't have the tools for it."

"We make pretty good correlations," he said. "Between what they do here and what's going to happen later on. You can't protect her from an ordinary life, Ray. Very ordinary. I mean if she doesn't go to jail. They let us know from the start. You can see it in their eyes. You've been around long enough to know that. They want it and they can't reach it, and most of them just give up. She gave up early, Ray. Why couldn't you see it like the rest of us?"

I imagined him there in his office, winking at Rose Edgar in private conference with him, swiveling next to her to assure her of his divided attention, perhaps touching her hand. "No," he went on, "couldn't handle the academic pressure so she stretched way out like they say, had a good time. If we gave grades for stretching way out she'd be a merit scholar. God knows, we could use a few of them."

"Pressure?" I said. "You call those standards pressure?" Somewhere in my long defense of Sonia he hung up, maybe after I called his school a hall of parrots.

Whatever Norentez was up to, he hadn't made it to Mexico. He was making mysterious calls to Lauranette, unwilling to say exactly where he was, but drawing her further into his story. We were still in bed one morning when he phoned. I could tell she knew it was going to be him.

Lauranette was rushing to hook up her recording device. It was a little rubber suction cup she could attach to the receiver, and it had wires leading to her tape machine. "What for?" I asked, surprised she'd be doing this.

"He knows. He wants me to," she said. She hushed me and sent me to listen in on the downstairs phone, maybe to prove the innocence of their odd communication. "Listen carefully," she said. "He's amazing."

When I said hello, he answered, "Yes, you listen too. I thought you were the girl's father. When they told me this other man, this Mr. Pless, came to get her, I didn't believe it. Maybe you are the uncle, yes?"

"Go ahead, Roberto." Lauranette was impatient. A minute later Norentez was sounding like a prophet giving us modern scripture. He was speaking of himself in the third person, his heavily accented English carrying authority and weight.

"The sheriff's men came in their cars with numbers on them, you know? Searching for the artist because of what he had done to their mall. He traveled at night along dark highways. A fugitive in the land he had painted. They were angry in the mall. He had fooled the people and fouled their ceiling. Afraid of his paint, they want the glass destroyed.

"They said a girl traveled with him. Too young for him. The one who had given herself for his work. If they found him with her they were going to fix him, let him rot in jail where real men could use *him* for a woman." His voice was steady, a driving monotone, as if he were reading this.

"The girl, she was a fugitive too. Pretty and bold. But now she is missing. She has to be found."

"Where is she?" I interrupted.

"Aren't you listening?"

"Keep still," Lauranette warned me, "or get off the line."

"Where is she?" I asked again.

"The girl went back to the rooms where she had modeled. The rooms had disappeared. She waited every day in the big hall, hoping for him. Watching the ceiling for her own body, which moved with the sun. And she wept. She was very careful. She cut her hair close to her head and made herself flat with boy's clothes. A disguise. This way, she looked for me. But the other men are coming after her."

"You don't have any idea what you're saying," I cut in again.

"I can tell you the girl is in danger."

"You're following her? Where are you?"

"I have seen the ones who want her. These men came to New York, but this Mr. Pless, he came first to take her home."

He seemed to want to protect Sonia, while he denied involvement with her. I wanted to trust him, but why was he being so mysterious? How did he know so much about this?

"The mall was my home sometimes," he said. "Her home too."

"That's not good enough," I told him. "What's your real interest in the girl?"

"By what right do you ask?"

"I was her teacher. I was very interested in her progress."

"You told me that before. So did she. I think you were more than that."

"What did she tell you?"

"That you watched her. That you took things of hers."

"What else? When did you talk to her?"

Lauranette broke in, asking me again to keep quiet.

Norentez said, "The police must hear this."

"Why aren't you calling *them*?" I asked him. "You're the witness."

"I can't," he said. "You know why. My papers are no good. I am illegal here."

"Then come here and tell us all about it. We'll take care of you."

"Let him finish, Ray. Go ahead, Roberto."

"The men the police look for at the mall—they don't just write the bad checks. They make movies. The very bad kind."

"Pornography?" Lauranette asked. "They were going to use her in pornography?"

"No, worse than that." Norentez's voice was fading.

"How could it be worse?"

"You don't want to know." He didn't hang up; his voice just disappeared. Lauranette thought she heard someone call his name but after a while there was only the buzz of the unattended phone. We assumed he was on the run again from the law and the immigration people.

Next morning I was waiting at the mall entrance when the doors opened. I ranged through the halls on all levels, alert for a boyish disguise, accosting several children got up in androgynous style. I was being watched by mall security; I knew their faces as well as they knew mine. They shamed me into a few small purchases. Early that evening I lost them for a while and was considering an overnight, thinking Sonia might come out of hiding by dark. I no sooner slipped behind one of the temporary walls than I was ushered outside.

Next day, back again. This time I confronted the first security man who caught my eye. "You don't have to worry about me," I told him. "I'm only here to admire your ceiling. It has to be viewed from all angles, in all lights." He moved off and kept a discreet detective's distance.

Richard and Sarah showed up, too, and one of the regulars

from the sheriff's department. That week our paths crossed several times as we went back and forth watching for our missing child. When this happened, Richard scowled, and Sarah pulled him away while Lauranette led me off in another direction. In the evenings she would drive down from the station to meet me for a drink at the Turning Night where we gazed out over the suburban landscape.

We all hoped Sonia was out there somewhere, hoped she was still breathing, even heavily if that was her choice of the moment. Any activity at all as long as she was alive. I always sat for at least one full revolution of the restaurant, from the mountain to the cathedral and back to the mountain again, taking comfort in the notion that, making a complete circle, I must have looked out over her hiding place.

All that week, then all of the next, strolling back and forth over the polished tile floors or sitting on the benches in the central atrium and gazing up from every vantage at the wonderful ceiling, waiting for Sonia's face and figure to shine from the glass and refresh the memory of what we looked for. She must have come forth and disappeared a hundred times.

I discovered two more positions for glimpses of my daughter. I was looking up one morning at a side view of her face and figure, enthralled by my sighting, chuckling in delight at Norentez's capture of a certain attitude, when someone nudged me from behind. I spun around, and Sarah was there beside me looking oddly contented, even mischievous.

Her hair fell carelessly across her face, and she turned her head from side to side to get it out of her eyes. In a light blue summer frock she was trim and quite beautiful, and as soon as she felt my gaze on her she did a fetching little shoulder turn like a model. "Do you like it?" she said. "I just bought it."

I told her it was very pretty, that she wore it very well.

"Lighten up," she said, "Richard's not here. What were you

laughing at? What's the matter? Is it the perfume?" I must have been backing away.

"Look up there," I said. I showed her the view of Sonia I'd just discovered. She was amazed—as if an astronomer had found a new star with the unaided eye.

"Richard just cannot believe it," she said. "The way Sonia comes and goes in the glass." One moment he was horrified by her public nakedness, she explained. And the next, he was confused, when the picture just disappeared. Maybe he was learning to trust whatever came into view. That it was actually there. Not just imagined. He could take comfort in that. For each disappearance there was always another sighting.

"Kiddie porn? Teen porn?" Lauranette's questions begged against the horror of what we'd heard in Norentez's warning. "She'd do anything, you know, if they flattered her," she said. "Take off anything. Perform any act. Wait, don't be angry. I know what you're going to say—that it isn't shameful to her. Just a kind of responsibility to love, and she's the honorable one, not shirking the duty."

"I'm not angry," I said. "You're right about one thing—her honor—and you're wrong about the rest. You can't mistreat her and be her friend. There's never been anything neurotic in her choice of partners. She kept them honest, all those boys. She never chased anyone who put her down."

"What about Roberto? All the way out of state, wasn't it? All the way to New York. And back."

"That's different. She sees something fine there. She wants to be part of something permanent."

"You're going to have to let go, Ray. They may have been your genes, but they're beyond your control. You never got close enough and you never will."

We were lying on our bed after showering. It was time for some gesture of affection before sleep. Neither of us moved for a while, and then I reached for my radio earphones. Lauranette grabbed them out of my hands and threw them across the room.

"I think Sarah's made another pass at you," she said. "Well, has she?"

"Not exactly." I moved closer to make peace. "It was more of a fashion show."

"That better be all," Lauranette told me, turning away. She wasn't fooling. "What are you going to do about her?"

"I'm going to talk to her when I have to." I rolled back to my half of the bed, and nothing was said until morning.

After two weeks we were still avoiding the worst-case jargon coming from the county police and the federal men who had joined the search. Sonia's face, her most beguiling smile, had been all over local television, her name repeated up and down the radio dial. If she was alive she must have known how desperate the hunt.

The Norentez tape, played for the police, gave me bad daydreams. I was full of the fate of black widow spiders and praying mantises after mating. I'd been forced to imagine the most horrible kind of film before I knew its name or heard it whispered. The police, more suspicious than ever of me, told Sarah and Richard they should not give up hope. Later, I learned from a town cop in Stilson that even before Sonia had been sought as a possible kidnap victim, she was already wanted as the thief who ransacked John Lambert's office and stole his files. The law had mixed feelings about her.

"You don't give up hope," I told Lauranette. "You just stop searching so frantically. You slow down and begin to hurt a little more."

I *had* slowed down. Still, I went daily to the mall and sat on one of the benches by the central fountain. If Sonia was alive, this was the place she'd come. The security men were becoming my pals. It was their job to watch dawdlers like me, and mine to watch for Sonia. We would sit and chat amiably about the ceiling, and I always looked for new signs in the work, suspecting Norentez had left something more if we only had the faculties to find it.

I spent most of my attention on the western end of the work, the mountain end, waiting for the mushroom cloud and fireball that would eat the survivalists' oxygen and make a mockery of the headquarters bunker. But all he showed us on the mountain was a shifting from the full-leaved green to the lacy interweaving of winter branches, changing seasons on us within the course of a single sunrise and setting. No easy political messages, only his clear-eyed perception of our sprawl, our commerce, our recreation, all the American activities that had caught his attention.

When a warning did show through his work it was not political, but right on target, aimed, I thought, at me. For some time I had noticed what seemed to be a hazy line of Gothic characters around the circle of an illuminated compass at the southwest corner of the ceiling—letters too faint to read. In the third week of our search for Sonia, they emerged as a legible line: A CHILD'S DEATH IS THE DEATH OF THE FATHER.

Amid all the loose talk of revolution . . . come the revolution . . . after the revolution . . . and the like, tossed with cocky certainty by the thousands of transient prophets roaming the highways over the last decade with rucksack and at least one stringed instrument, and with my blessing, since their antagonists seemed so much more dangerous and deceitful, Norentez had found a smaller way to warn the world of trouble coming.

Lauranette saw it, too, whispering the line in fascination. "He meant that for me," I told her. "For people like me."

"Nobody's dead," she argued, thumping her leg for emphasis.

"A lot of people are dead. Don't you understand what those men do?"

"Let's not stay long, Ray." She was looking over her shoulder as if someone might be listening or just watching us. "The ceiling's not so good at night. It needs sunlight to really work." We were on our way up for our nightcap at the Turning Night when someone reached over from the down escalator criss-crossing our path and touched Lauranette's shoulder. It was a girl with a shaven head. I couldn't see the full face. With crowds coming behind us it was impossible to turn and race against the rising stairs. We pushed our way to the top, then dashed down the descending case. Whoever it had been was gone.

"It was her!" Lauranette said. "I know it was!" It was the familiar way she'd been touched and then the rabbitlike flight that convinced her. I didn't believe it was Sonia. If, in fact, she was hiding from us, not captive somewhere, why would she risk discovery?

"Impulse," Lauranette thought, "then realization of her mistake." She insisted that I call Richard and Sarah, and this set everyone frantic with the news of the sighting. Minutes later police were roaming the mall, looking for a girl with a shaved head and tattersall vest. Flashing red and blue lights danced in the parking areas. Another night of official questions, recriminations from Richard, tears all around and a final concession from Lauranette that perhaps it hadn't been Sonia after all. "But what if it had been?" She wasn't sorry she'd raised hopes.

I made the only act of contrition. Before the floodlights were turned off beside the central fountain, I gazed up at the panels where Sonia would always come and go—robed and disrobed, pleased and petulant—and promised her changing faces that if she would only come forward, be alive, I'd never frighten her, never invite her contempt, never cross her sight again.

Against my premonition that she was dead, my promises seemed weightless and easy, more eulogy than benediction. The lights were dimmed almost to darkness but I stayed a moment longer to wonder in the shadows.

"We don't need you in this." Richard was behind me, leaning against the trunk of a palm tree, watching my meditation. "You don't fool me for a minute, always staring at the ceiling." He came toward me, fists tight at his sides. "I think she could have told us a lot more. This is pretty convenient for you, if she doesn't come home."

"Nobody puts anything over on Sonia." I stepped forward, within arm's length of his anger.

"I think there's a story about you that your radio woman isn't playing for us." Richard was looking quite haggard. "What I don't understand is how you could have been at that school for so many years without someone catching on to you. An older man and children."

I could only think he was the wronged one in all this, the only one acting completely candidly on the things he knew. There was no more time for him to goad me because Sarah was calling from across the fountain, "Come on, you two. They're waiting to lock up."

"You two?" he asked himself testily. "Where does she get that 'you two'?" Then she was beside me, shaking my hand good night quite warmly with an extra pressure, a little secret.

"If I ever find out . . ." Richard said.

"Oh, be quiet," Sarah told him. "You won't do anything of the kind."

He raised a flat hand at her, and she defied him with a squared stance and narrowed eyes. They walked stiffly away, a fight waiting for privacy.

———

When the security men told me to stay away from the mall, it was like barring casino doors against a man who hasn't cheated but has a system. Totally unfair, though I learned they were within their rights. It had to do with public disturbance and loitering. Now, along with the old mug shots, I had a mall dossier to match my school file. There were reports of my touching several women; vague charges based on a tap on the shoulder, a calming hand on a teary child, a nudging in a restaurant line. They were presented to me not as formal charges but as questions. Did I do this and did I do that?

I roamed the county in my car again, taking the search to the back roads. There was little point to the hunt. If Sonia was alive she'd be looking for bright lights. This was just anxiety burned off on gravel, out of everyone's sight but farmers and star-route mailmen.

When Sarah phoned again asking for another circle, I didn't tell Lauranette. Sarah made it difficult to refuse, calling Sonia "our daughter." We wouldn't have to stop in the woods this time, she said. Her pleading was full of the promise of sweet trouble. I couldn't say anything that might cut me off from news of Sonia. "Not just now," I told her.

I was having bad nights. Lauranette had to wake me from what she called flapping dreams in which, she said, my arms rose and fell like goose wings. One night she woke me and said, "You were flapping and talking, too. You said, 'She's buried in the glass.'"

Lauranette wanted me. And she wanted me to put the gun back in the closet and get off the back roads. She wanted me to stop wasting gas. She sat me down on our sofa before she left for work one afternoon and made a very short speech. "You can watch them, but you're living with me. I'm not settling for parts of you."

A few days later, she talked to me sweetly on the air, defying the Morancys' warning against private jokes and intimacies. "Has anyone seen into the teacher's mind. I see him. He's alone, listening to me, driving beside the river, thinking of ways to bring the survivalists out of their cave. He's thinking of a national holiday for the mall artist. He's wondering why he can't keep his preoccupation with me confined to his head."

It was a little fast for our town on the Potomac, but Lauranette says, in radio those things slip by almost unnoticed. She was wrong about where I was. I was on our bed with the headphones on, and almost didn't hear the telephone. I *had* been thinking of her though, and the way she'd cocked her head a little sadly when she told me she couldn't expect me to renounce my half of the other family, but that someday I might find a quiet honor in my distance from them.

"She's not here," I answered.

"No, this is for you." It was Norentez. He wanted me to meet him at the mall. He was going to show himself at last.

"I can't," I told him. "I'm not allowed there."

"You can buy me a sandwich in the turning restaurant."

"You don't understand. They won't let me come in."

"Believe me. They won't bother you," he assured me.

When I arrived I was surprised to find he'd been right. No one stopped me. I was obvious enough, my head still covered with the dark lines where the stitches had been removed. It occurred to me that I was just another troublesome customer, someone to be bluffed, but not taken to law unnecessarily.

In the restaurant I didn't notice Norentez until he signaled me. It was an old man's gesture, his head tilting forward when he raised his arm. Almost arthritic. I'd been looking for faded flannel and jeans. Instead he wore an old-fashioned dark suit with light pinstripes. Overlarge and padded, with wide lapels, it was clownish.

"My disguise," he explained, running his fingers over the odd clothes. "They're not looking for you. It's me. They're coming at me from both sides." He seemed very tired though alert, even furtive, as he began to explain himself. "I can't find her. She can't find me. I think they have driven her away in the big car. You see, they are preparing her for the final movie."

I ordered club sandwiches for the two of us and pointed out landmarks as we turned over the landscape, waiting for him to tell me more about himself and Sonia and the "bad men" as he called them. When the food came, I said, "Come on, get on with it."

"No, we don't talk while we eat," he told me emphatically. "We think about what I have already told you." He ate his sandwich in several bites, like a starveling. When he was finished he patted his scrawny chest with both hands to prove he had no wallet. I thought the whole thing might be his way to cadge a free meal in a plush booth. And I was more than willing to pay.

He started in again on the thing he knew would hold me. "She thinks it will be so important. More than taking clothes off for the painter."

He wasn't even thirty, but seemed so much older now, his hair matted, his thin face weathered. I thought of him traveling the country, one step ahead of the immigration people. But why had he come back where they'd be sure to look for him, and put himself at risk? He clearly felt a duty to protect Sonia.

He was leaning across the table, trying to get closer to my ear. "The police are no help. Even if we could go to them. They would not wait for trouble in a little place where it smells of hog blood. Yes, and why should they believe us if we don't give our name?" He looked up at the angle of the sunlight falling through the windows. "I think it is three o'clock," he said. "Time to go down."

He wanted me to follow him to the central fountain. There was one more thing he had to show me because, he said, I knew how to read his work. It was something I wouldn't like.

"I know the ceiling almost by heart," I told him. "It's not a question of liking or disliking. It's accurate enough if you know how to see, if you don't try to make it hold still. If you just let it move, let it teach you." I couldn't help flattering him.

"I know that's what you think. Your Lauranette told me how much you watch it. That's why you should see this." He looked up again at the column of sunlight falling into the room, and said we should hurry.

On the way down the escalator he kept one hand on the moving rail and one on my arm. How did he get around, who helped him? It occurred to me that he could, in fact, have some hideaway in the mall, some place he crawled into at night.

When we reached ground level he said he was going to sit down for a while, and gave me instructions. I was to stand facing the water with my knees against the fountain wall, then to move clockwise around it, all the while keeping my eyes on a glass panel in the ceiling. There was a girl up there in a bathing suit with a beach ball under her arm. When I was finished, I should come back to his bench and he'd have more to tell me.

I did as I was told, and before I was a quarter way around the circle I sat stunned on the wall. The beach ball had become a fine likeness of my daughter's head in ecstasy, thrown back, hair dangling. As I had moved around the fountain, Sonia was seen radiant in a body-tight suit, and in the next instant her severed head had fallen under her arm. With each step I took, the beheading repeated itself, on, off, on, off, until I looked away. It was like one of those children's novelties, a picture that moves as you shift its angle.

When Norentez saw that I couldn't finish, he walked over and calmly told me this had been done from imagination obviously, not from life or memory, and if it helped me at all, I could think of it as another kind of warning. "Believe me," he said. "When I did this glass I didn't know anything about these people she goes with now."

I grabbed him, shook him by his silly lapels and only then

realized how incredibly light he really was. It was like bullying a mind that had almost no body to support it. And when I was finished berating his sick, ghoulish suggestions, I was shamed by my outburst and his patience. He said he had been troubled by the vision, and that's why he'd gone to such trouble to disguise it. "I have to show it," he said, "because it is in me. But I want to show it under joy.

"Accurate enough if you know how to read it?" he asked me, not unkindly. "If you like the girl, this is very hard for you, I think. Maybe this is the end of her kind of dance."

"What kind is that?"

"The thrill beyond the pleasure," he said. "Do you understand? She will offer anything to see what will be returned. People like this are chosen. But it's very dangerous, you see? It brings the bad man!"

My nervous string of "yes, yes, yes, yes," was not assent but impatient command to continue. He hadn't wanted to scare her, he told me. What he put in the glass was really out of his own history, his grandfather's recounting of rituals from the old days on the mountain above his village. It wasn't clear to him whether a young woman selected for death was being honored or punished, but they had never picked a virgin for the sacrifice. That was only myth. Just the opposite was true; it was always the young woman of wide experience.

I stood to look at the glass panel once more but the light had shifted. Norentez touched my arm. "You didn't imagine it. It was there. We will try to keep it hidden in the glass, all right? It doesn't have to happen." He was going for some fresh air, he said. About two minutes later, when I looked for him outside the mall entrance, he had disappeared.

Lauranette envied me that last session with Norentez. Her questions about him were mostly unanswerable. Had he been optimistic? Did he have enough money to survive? Where was he going next? "The question is," I said, "is Sonia still looking for him? Would she take his advice if she found him?"

I was riding with my little rifle under the seat, cruising for the filmmakers. As if I might stumble onto their set while they were filming. As if there would be time to save Sonia before she was written out of the script.

I found myself going back and back to the abandoned farm where Norentez had lived. A pack of wild dogs had been meeting me at the cattle grate, snarling and jumping at the car, biting the tires. They'd chase for a while and then retreat into the woods before I reached the meadow above the slaughter shed. I wondered what godforsaken flesh sustained them. Usually I drove up the meadow to the tree line and parked there for an hour or two. This was the high ground from which I put myself in command of the shed's door, the target for my little rifle.

Day after day, no one came. Imagining a dark man in my sights I shot at the empty doorway and had no idea whether I was even hitting that generous rectangle. After spending a small box of ammunition I'd sit a while longer at the wood's edge. Trying to forget that if something foul had been planned for my daughter it had probably already happened. My daily visits to the shooting ground were private services to Sonia, fifty-shot salutes. Lauranette didn't need to know about them.

Two weeks of this routine before I missed a day. John Lambert called again. Still wanted his papers back. In his off-season he was trying to find out where he stood with the other teachers, whether he'd be facing a mutiny after they saw their files. Maybe I could help him. He was breezy on the phone, quite casual, an old friend.

"A conference?"

"Sure," he said, "if you want to call it that. Lunch. I'm buying."

"It would have to be quick," I told him. "I'm quite busy."

"Another edition of that book, I bet. It was never really a textbook, was it? That's another thing. Some of these new things. You probably want to steer clear. For your own protection. Not the libel thing so much but out of fairness to everyone. We'll talk. Bring the papers."

When we met, I handed them over first thing. That way we could hurry lunch and we'd both be away faster. He glanced quickly through the file, and seemed relieved at what he found, or didn't find. He patted the folder. "Nothing too serious here. I'm sure you've had a look. Really just quick, undigested impressions of what was going on at the time. Mostly gossip with myself. Have you had a chance to talk to Rose Edgar lately?"

No, I told him, I hadn't had occasion to call Rose.

"Well, I've been trying to reach her. We all have to learn how to take criticism."

I saw the extent of Sonia's mischief. Even the favored few had been treated to Lambert's secret opinions of them. Rose, too, and I imagined her stepping back toward me in solidarity with a colleague and peer. It made this whole awkward session with Lambert worthwhile.

He started with a beer, then made it two, and when he finally ordered food it was the big steak, for both of us, something to linger over. He wouldn't hear of my having just a salad. When we got to pie and coffee he still wasn't satisfied. There was something he wanted me to admit, and more he wanted me to know.

"I think it was your mission to make everybody different, Ray. To make them all special cases with their own agendas. And we let you, up to a point. I let you alone for years, don't deny it. So why can't you have some understanding of my job, my duty?"

"To make them all the same?"

"To get them all through. To make sure they could all meet minimum standards. Which your Pless girl never did. We have a building full of people doing the best job they can. Not all of them clever as you, Ray, but dedicated. They're not getting rich, you know. You strayed from the texts and got away with it. But there are some practical things in the old books, things your favorite student never grasped. You know, I date your real troubles with us from the day she entered high school."

Lambert was ordering more coffee, warming to his argument. Instead of protesting I drew him out with my hand, like a chef over a pot, pulling on the aroma. "You want more?" he said. "All right, let's talk about the Pless girl some more. Her own father said, 'If she can't do biology, why isn't she in home economics?' What could I tell him? That she was giving her own life classes in biology down at the mall? That her lab notes were one long sex diary? That her brain wasn't made for numbers and letters? That her teachers had given up on her, all but you?

"Oh yes," he went on, "her father was asking for home ec courses, but do you think we could coax her into any of Rose's classes? It was like we were insulting her. Couldn't we all tell by the way she looked, the way she dressed, the way she walked, that she was meant for the big ideas, the grand concepts, the ones that must have been beyond us because we weren't teaching them?"

"How would you have known if she *was* beyond your school? Floating above all the nonsense?"

"No, Ray. She was a hum-brain. By the time she got to you, it was just camouflage on failure. As I told you before, she tried early and found it was no use. After that, you wanted to carry her but she was too heavy. Even she saw the dishonesty in it. She didn't want any favors.

"I don't know how far out of line you stepped with her. I could forgive almost anything. I was sorry to hear what happened."

"What did you hear?" I asked too quickly.

"That the police can't find her. That she might have run off with some unusual people. Some kind of movie gypsies. Look, I'd like your opinion on something. We have to find your replacement for the history course. Do you think Rose Edgar would be any good at it?"

He saw me staring at the file he was gathering up. "Oh sure," he said. "She's wanted it for a long time. But you know I still value your opinion. Think about it and give me a call if you have some ideas. It's the children I think about." He started off in another direction. "The way society is structured today . . ." He caught himself at the edge of this philosophical chasm, stood up and smoothed down the front of his suit jacket. Now that he'd talked himself out, it was too late for me to get to the shooting ground. I had to skip memorial target practice for the day.

Next morning one of the wild dogs was lying dead beside the cattle gate. I didn't want to look closely but from the car window I could see that one of its legs was missing. There were tire tracks running through the meadow grass all the way to the shed. Whoever had been there was gone. I stayed for two hours, cursing myself for the day I'd missed. On my way home Lauranette interrupted "Tumbleweed" to say, "Teacher, don't come home. If you meet me at the Double Twin in the mall, we could catch an early show."

The movie was only a little sad. Not enough to make Lauranette so blubbery. And she was the kind to disguise cheap emotion. At the end of a picture she'd sit through all the closing credits and stare at the dark screen, giving her tear ducts time to swallow back what they'd spilled rather than let me see brimming eyes or a streak on her face.

With her head on my shoulder she told me, "It isn't the movie, it's you. You don't see anything. You're not here." I mumbled and held her while the theater emptied, and then confessed to my daily shooting habit. When I came to the dog with the missing leg, her eyes were dry again.

"Sometimes they lose them in traps," she said. "That's what happened, I'm sure of it." Lauranette was looking sternly into my eyes, forcing my attention. "You're going to have to put down your fantasy, and put down your gun. And stay away from that place. You're lucky you haven't already shot yourself in the foot."

I should remember, she said, that Norentez's stories were his way of reducing life to the world he colored. "If you're going back there, I'm going with you." She thought her being with me while I pumped the .22 bullets into the shed door would bring me back over the line.

"It's on the ceiling," I interrupted her. "And it isn't pretty."

"Show me," she said, feeling my brow.

I took her from the theater to the central fountain and put her through the clockwise routine Norentez taught me. But of course the light was wrong. There was nothing in the death panel but the shapely suntan with beach ball. "You don't need your eyes examined," Lauranette said quietly, "you just need them refocused." And she led me away by the hand, nurse and patient, down the halls of my private bedlam, into the night. We had both our cars there and she insisted that I drive in front of her, all the way home.

On the way she'd had a slight change of attitude. "You're getting careless with my life," she said when we were back. "And you're being reckless again with your own." Her head was tilted to the side, an attitude begging my sincerity. If spontaneity could be ordered up, she deserved it. I couldn't do it. I was hearing my voice, listening for my effect, measuring my words against secret plans for more surveillance, when I told her:

"I want what's right for both of us. I know what I've been doing seems mad. I'll be getting work again. We'll be together if that's what you want. Is that what you want?"

She nodded.

It was all true, and still a mask, and I wore it all that night of love and even the next morning as I drove down the east-west highway alone, and through the woods to the farm; playing with idle superstition: if I can steer between those two potholes, there'll be no heart attack; if I reach the water tower before the man on the morning show spins the next record, it will stop drizzling; if my windshield wipers move back and forth six times before the rubber squeaks on the glass, Sonia is alive and well and somewhere in this county.

One of the wild dogs was hanging on the fence beside the cattle grate, strung up between rusty strands of barbed wire. I stopped to lift it down and saw where bullets had torn open its belly. The sound of a motor came drifting across the meadow ahead of me. Dropping the dog, I went for my gun. I left the car blocking the grate and ran into the meadow.

The noise stopped. I dropped to the ground as the shed came into view. I was bellying up to the tree line, taking high ground again. There was a gray pickup truck beside the little building and beyond it some huge logs that had been dragged out of the woods, a tractor parked beside them. No sound.

I stood and began to walk down the hill, rifle ready. When I was still fifty yards away, a man came out of the shed with a big yellow chain saw. I fell to the ground again. The man looked around furtively and headed for the logs. He had a slight limp and was got up more like a mythical lumberjack than a film-maker, in a red plaid shirt, black suspenders, and baggy trousers tucked into high boots. I was trying to make the little bead on my rifle sit still in the V, his chest behind it, moving around the logs.

The lumberjack pulled at the starter cord for a long time, then fiddled for a while with the controls. There was nothing to hear but my own breathing until the motor caught and then his voice was riding clearly to me. "All ready." He turned back toward the shed with the running saw and was halfway there when I snatched at the trigger. He looked up.

Pump and pull, pump and pull. Fast as I could. Getting off that many rounds there was a good chance one of them hit him. He dropped the saw and it hopped along in front of him till the motor died. He hurdled it, going as fast as he could on his bad leg toward the far woods. A second man came out of the shed with a black carrying case, and chased after him. And then she was in the doorway, probably terrified. I knew it was Sonia though the face was hardly recognizable, apparently covered with rouge and other makeup.

She was only half-dressed when I called out and came toward her. It was some sort of costume she was in, a frilly Victorian blouse that had been torn from her shoulders, and a bustle skirt. She was barefoot. Trying to do herself up, she didn't wait to see what I had in mind, but made a dash for the pickup and jumped into the cab. The engine sputtered and turned over and the truck went careening wildly across the field. I ran to intercept her. Sonia never slowed at the blocked grate. Snapping off a fence post, she smashed through the wire and was gone.

I wanted Sarah to hear this first, before the police. When I phoned, Richard answered. "She's alive," I said. "She got away." I was elated with the rescue. All he wanted to know was where I had last seen Sonia and which direction she was going. Before he hung up he called me a damn maniac.

It was no better with the sheriff's man, stiff with his suspicion. I went with him in his car to the scene, showed him the dog, retraced my steps. He took my statement. "Of course she was in trouble," I said. "Wasn't she two parts naked?"

I admitted I hadn't seen her face clearly. But didn't I know how she moved, how she ran, her gestures when she was frightened, the way her head bobbed and shifted. What about the hair, he asked me. Of course, it wouldn't have grown back that quickly. The moviemakers would have insisted on a wig.

"Why did he come outside with the saw if he was going to use it on someone inside? Why did he carry it to the logs if he wasn't going to use it on them?" The deputy's literal mind couldn't get into the movie at all. He couldn't accept the idea they were only setting her up, allaying her fears right up to the end. "And lots of people wear suspenders," he said. "Why would he have such a big saw if he was only going to use it on someone's neck? You had no right to shoot at them. Wouldn't you run if someone started shooting at you?"

Without spelling it out, he made clear what he thought had happened. One of the men had been in the shed doing the girl, whoever she was, while the other was getting ready to cut and steal cord wood from trees that had been sold for lumber. Back at his office, the deputy gave me a receipt for my rifle, which was being temporarily confiscated. A disgraced teacher, not worthy of more of his valuable time, I was sent on my way.

Several days passed with no news at all. Then Sarah phoned. "Sonia's all right!" she said. "She's alive! But she wouldn't say where she was calling from. She's not coming home."

The official search was over and the period of Sonia's wider wandering began across unknown states. With unknown companions. What Lauranette called "gypsy time." Two years, as it turned out. Without a clue to her whereabouts. I believed I had saved her from death at least once, maybe twice. No longer young enough to be called a runaway, Sonia was on her own.

V

WALKING NAKED

I made my song a coat
Covered with embroideries
Out of old mythologies
From heel to throat;
But the fools caught it,
Wore it in the world's eyes
As though they'd wrought it.
Song, let them take it,
For there's more enterprise
In walking naked.

—W. B. YEATS

There's a reunion and you're invited. Everyone would love to see you." My invitation came over the telephone from Linda Shradey, one of Sonia's former classmates, a member of the first circle. Linda had moved up to the house on the mountain abandoned by the old Sky Meadows people. "Not really a commune anymore," she explained, "just a common house and garden for a bunch of us." Linda said she had a letter she thought I'd like to see, and made me promise to be at the reunion at the Stilson Motor Inn.

It was two years after Sonia's class had graduated, and my scar was a thin white line. I supposed that in their premature nostalgia they wanted another look at me. The time was convenient, a Friday evening. Any time would have been. Of course I already knew what was happening to most of them; which ones had stayed here to pump gas, or check out groceries, or frame houses. Which had mastered keypunch, which had already moved closer to the Beltway to learn how to maintain or program the computers that were going to put the keypunchers out of business. And I knew the names of several dozen who had gone on to college.

My attendance at the motor inn that evening wasn't to take career census or indulge my sense of having helped children into useful lives. I wanted the letter, her handwriting, her news. Who else could it be from?

Lauranette tried to steer me away from the old insults. "You can't go back and let those people walk over you again."

As if, after all this time, pride could keep me away. When she saw I couldn't be dissuaded, she decided to come too. She was afraid some new clue might set me off.

I had gotten a job as I'd promised her, at first as a volunteer, in charge of a county hotline, helping victims and the needy in their struggle with the little bureaucracies that tormented them, maybe saving a few people from their own dangerous hands. "You're good at talking your way into other people's lives," Lauranette told me. For some time we'd been living frugally and contentedly, building our shield of passing weeks and months against the old grievance—my preoccupation with Sonia and the Plesses.

Sarah and Richard were inhabiting the same house again. Holding things together for Rita, Sarah said, until she was out of school. Satisfied that I had drawn back from the edge of Sarah's enticing circles, Lauranette thought it was important that I stay clear of Lambert and the high school faculty. Why should they accept my story now if no one believed it the first time? She predicted they'd draw me out, and recall the old insults, make me their fool again.

"You're not just going there to see what's in the letter, you know. You want more. A celebration in your honor. That's not what they have in mind."

"I'll just drop by for a while. Some of them feel very bad about what happened."

"No. They're asking you as a freak. You'll be a little side-show for them." Come and look at Sykes. He'll probably get up on a chair and tell us what happened to Stilson County while we were sleeping. Maybe we'll get him to talk about the day he shot at Sonia Pless. Lambert doesn't think we should ask him. Let well enough alone, the principal says. He doesn't tell us what to do anymore, we're two years out, we're asking Sykes. And you know, he'll probably come. I knew it! He's here!

In the motel lobby a big sign in gold sparkle paint said WELCOME '75 and RIVER HIGH WE STILL LOVE YOU. Lauranette offered a last chance to escape. "You don't have to go in there." There was a crowd, several hundred of them, milling around three kegs of beer in the ballroom, and I went in to drink the warm foam in waxed cups with them. Before the class president said his pleasantries I already had an audience of a few dozen hanging back at the edges, watching me like keen chaperons.

"Rose Edgar!" She was very bright and cheery. Flourishing, even a little flesh-proud, wearing two shades of aquamarine to complement her tan, and chatting up her old favorites. When she saw me she came pushing forward, sloshing her beer. "I didn't think I'd see you here, Ray. We've missed you a lot," she said searching my face. "You knew they'd given me your old job?"

"I knew you were interested in it."

"I suppose I didn't hide it very well."

"Not badly."

"Well, you look better, Ray. You seem rested."

"Tell me everything," I said. "How's John Lambert?"

"I'm worried about him. He doesn't exactly have a child's cardiovascular system." She was enthusiastic, even with bad news. And she was giving me nothing to aim at, not a hint of guilt.

Rose followed us to the potato chips and said quietly, "You suffered a lot for something that didn't turn out very well."

"What didn't turn out well?"

"You know. Our little Miss Sonia. She's been with some

young saint living on nothing a year in the woods. They've got a letter from her they're passing around. Maybe they'll let you read it."

"Are you going to let them have you, or get up and walk?" Lauranette whispered in my ear. A few minutes later I had the letter in my hand. I didn't have to ask for it. Linda Shradey, pleased to see me, pulled it from her purse, unfolding two dirty pages in a careless scrawl.

"This isn't her," I said, annoyed. "She didn't write this."

"No, she didn't write it," Linda said. "He did. She's with him. Lois is. That's what she calls herself now."

"This isn't her. It's not her," I insisted.

Lois brought your name up. Thought we had things in common with you folks. Just doing our work each day, no rush, lots of lessons, feeling this one out. Left a fine place in Arkansas, a small farm commune in the woods. Good people. Really good people. We miss them but it was time to go.

Property was promoting a spoilage in the best of us. Great place for IT to happen but possessions were pushing energy in another direction. Loved them but we were losing sense of intimacy with the land, subsistence, necessity to deal directly with first priorities. Really dig watching and anticipating.

Helped them start a school. Tried to keep it clean and personal, direct and generous, always tough (smile) but in the end we were just "those funny people we love who have their weird ideas about animals and conveniences." Walked the two miles to the gardens every day and really knew why.

Were they ever surprised when we let them have everything! Even the cabin we built. Don't claim to be beyond a damn thing, but wouldn't give up this great leap we make each day. Lois and I feel the urge to unite with more people who feel the way we do.

Never thought I'd come to this. Always out on the point someplace. Moving now, looking for the place the energy is right.

In Nature,
Cal, Lois and pups

"You have an envelope?" I asked. "An address?"

"It's her," Linda said. "Believe me. No address. They're traveling."

"No, this wouldn't be her," I said again. "This kind of thing's already out of date. She wouldn't have any part of it."

"So who else do I know who calls herself Lois?" Impatient with my doubt, Linda took the letter back.

"Are they coming here?"

"I don't think so. Her family would probably come after her again."

I asked if I could come up to the mountain place sometime. Linda was smirking at Lauranette's grip on my arm. "There aren't any gates at Sky Meadows," she said. "Anyone's welcome for one meal. After that it would just be a question of compatibility and commitment. Actually, we *are* looking for an older person or two, for balance, you know."

"Nothing like that," I assured her. "Just to look around sometime."

"Whatever," she said.

I saw Lambert come in. He circled the floor once before he started to work the room with handshakes and brief greetings. We acknowledged each other's glance, but some time passed before he approached me. Rhonda Blay, still an algebra teacher, the one the students used to call Blue Gums, noticed my reticence.

"Say something to him," she said. "He's lost some of his best people. He's not a bad administrator, he does have standards."

I reminded her of the time he had asked her to let pi equal 3 because 3.1416 was too many numbers for some of the children to remember.

"That?" She laughed. "It was just his little joke. He knows some math. He's been good for the school. He has a sense of humor."

He must have seen us looking his way because a moment later his hand was on my shoulder. "I thought you might come to this, Ray. I'm glad you did." His eyes were darting about as he spoke. He couldn't afford too much time with me. There were a couple of things, though.

When he had me away from Lauranette, he said, "Something happened the other day. I was in the office going over next year's schedules when I had this little pop in my forehead, right between my eyes. I was dizzy for a while. Have you ever had something like that?" He hadn't told his wife. He wasn't sure if he was mispronouncing a few of his words, saying little things out of order. "Do you notice anything?"

"No," I said honestly, "probably nothing to it. Your imagination. See a doctor, just in case."

"You can make yourself sick going to doctors," he said. Though two years had gone by, it was as if we had just gotten up from the luncheon we'd had together. Again, he wanted me to admit something about the loose life the hippies were still leading, something finally damaging and irreparable. His words were "the line of long men." He meant the long line of men, and had to correct himself. He looked suddenly worried and I encouraged him again to see a doctor. Lambert wanted my information, not my advice. It was a tacit insult, taking me for a store of knowledge now with not much common sense.

More old students and colleagues were gathering around

me. "You have nothing to say to them," Lauranette whispered, a little desperate. But a few were asking sincere questions. "Did you know you always used to get my name wrong. It wasn't Terry. It was Terri with an i." I looked over the room, wishing I could make them all understand. They gabbed in contented ignorance of my daughter while she roamed the country, and the artist might be back in Mexico or instructing another community on the ceiling of its mall. Some of these twenty-year-olds around me were already taking wives and husbands. Bashful ones, too, their hands busy with cigarettes and beer when their mouths fell on silence.

Then the question I knew was coming. Derek Stevens was asking, "Did the guy really have a chain saw?"

"Yes."

"You shot it out of his hands?"

"I don't know. He dropped it."

"How did it all start?"

"Listen, that's history."

"Your subject!" Rose Edgar said. She was trying to hush them so more could hear my story, when one voice got the old name rolling across the room. "Chalkman." In a moment a soft cooing filled the place. Lauranette picked out one chanting face and threw her beer directly into it. The boy looked at his dripping shirt and pants.

"Hey, bitch. Hey, what's the matter with you?"

I went after him, swinging at his mouth, and left him with blood on his lip before we were both restrained and pulled away to our cars. "Who invited you anyway?" he called.

I drove up to Sky Meadows for my visit. Cal was there but not Sonia. Cal was healthy looking with a radiant smile; the garden soil under his fingernails like ten little flags of his industry.

Tan and muscled from his natural labor, a man with a hoe and college, too. The others were quiet around him, and I gathered that he and the pups were not going to last long here, that his brand of community was too rigid for them.

He was eager to talk, though not about his Lois. "I don't think it was her real name anyway," he told me. "She was very young. Had a lot to learn." When I asked what had become of her, he said, "I don't know where she went. I don't really care."

Gliding down the mountain to Lauranette again, to supper, I knew Sonia was unbound. Not with Cal! Had never really been with Cal. She was on her way once more, one step wiser, moving ahead, keeping us waiting.

Sarah never got used to the waiting. The summer after the reunion she started calling me again. It was usually in the afternoon when Lauranette was at the station, and Richard still at work. She was asking very stale questions. How could a child stay away so long, how could she be so ungrateful.

After so much time, I said, there was bound to be some embarrassment, some difficulty in dealing with the desertion, with what she'd already done to them. "She could have made herself a mother by now," Sarah complained, "and we'd never know it."

So Sarah, too, like Lambert, had been stuck on the promiscuity. And when I told her to read something I thought would ease her mind, she said books made her sleepy. "And Richard gets so tiresome!" She was worrying full-time about Sonia. "I don't know what made her that way, what made her want all those boys."

"She didn't want them all. Think of it as an experiment." But Sarah couldn't help herself. She had started thinking about Sonia's long line of men, of those she'd already been with and those still in store, of the wound these men, some of them not so young, had made in Sonia, as if each one deepened the sexual scar.

We were in our third year without a view of my daughter, or the sound of her voice, only the revealing glimpse on the mall ceiling which came and went with the changing light of the sun. Lauranette and I were settling in for life, I thought, watching ourselves drift forward without alarm, in equilibrium; the worries of aging balanced by a new contentment.

We no longer pushed one another toward more love or more achievement. It seemed she'd go on forever as the easy voice of Home Town Radio. She had never sent a tape to a larger city, never tried to move up, but maintained her truce with the Morancys, who would always like her numbers though they called her in now and then to remind her of current community standards and her guest status in our county's living rooms.

She slept in every morning while I went to organize the hotline volunteers for the day. I returned for lunch with her, and we discussed ideas for her afternoon program. When she left for the station I went to my room to make notes on Sonia's life.

"It's all right," Lauranette said. "It's honest labor. So what if it can't be published?" It could be a diary discovered when this decade was a curiosity. In her generous way she left me free to be apologist for the nonperson, for the daughter who wasn't.

Another year, and then two more in our quiet town on the Potomac where people called me Ray Sykes again, and were apt to ask me for any kind of information when they passed me on the sidewalk. I could as well have been a librarian or a telephone operator, a data bank going to waste. Somewhere in America, Sonia was twenty-four. Did she vote?

We made a special effort over dinners, not heavy sauces so much, usually something sautéed with the right herbs. And wine, or beer in a wineglass. And candles because, as Lauranette said, this was the meal that bound our lives together, the transition between those hours when we ignored one another and the hours we might ask each other for anything. A reacquaintance after the day's estrangement.

After supper there was radio again, Lauranette listening for new voices, new sounds. She'd roam over the spectrum, AM and FM, after dark, when the talk-show hosts came out like chatty elves all over the dial. They were bouncing everywhere off the cooling atmosphere. We never knew from what direction or distance the next signal might arrive. But we had an extra sensitive tuner and special antenna to capture them.

Lauranette made a game of it. We each had fifteen minutes to find the most distant signal and after that the winner picked a favorite voice, and we'd listen for a while to a political scientist in Toronto or a sex therapist in Chicago, whatever was under discussion for the evening in whatever community. Then we'd turn to something closer, Winchester maybe, or even Washington, so that after communion with so many distant cities, so much rapid travel over our nervous continent, we gradually had shrunk the world to our bedroom again and could fall gratefully asleep against each other.

We were going after distant signals one night when we heard a woman with a pleasant, untrained voice struggling to hold key and range in the last line of a folk song, a lover's complaint:

Soon you will meet with another pretty maiden,
Some pretty maiden, you'll court her for a while.
Thus ever ranging, turning and changing,
Always seeking for a girl that is new.

In a cacophony of night air Lauranette tried to hold the signal but it faded away, or another voice rode over it, and there had been no chance for station identification or the name of the singer.

"You can't identify someone on the air if you've never heard their radio voice before," she told me. "It's almost impossible." Broadcasting doesn't just change the pitch, she explained, it changes the timbre, the whole quality. But if that was so, why did Lauranette go back each night for a week, searching in the same area of the dial? Did she think she was going to reach some outpost neither of us had heard from before, someplace west of the Rockies?

"It wasn't the voice," she said, "it was the words. And the tune. It was lovely." I kept looking and a week later found it again, the same voice laboring with the same song; a whole verse and another line this time, before a local man bumped into it with weather.

Early one morning, just as the sun was rising,
I heard a maid singing in the valley below.
Oh, don't deceive me, oh, never leave me.
How can you use a poor maiden so?

Remember the vow that you made to me truly,
Remember . . .

I fiddled with the dial for a long time before giving up. There was too much there, too many sounds, too much static. I guessed wildly. It was Friday again. Our first contact with the singer had been exactly a week earlier. It was the theme song of a weekly radio show. We didn't have the call letters; the station might be anywhere in the East, but I couldn't hide my excitement.

"Is that what you've been looking for all this time?" Lauranette was incredulous. "She was never a singer. What makes you think you'd ever find her on radio?"

Even so, she steadied the ladder for me when I climbed onto

the roof to adjust our antenna, searching for the Friday voice. Whatever I was doing wasn't helping. We lost the thing altogether after that and gave up. I confessed to the wild improbability of my dream. It was like the figure of the girl with a beach ball on the mall ceiling. I hadn't been able to turn it into Sonia again in any light, at any time of day, and I came to think of it as a warning that had disappeared, an artist's trick accomplished with vanishing colors in a mall of so many other diversions.

The Whole World had become comfortable with a moral interpretation of its ceiling, and heavy crowds helped to make the work quite legitimate. But Norentez had never been asked back for a celebration of his art.

My volunteer work had become a paying job. There were people in government saying this was important stuff—helping victims redress grievances. For a while there was federal money. But now the county was stuck for my whole salary—probably wondering how they could be paying me again, getting their money's worth, though.

Lauranette was helping, too. We rounded up groceries for holiday meals, and worked overtime on the emergency phone. We even put up battered wives in our home. There were things said about that. All we could do was joke about it.

"From Chalkman to parlor lizard."

"A rogue's progress."

"At least your women are older."

"If you could have had children," I asked Lauranette, "how many would we have by now?"

"A half dozen anyway," she said without hesitation.

"Intentionally? Out of carelessness? Because we're naturally reckless people?"

"Out of passion."

"Whose?"

"Mostly yours. Not just that, you," she said, removing my hand. "With one, you would have hovered. With six, you could have let them go, one by one, as they grew up."

"There wouldn't have been enough money."

"Scholarships," she said resolutely, "or into the work force."

"I would have wanted another daughter for you," Lauranette went on. "At least one. And as many sons as you could stand."

Nine years after Sonia's high school failure we weren't afraid to talk about her anymore. She hadn't called her home in months. I knew Lauranette thought of Sonia as the wild gene that had vanished for good. And when I saw Sarah at the supermarket, or we sat in our cars on opposite sides of the gas pumps at the filling station, there were long looks and quiet words. For me, just another way of waiting for news that had to come.

On the evening of July 20, 1984, Lauranette reached over my shoulder and covered my fingers on our radio dial. We had heard a soft voice coo "Mr. Chalk" three times, and then the laughter of a studio audience. "Hold it right there!" Lauranette urged, her hand tightening on mine. "It's drifting. Follow it, follow it! You can't just sit in one spot and hope!" I think I could have held the signal a moment longer if she hadn't been trying so hard to help me. Afterward, she sat beside me, ashen, as if our radio had caught a ghost.

We found ourselves in the car heading for the mall, and then under the glass canopy, wandering. Over the years the mall had become a museum for us. Lauranette was trying to steer me through the crowds to prevent my bumping into people as I stared upward. It was difficult to catch much of Sonia at night-time on the floodlit ceiling.

"You do admit it was her?"

"The other was so long ago," Lauranette said. "It wasn't the same station you used to look for. Much lower on the dial."

"She wouldn't have stayed in one town. Besides, we both heard her say it."

"But why would anyone bring that up again. Why would anyone think it was funny?"

"We missed the first part. Any word can be funny depending on what goes before it. I think she's close."

"You're guessing," Lauranette said. "Wishing. Will you be calling the Plesses about it?"

"It seems only fair. But we might not have to."

"Yes," she said after a while, smiling at me as I stepped quickly across the atrium to another of my customary viewing positions. "Yes, I think it was her. I'll help you look," she said brightly. She didn't seem to mind that our lives were opening to the old problem again.

"You know what I hate to think?" I said. "What I can't stand? That someone knows all about her already. We're getting static but someone else is getting her clearly. She's already known."

Taking us completely by surprise one night Rose Edgar came to our house with bad news about John Lambert. Another cerebral incident, probably forcing retirement this time. He was home and didn't want visitors. I heard all this from my bedroom. I was on the bed beside our best radio, wondering if I was going to be interrupted in my search. Silent, arms around my knees, I was waiting to hear Lauranette dismiss the uninvited Rose.

They were on the stairs, coming up, though Lauranette was trying to discourage her. "This is a bad time for him. Friday nights. There's something he's been trying to get on the radio." They were in the doorway, and Rose was asking what it was that could be so important.

"Ray! I'm afraid I've brought bad news! But what are you trying to get? You look like one of the kids with your legs tucked up like that."

"It's nothing," I said. "Something we've heard a few times. Just a song I can't get out of my head."

"Oh? What song?"

Lauranette tried two lines that had stuck with her with an approximation of the tune:

Thus ever ranging, turning and changing,
Always seeking for a girl that is new.

"That?" Rose said, sitting down beside me. "It's the 'Shenandoah Journal' theme. But you're trying in the wrong place. You can get her from the city. Not a beautiful voice, but a pretty voice. So relaxed. And she might as well be talking about us."

Rose was trying to help me find the station, her enthusiasm riding over my irritation while she went on describing this music and variety program she said was full of gentle reminiscence.

"You know. Rock Falls, Virginia. No, no, the other way," Rose said, taking over the dial, and a moment later we were receiving Sonia's uninterrupted voice with absolute clarity.

"You know who that is?"

"Lois Rengert," Rose said.

Sonia had been calling herself Lois and using her mother's maiden name, Rengert. Maybe her past troubled her, or she thought the old, raw evidence on the mall ceiling could come crashing down on her head.

It wasn't a wild fame, she was no household word. According to Lauranette, Sonia knew the secret to radio's victory over television, letting her audience make their own pictures, infinitely more intricate and satisfying than camera images.

She was working slowly and casually with a thirty-year swath of history. Cut into small, closely examined pieces of time and territory, her material could last forever. And soon enough her list of stations was growing, pushing her small fame westward. She reached the Mississippi and crossed it.

Stilson County began to wake up to what was going on, and reclaimed her. She was their little celebrity, visiting but not quite home. Richard and Sarah had to listen with the rest of us each week if they wanted to know what was happening in Rock Falls, Virginia. And it was possible to see her! If you got tickets early in the week, you could watch the live show being broadcast from the old James movie house in Winchester. For some time now, Sonia had been right here in our territory.

Her voice was quiet, almost an apology. I didn't have to throw her up in anyone's face. People were listening with admiration and some apprehension to the weekly reports from her make-believe town.

A Friday evening at the broadcast hour, unable to resist, I called Lambert. His wife said he couldn't come to the phone. He was in bed. Not allowed to get excited. "There's something on the radio," I told her. "If he could listen it might cheer him up." She promised to look for the program when she took his supper up.

"Right away," I urged her. "She's on right now."

I was worried each broadcast might miss its special target, might disappear in the air. She was just finishing her theme song, apologizing for the little frog in her throat. She paused for a sip of water and began:

"It's true. What you've heard. In Rock Falls anybody could have a reputation . . ." There was a ripple of soft laughter in the theater, applause that wasn't quite earned, I thought, more in honor of her little fame than the substance of the moment. "They were there for the taking . . ." she went on. "I had one . . . worked quite hard on it . . . a lot of tongues helped in the project. . ." General hilarity. I was glad her people were having a good time, but I wanted them to wait for something a little stronger. They were begging for it, anticipating their own delight.

"A reputation you wouldn't want to take out in public with you . . ." When the tittering stopped she said, "Wait a minute. Not mine. This one belonged to Carl Testamen." And she told a story of a dyslexic boy, whose intelligence, hidden somewhere under his reading disability, was eventually revealed in horticulture. "He could make things grow that had no business surviving in our climate. Latin names, which he could neither spell nor pronounce, sprang from his garden."

I knew she was talking about one of the boys in her old circle though she slid away from positive identification. The suggestion of promiscuity in her introduction was turned aside and ignored. In her town, dalliance was shy and led to amusing failures. Rock Falls seemed to repopulate itself without sex.

"He called his mother 'Mummy,'" she said. "But I always liked his herb garden. The herbs were for Mummy's kitchen . . . come to think of it he did pinch some basil under my nose and ask if it made me feel . . . interesting. Carl Testamen . . . settled right there in town . . . got a job over at the Green Thought Nursery. It was his story, he could live with it. A bachelor for quite a few years . . . almost eligible . . . working over there at the nursery . . . doing what he always did best . . . fertilizing . . . trees . . . and things."

They loved it, but this version of Carl didn't quite suit her either. In the next fifteen minutes she reinvented him once more. A boy who wore knickers until fourth grade, was faithful to his paper route, always folding tightly before throwing, saved his money for necessities, and was polite to all his teachers with the possible exception of Mr. Chalk.

"Mr. Chalk," she said, "had trouble keeping his eyes to himself. How many ways could he look at you? Well, he had the fox eyes of a disciplinarian. The knit brow of a confessor. The glance of a spy. The gape of a voyeur. Sometimes, the honest gaze of a teacher waiting for anyone to answer. But more often, the dilation of the moonstruck."

I knew she wasn't reading this. She paused, as if exhausted with the kinds of attention I'd paid the children, then thought of one more. "Angry slits leaving only enough light for revenge." That was it. "More about him next week."

She backed away from that promise. There was nothing about me in her next broadcast. All of Stilson must be listening, I thought. Richard and Sarah must be by their radio, too, or even in her theater audience. Maybe a red light had gone off. Privacy invaded? A libel judgment? These were Lauranette's suggestions. Law hadn't occurred to me.

Sonia's references to Mr. Chalk in the weeks that followed were brief. He came and went like a cloud of dust in the school hallways. She gave him no more personality than a piece of chalk, though she kept him around long enough to teach her mother and herself. Once, she defended him against the cooing of his name in the classroom, and rescued him from bullies in the parking lot, even apologized for his threadbare sport jacket, which she hung on a clothesline and let schoolchildren beat with a broom until the yellow dust had all blown away.

At the same time she created a school principal who could steer his faculty in a straight line and keep discipline among his students with no more than a slightly raised voice. Who could she have in mind? She created teachers, honorable and sinning, and workaday townspeople with endearing tics. There were fathers and mothers who scolded and adored, some deceiving themselves in false cohabitation. Still, she gave them full lives while she gave me no part.

"A fitting punishment," Lauranette said. "Why don't you go and watch her do the show sometime?" But I knew she didn't really want me to.

"It could upset her," I thought. "She might stumble, forget what she wanted to say."

"That's not it." Lauranette made her own fox eyes. "You think if you stay away she might say something to redeem you."

It was more than that. Listening to her voice from afar was one thing. But going to the theater? That would be spying. In the small auditorium she'd very likely see me. For the time being I preferred invisibility. Let her wonder if I was listening. Let her decide, unprovoked, what to do about me.

As life in Rock Falls began to charm a nation, Lauranette grew more wary of my smug silences. She could support me in Sonia's rediscovery only up to a point. She saw through the little excursions of my imagination, the satisfied set of my jaw, the grin held too long, the audible daydreaming. She heard me say, "She can sing a cappella, she can sing with the poets."

We read in the paper that Sonia was living with a man who worked on the program with her. Followed her everywhere, by the slant of the article, worshiping and adoring. He was the one who knew where all the wires should go and which knobs to turn to make her voice please us. He screened guests, too, and kept her public at a polite distance.

Sonia began to weave Roberto Norentez into her Rock Falls mythology. No danger in that; he was a hero beyond criticism, and out of the country. And there was nothing about the way she'd been painted into the future on the mall ceiling or warned about the movie she'd been meant to star in. Lauranette chafed with the continuing insult, the treatment of me as a buffoon.

"You're forgiving too much," she said. "That girl owes you something."

Eventually I wanted to see the thing for myself. How it was that Sonia could reach California from a microphone in Virginia. Early on a Friday evening I drove alone to Winchester. Circling the theater, I watched the parking lot fill and the crowd gather on the sidewalk.

Leaving my car on a side street I walked around the block several times, scared to approach the place. The line in front had suddenly taken serpentine form, doubling back on itself. People ahead of me were already despairing of getting in. When the man came out to announce a sold-out performance it was almost a relief. I retreated to my car where I could listen to Sonia in private. Happily hiding on a back street in Winchester I heard my daughter speak again to her growing faithful.

This time she began, "Peter Holzgrefe loved Mary Connors on Wednesdays." She stopped to let that sink in. My God, I thought, she's going to tell about the circle club. She'll disgust them. "Peter loved her on Wednesdays because that's the day she knocked on the cement hatch of his shelter and dropped in mail and supplies.

"The trouble was," she said, "Mary loved Peter Holzgrefe every day." His quarters were dark and foul, he couldn't invite her inside. She loved a survivalist who only came out to relieve bladder and bowels, always in haste and rather too close to his entrance.

Mary had coaxed Peter to dare one day a week in the open air. On Sundays they would drive across the county, into the city, to services at the cathedral. And in the afternoon they debated his return. "Live with me," Mary argued.

"This is dangerous," he told her. "I mean you don't unbuckle your seat belt one day a week, do you?"

They dawdled on their way west, stopping for refreshment in the turning restaurant over the great mall. And there they sat for hours on a crystal evening, watching first the light in the cathedral tower, then the light over the mountain. Wondering which signal to follow, Peter sat for full revolutions of the Turning Night, letting an engine shift his allegiance.

She got this from me, I thought. "She's making it up as she goes along," I blurted out, glad again that I wasn't in the theater. Then, out of nowhere, Sonia brought Mr. Chalk onto the scene. This Mary sees him in the restaurant. "There he is, my old teacher," she says. A cue for mirth in the audience. Mr. Chalk didn't have to speak. They were already breaking up.

At the end of a monologue, when laughter subsided, she usually offered a sobering thought, something leveling and kind, something to chasten the smug or resurrect a fool. That night, I expected her to tell everyone how her head had been turned to the warning lights. I was waiting to hear it from her. Let her honor the Chalkman. But nothing this time. Mr. Chalk drifted offstage in his own dust.

Instead, she spoke of an outer Beltway and children driving circles, switching orbit in a game grown out of human scale. "A concrete cyclotron," she said, "young people spinning around it with a young people's faith in soft collisions."

At home, Lauranette couldn't believe it. "You liked it?" she asked. "I was listening. How could you have liked it?"

"Like it? It's extraordinary!"

Toward the end of a dry August, when the unrelenting sun could be appreciated only by our two tomato plants, a phone call came to lift the weather's pall. On the other end of the line was the voice of the "Shenandoah Journal" calling for the hostess of "Tumbleweed." With ingratiating modesty, Sonia said, "I'm in radio, too."

"Yes, I know," Lauranette replied.

"You listen to me?"

"Occasionally."

This stopped Sonia only for a moment. "Are you still with Mr. Sykes? The same house and everything?"

"Yes, as a matter of fact I am. He's very proud of you, by the way. What you've done."

"I hope he isn't taking the program too seriously. I'm not trying to hurt anyone's feelings."

"Of course not."

"Listen, would you like to get together sometime?"

No plan was made. Lauranette wasn't sure she wanted her coming to the house. She was fascinated by Sonia's sudden prosperity, but after so much time, she saw my temptation to get too close to my daughter again, to reveal too much.

Everyone knew where Lois Rengert lived, a little antique community, old houses and a buffering green space guaranteed for a time by easements and covenants. Too expensive to be quaint, but a kind of refuge from progress. An easy detour for me on my way to work. Her small brick cottage on a lower street had a tidy yard and shiny red door that was always closed no matter how many times I drove by it. If I couldn't see her I assumed nobody was noticing me. It wasn't unusual for day-trippers to cruise the village ogling the architecture of a dead past.

This went on for a few weeks. Like a clumsy fisherman I trolled by, my motor a little too loud for the scenery, but think-ing, if I throw out my line often enough, one day the speckled beauty rises, even for a lump of bread. And if I persisted, if I set the hook, I'd be obliged to remove it. That's what I wanted, to see her startled eye turn to trust. The tricky part would be letting her go soon enough, without damaging her.

The day she drove out in front of me in a little convertible roadster I hung back, ready to follow in any direction. Out on the main road I stayed at least two cars behind. Why we finally ended up at the mall I'm not certain, but I think she was aware of me from early on in the trip. On the east-west highway I thought I'd lost her. Then, at the end, she was behind me, following each turn I made in the parking lot until she came to a stop right beside me.

"Mr. Sykes," she called to me. "So we meet again."

Sonia at twenty-eight! Of course I'd counted the years. A mature woman of wide American travel and experience. Medium height, a full figure, surprisingly full. My imagination had insisted on the slight frame of her childhood. On the radio she'd been so trim for me. It was exciting, endearing to know she was capable of change like this. The simple fact of a difficult metabolism reconfirmed her humanity.

I wasn't disappointed, not at all. It was just that all the wise observation of her program, her mastery of life, even her voice, had suggested someone less rich in flesh. Perhaps I was afraid she was so ripe that she couldn't last. Her hair, slightly darker, had grown below her shoulders again. She was larger than her mother now, and softer.

"It's Sonia Pless!" I said, getting out. "What brings you here? How've you been? Of course I know how you've been . . . wonderful! What a surprise!" I reached out to take her hand. She looked at me wisely, shaking her head.

"Surprise?"

"Not really."

"No. Not really at all," she said firmly. "I hear your muffler almost every morning. I look out through the curtain and there you are, slowing down, staring at my house."

"I do know where you live. Everybody does."

I admired the cool stance she had taken in front of me, the way she examined me for deceit. "We never miss a program. It's really a wonderful thing you're giving people. A gift." Naturally I was curious about her. Anybody would have been.

She shed the compliments and bore in on me. "Are you still a bit of a prowler?" Sonia looked down at the pavement, maybe considering what to do next. "If it's the program you like, you could just listen to it."

"We do! We do! Very closely. I hope you're being careful. Libel is so tricky now, such a hair-trigger thing."

"You're not threatening me, are you?"

"It's nothing like that. You can say anything about me you want to. It's the others you have to be careful with."

Some hair had fallen across her eyes. A strand was caught in the corner of her mouth. I reached slowly with a finger to clear it. She turned aside.

"Not me," I said, stepping back. "But there are people around here who still can't forgive you for ignoring the rules. Where is your . . . ? I don't know his name."

"He's a friend," she said, "a colleague. We share a house."

This Carl had gone up to New York to arrange a broadcast there. She'd agreed to be videotaped, and wondered if she'd made a terrible mistake.

"It's so boring to see," she said, "what we do. Not for television at all."

"You'll do fine," I said.

"I suppose you're prejudiced."

"Yes, I am. Do you come here to look at the ceiling?"

"Sometimes."

"You're in it in so many places. You must know that."

"How many?"

"I've counted eight."

"Your eyes may be playing tricks on you. What do you mean eight places?"

"Of course they wouldn't all be visible today."

"There aren't any real people in it."

"Like in your Rock Falls?"

"Yes, if you like. But this is different. The people in Rock Falls never hide. You can always see them." She declined to go inside with me to admire the ceiling, and I couldn't blame her.

"But there were only seven," she said.

"That's what I used to think until your artist showed me the last one. A bathing beauty with a beach ball. And something else I figured out. Each scene he did with you has one good month for viewing, the same month he painted it, because that's the way the light hit the glass when it was done. He started you in the changing room and then moved you back and forth. You're in all the months with R in them."

"Like an oyster?"

"Yes, Venus on the half-shell. But the last one he did isn't easy to see."

I must have been reviving her old suspicions. To her I could as well have been a man with a garage calendar, dog-earing the pages on which she appeared.

"Well?" She was about to leave.

"Were you at the mall the day Norentez left for good?"

Her head jerked up, and I thought, God, am I dredging up something too awful?

"Roberto," she said slowly.

Sonia was wary. She looked around her at the vast acreage of cars, maybe preparing an escape route. I wanted to let her go. "We admire you very much," I told her. "You must know you're reinventing radio."

"You're reinventing me," she said. "Don't. To tell you the truth I'm a little sick of it all."

"Tired of Rock Falls?"

"Wouldn't you be?"

"But if you gave up your program what would you have?"

She seemed amused by the parental panic in my question. "What I always had," she told me with a cold certainty. "It's too small for a sign. There's hardly a road. Anyway, you were talking about Roberto."

"He was looking for you, you know? But you left."

"I was looking for him, too. But they were giving me the rush."

"They?"

"The people I was making the movie with. Not really a movie. I thought I could make a little money. I needed money to travel."

I stepped toward her, eager to hear more. "What was the movie about?"

"Love out of control. Ultimate sacrifice. That sort of thing." Her story took hold of her. She seemed calm again, satisfied with this way of dealing with that awful day in the slaughter shed. She was almost talking to herself, the way she did on the radio, creating something palatable.

"What part did they give you?"

"You don't understand. I was in charge. I was the whole show, if you want to know. They were all right with the camera but they didn't know anything about acting. I was making it up as we went along, doing the script myself."

"Did the movie get made?"

"You know, it didn't work out."

"Are you going to put all this into Rock Falls sometime?"

"I wouldn't know which way to go with it."

"You could make it up as you go along, like you say. The way you're doing now."

"Look," she said, "you could do something for me."

"Wait, I want to know just what happened." I wanted more about her moviemakers.

"What you could do," she persisted, "is tell Lauranette I'd

be happy to be her guest on 'Tumbleweed.' I mean if she'd like to have me."

I was thinking of a dinner—all together maybe. "Do you see much of your parents?"

"Actually, we're sort of friends again."

"Do they ever mention me?" I asked.

"Funny how your name never comes up."

We laughed together for the first time.

Instead of approaching cautiously, I came right out with it.

"But she hasn't earned your pardon," Lauranette said.

"I haven't earned hers either."

"I'm not making her legitimate in this house. Besides, I don't put on celebrities."

"That's not her angle," I said. "That's not what she wants."

"What does she want?"

"You won't believe it," I said. "She's not just beautiful, she's softer. Reflective. Generous. I couldn't expect her to admit everything. The thing is, she respects you. She'll tell you anything you ask."

"What would I ask?"

I couldn't say exactly, but I kept after her. If she was saying no out of loyalty to me, she could be most loyal by taking Sonia on her program. "I want to hear what she'll say to you."

"All right, all right!"

Afterward, I wondered how she'd treat Sonia in the interview. The way Lauranette saw it, the girl had survived her casual wandering, almost unaware of her luck, and with no respect for those who had watched over her. So: let Lauranette be provocative, I thought. Let the conversation begin in temper. Or let her tease Sonia into candor.

Lauranette didn't want me in the studio for this, and I didn't argue. I made my own plans for the broadcast. A high place where there'd be no danger of interference with the signal. My portable radio. No picnic, nothing to distract me.

I left myself plenty of time that September afternoon, driving west onto the ridge road up the mountain. There was one helicopter beating its way over the valley toward the government bunker. After that, no sound of engines. I parked on the side of the road and carried my radio to the edge of the woods over Sky Meadows. There I had line-of-sight contact with the WHTR tower far below me, the signal as strong and clear as anywhere in the county.

Across the flatlands beyond the hills the glass roof of the mall twinkled like a tiny blue jewel. If they knew where to look and from what angle, this was the season and hour people could catch Sonia in the changing room of her childhood. When the Sons of the Pioneers began to sing "Tumbleweed" I was in my headphones, against the chance that even birds or squirrels would interfere.

"Today my guest is Lois Rengert of 'Shenandoah Journal' and Sonia Pless, who started right here in our own high school. One and the same person. So many people here want to know how Sonia became Lois. Maybe she'll tell us." Lauranette sounded arch, vaguely hostile.

There was no answer, and she began again. "You can't see Sonia but I can tell you she looks pained, as if the topic I've suggested is a little tedious. Is that it, Sonia?"

Again there was no answer and I thought Sonia must have walked out. Lauranette said, "All right, let me try again. For some of us, Sonia, you're a prodigal daughter. It seems fantastic that you've returned to us as a celebrity. Not to say a little undeserved. Do you want to explain the transformation? Tell us how it's done? That fascinates people, I think, the chance of their own fame. . . . Nothing? She's shaking her head. Sonia, in radio you have to move your lips."

I fiddled with the volume as if this could force the first sound from my daughter. Lauranette was unrelenting. "I've heard you say you never really had a family. Where were your loyalties when you were growing up? Where are they now?" Another long silence. "Some people don't really know their own story," Lauranette suggested. "Maybe it's better to say nothing than to guess."

Not a murmur. And then, as if Sonia had heard none of Lauranette's questions, she began to speak. "It just makes us look like damn fools. The arrogant way we deny visas. We're paranoid, a laughingstock to other countries." With concise, impassioned argument she drew Lauranette away from Lois Rengert and into a discussion of immigration policy. And I knew at the end of her well-reasoned trail was a green Mexican village and the artist.

They had gone on talking for a long time after the radio program was over. They were still in the small lot behind the station when I drove in to meet Lauranette. They were leaning on Sonia's convertible, speaking to each other across the top. The canvas roof was being slapped like a drum as they made their points.

As I approached them, Sonia's vitality and emergence as a full woman struck me all over again. It had amazed Lauranette to hear that she had taken four trips to see Norentez and that one of these visits had lasted several months. But now they were talking about me. And I walked right into the discussion, putting my arm affectionately around Lauranette.

"This is about you," she said, annoyed.

"Oh, he can stay," Sonia said lightly. "What harm could there be in that?"

"All right then," Lauranette said, ignoring my caress. "Why

don't you just look this man in the eye and tell him what he did for you?"

Sonia had nothing more to say. She nodded once to each of us as if that were a sufficient good-bye to rudeness, got into her car, and drove away.

"It's quite smart the way she's kept herself off television," Lauranette agreed one Friday evening after another entertaining "Shenandoah Journal." Though I felt in her heart she didn't want Sonia on television for more than altruistic reasons. As if my daughter's celebrity itself was dangerous to all of us. When Lauranette called up to me from the living room the next night, "She's on! Come here! She's on!" she didn't have to say Sonia, and she didn't have to say television. I rushed down, a little panicked to think this could have happened, and was relieved to see it was only an interview. One of the national late-night faces asking her questions.

In black and white. We didn't need colors running out of register over the gaudy baubles and makeup of the medium we shunned. Poor reception too, fuzzy pictures, but suddenly Sonia was the only light in the room, a serene presence arriving from New York where she sat next to a nattering interviewer of irreproachable handsomeness. A still young woman in a dark dress buttoned to the neck answering arch questions, this time with precision. All those dots of light, shadowy and blurred, and at the same time so distinctly my daughter; how careless a shading could produce so certain an identity; her face as puffy as a cortisone patient's, the true outline revealed somewhere between the indistinct boundaries, familiar gestures and attitudes emerging from the murky screen.

"The population of Rock Falls?"

"Six thousand and ten."

"Do places like that still exist?"

"Rock Falls does."

"These people you talk about. Are they modeled on your childhood acquaintances?"

"They are my childhood acquaintances."

"You grew up with them? You played with them?"

"I played with my imagination."

Lauranette said, "This is bad for our eyes. Let's put some lights on."

"No." A corona of blue surrounded the set as I tuned multiple images closer to a single portrait. At 11:35 p.m. Sonia was princess of America. And not especially congenial with her host. Her attention began to wander.

"Where actually did you graduate from?"

"From? I didn't."

"You don't have a college diploma?"

"I don't have a high school diploma."

"And yet here you are on the . . . well, on national television as a . . . what would you call yourself?"

"A label would be reductive, wouldn't it?"

"You've been compared to some of our best humorists."

"It's a national failing, don't you think? These silly ratios. Equating the franchise with the talent."

"Pardon?"

"I mean speaking to some millions every night at the same hour doesn't confer intelligence, does it?"

The host shook his head as if to clear it after a sucker punch. "You just sit there," he said smiling. "Let me ask the questions. You do like all the attention, don't you?"

She thought about that for a moment and said, "I think it's gotten to the point of people overreacting to the material. Feeling obliged to laugh at everything. Sometimes at targets that are too easy. As if this thing was scheduled to be funny, and they're not going to be caught not having a good time. What I'm trying to say is, there's some unearned flattery. A faulty applause meter. It can be corrosive."

I was pacing in front of the set; Lauranette told me to sit down. The host said, "You've called your early travels around the country a pinball journey, I think. What did you mean by that?"

"You just roll," she said. "Carom off one state into the next, sort of bouncing off society's natural bumpers. Most of them are elastic . . . the police, or just the people. Not so risky as you might suppose. I think you can absorb more when you're passive."

"Punishment?"

"No. The world around you. The things you'll be using when you settle."

"You ran away quite young, didn't you? Were you ever in any real danger?"

"Yes."

"Can you explain?"

"Not really."

The man shook his head as if he'd been hit again. "What did your family think of all this?"

"I didn't have one."

"Your parents would be surprised to hear that."

"Oh, we loved each other, I think. But there were ways we just didn't exist for one another."

"No similarities? Common traits?"

"With my mother, maybe. We both wore a lot of red. But my father, that's a whole different set of genes."

"So who financed your journey?"

"For a long time I was one of the traveling poor. There was some waitressing."

"Tell us about it."

"You know, selling charm and service at the same time."

"You had lots of charm to offer." His eyes were on her breasts. For a moment the camera focused there, and then our late-night man spun his head back to the audience in mock astonishment.

She rode over the interruption gracefully. He said he couldn't imagine her living in a commune. Yes, there had been some time in a commune, she said, "when baths were out of favor with God."

"Then puppets?"

"That's right. We had a traveling puppet theater. A school bus painted like a field of wildflowers. Very political."

"Is that why you left?"

"Actually, it wasn't the politics that bothered me, but the assumptions. Throwing ourselves on the kindness of people. Sleeping on their property, putting a big strain on their toilets. We assumed they were as sure of the issues as we were. They owed us accommodations because we were fighting their fight, because our answers were the right answers. Maybe they were."

"There are a lot of gaps in your story."

"You could say I'm fond of Mexico. I go there from time to time."

"Mexico City's incredible, isn't it?"

"I don't know."

"But where do you go?"

"A village. A place that doesn't need to be discovered."

Suddenly she was gone and we were watching a lady's razor that hummed in orbit like a satellite clearing a swath of sky, stars flashing behind it, then stars twinkling on teeth, these made possible by the new formula of a toothpaste. When the magic was over, she was still there next to him. He was leaning toward her, smiling congenially before he sat up straight to his role.

He reintroduced her as the creator of Rock Falls and asked

her to take us back there for a moment. "Weren't you inspired by a radio personality from your own home town?" Sonia's lower lip moved forward slowly like a deliberative device, distorting her face in the most artless way. Lauranette's hand dropped from my back.

"There was a wonderful woman there, yes. She could have gone so much further, could have made so much more of it, created herself maybe. There's honor in staying put, though. Don't you think? A silent victory over this sort of thing."

The host looked down, then raised his hands toward his chest, as if to ask, "Me?" I saw the blue corona of the television as Sonia's halo as she preached beyond the lives that had preached to her. And miracle, she would be here until 1:00 a.m. when the man would raise his arm and wave it like a wand, bestowing sleep on America.

"Can you tell us her name?"

"That wouldn't be fair, would it? Haven't I just explained?"

"But don't people know already? I mean they know where you came from."

"We're talking about Rock Falls. Look, until you understand that your imagination has a weight, you only half exist." The man looked at his hands as though he might be disappearing.

"There's a teacher in your town. A Mr. Chalk. When the newsweeklies wrote you up I think one of them called him a 'pedagogical Babbitt.'"

"Typical."

"What?"

"Reaching for a clever formulation. Totally missing the point."

"Well then, how would you define him?"

"I wouldn't."

"All right then, real or imaginary, what could you say about him?"

"He was zealous. His commitment to his work was a kind of lust. He's laughed at for that. There's always an injustice in mockery. But there's a lie in applause, too. Remember? We discussed that earlier."

"Fair enough. What about the helicopters you have him talk about? The bunker? Was that the dark side of growing up in Rock Falls?

"Not really. In America we all think we live in the bull's-eye. Seaports, prairie silos, mountain bunkers, business capitals. We all carry ground-zero badges. Everywhere you go, people tell you how lucky they'll be to go first."

"So Mr. Chalk was wrong about that?"

"Not wrong, maybe a little myopic."

A new guest was introduced, actor and dear friend of the host. Sonia politely moved down a seat, yielding her place to him, but the cameraman kept coming back for her reaction to everything that was said.

In November of that year I received a short, sad letter from John Lambert. A letter because it was very difficult for him to talk.

Dear Ray,

If you don't know why this is typed, I'll tell you. My handwriting looks like a child's. I won't let anyone see it. Food and soup all over the table. I don't let Alice feed me. Sorry this is such a mess. I see very few people these days.

Thanks for telling us about the radio program. Our own Sonia Pless! Who could have predicted? You'll admit she was a wild mare in the old days. And always in season. To think she was actually learning something! She certainly kept it a trade secret.

What was her trade anyway? Romantic notebooks as I

recall. Good God, man! We couldn't let that pass. Where did she go on to study?

She's made us all famous, hasn't she? I must say I'm very flattered by her treatment of me. But you, Ray. It's not fair to you. No matter what happened. I've been thinking about our refusal to graduate her. Do you suppose it might have cleared her head?

When I went to see Lambert for the last time he was just able to speak, and he wanted to know where she did her graduate work. As if some academic miracle had occurred.

Sonia was keeping her Mr. Chalk a figure of fun, making him ask ponderous questions. Still, her answers were often my answers.

"People, what is your Manifest Destiny?"

"The right to a rectangle of land by the hum of an interstate highway," her student said. "The right to plant grass and ride in dominion over it on top of a whirling blade. The right to make larger croquet lawns unencumbered by trees, or even wickets." I doubted she knew what part was memory of my instruction and what part her own invention.

"Be there."

Sonia telling Lauranette to come with me to the James Theater for the next "Shenandoah Journal" struck us as an odd command and a rude way to hang up a phone. She'd been trying to get hold of Lauranette for most of a week, she said, but they wouldn't put private calls through at the station while "Tumbleweed" was in progress.

Why hadn't Sonia called our house earlier? She couldn't

really answer that. Perhaps she'd preferred to reach me through Lauranette, and, as it turned out, Lauranette answered the phone anyway.

With or without Lauranette, I was going through with it this time. No hanging back at the door. Without argument, she agreed to go with me on the condition that we not discuss it between then and the Friday evening of the broadcast—a rule she broke repeatedly, wondering what does the girl want, what is she up to? Like so many others around here Lauranette was eager to see the prodigal in performance, though she still took the part of a buffer against damage Sonia and I might do to each other.

Our complimentary passes from the star were delivered to the house the day before the program by one of her production crew. A note said, "Third row center, just where I want you."

Lauranette was wavering.

"Sure it's revenge," I admitted. "It's exactly where I used to make *her* sit."

No crowd problem this time. The color of our passes gave us quick entrance to the theater. We found our places easily, settled in, and began to count the house. Forty rows of twelve on each side of the center aisle, and every seat taken. Almost a thousand with those standing in the rear.

Lights down, a wine-red curtain parted. Stepping jauntily across the stage came Sonia! The people erupted, whistling, shouting. She was holding a microphone, shaking the attached cord into obedience behind her as she came forward, beaming down, in bliss it seemed. Waiting for order, for a chance to begin, she saw us.

Sonia was radiant! She looked even larger than I'd noticed before. It might have been her dress, a gown of rich purple with silver embroidery around its deep neck. It billowed like a maternity shift. People were calling out "Lois, Lois," pleased with themselves, a regular cult. Time for her to speak.

"Tonight it's different. Some things need to be said. Things that actually happened to me." A soft chuckling ran through the audience. Obliging Sonia, letting her know they were on to her weekly confidence game. "Really. I want to tell you what it was like having Mr. Chalk around all the time."

More tittering, the same people uncovering another layer of her charming deception. "We have a problem here. Maybe I've gotten too smooth at this. Actually I want to be serious. No tricks. Just listen to the words." They weren't giving in.

"Can't you tell the difference?"

"No!" from somewhere far behind us.

"You won't surrender." She shrugged. "I'll go ahead anyway."

Lauranette was asking if I wanted to leave before this went too far. We couldn't get up without embarrassment. We were trapped with Sonia looking down on us while she promised, "Not a lecture, just a little local history." Lauranette stared right back at her, ready, I think, with counter-insults to hurl at the stage.

True to Sonia's word, it was about me this time, and remarkably accurate, as close to the truth, I suppose, as she was able to come. She went all the way back to her first year in high school, to her discovery of her class schedule in my notebook. "He wasn't even my teacher yet." And when she'd finished her portrait of a lurking chalkman, "a teacher cursed by his teacherly passion, his need to follow a student into her most private world, even into her diary," when this was done to her satisfaction, the people were finally silent, tuned for sinister news of me. Which she then refused to give them, shifting the story to herself and her circle.

"Who wouldn't have been surprised by us? We did things that would make a parent's hair curl. And he knew about it. Mr. Chalk had our social calendar.

"This guy was telling us things we didn't want to hear. Prophecies of trouble coming. 'When your landscape is gone, you'll have no history.' What could that mean to us? We'd been happy in our mall. Busy with love. He could only bring us down with all his watching and warning. Always selling history. Around us too much. Hovering. As if there wasn't enough time in the classroom to give us what we'd need just to survive.

"And you know, he was right." I think she was looking directly at Lauranette when she said that, choosing her as confessor. Sonia went on, with a slow, detailed account of the night a man had been hiding in her car, and I had chased after her. Off the highway, along the dirt roads, and through the woods to the slaughter shed. Until there was nowhere else to turn. When at last she saw the person who might have harmed her, she said, he was gone before there was time to be terrified. "Besides, I was still scared of Mr. Chalk."

She was leaving the audience no room to laugh. Lauranette had a viselike grip on my hand. "I suppose," Sonia went ahead, "I should have pitied Mr. Chalk by then. But I was out to change the world with my social sabotage. And he kept appearing like a tiresome chaperon."

Before she began the last of her confessions she turned her back to the audience for a moment, perhaps wondering where to begin. "I was in films once. Not actually film. Tape. I had two partners who'd come drifting into the Whole World. Looking for talent, they said. Pretty soon they were working for me."

It was very casual, the way she was getting into this, pacing the stage, like someone putting her memory in order, making sure of the facts. "Production costs? Think of it this way. A stolen video camera. A bad check for the tape. Costumes by the Not So

New shop. We were our own talent. Taking turns as star, cameraman, director. A rotten little corps of cinematographers out to make a shocker. A spoof on one of those chain saw things, an outrageous comedy. I don't know where they got the chain saw. It wasn't even supposed to start.

"Let me set the scene. A lumber camp. I come in dressed like a harlot, looking for my man. The men play incompetent lumberjacks. When I show up strutting and whining, they plot to saw me up. Then a Chaplin-like routine. The saw won't start. One of them holds the rope, the other pulls on the saw. They're wearing themselves out. And you hear my voice. I'm getting interested in their problem, telling them how to get the thing going. But we're laughing so hard, we have to keep starting the scene over."

Lauranette was nudging me. "This isn't Rock Falls. I think she means it."

"We had to get serious or blow the whole project. One of them took the saw outside, and the other said, 'Let me tie your hands. This has to look real.' I was about to let him when I heard the saw motor that wasn't supposed to work, didn't even have gas, they said, and the man was hurting my wrists, advising me to hold still, his mouth suddenly twisted.

"There was the rising whine of the chain saw outside the shed, and someone calling, 'Is she ready?' I was fighting, my dress tearing, when these sharp explosions arrived over the noise of the saw, like a slow string of firecrackers. I was freed, and a moment later my partners had disappeared into the woods.

"When silence returned there was Mr. Chalk with a little rifle, standing alone on the hillside. No telling what he might have in mind. I didn't stick around to find out."

She was finished, and getting no response. Just what she'd asked for, though I felt she wasn't comfortable, not sure where to go next. "Ah, persistence," she sighed, as if this were the key to her story. And the time had come in her life, she said, when she really ought to be working on an obsession of her own. I knew then she was saying good-bye to her "Shenandoah Journal."

Sonia began to clap slowly, softly repeating "Chalkman" on a double beat. She was smiling down on us as her rhythm and the name found a few scattered takers in the audience. They clapped slowly with her, calling "Chalkman, Chalkman," and others joined them.

The name spread through the front rows with a low rolling resonance, washing around us like a dangerous tide, Lauranette holding on to my arm to save me from the undertow. She looked frightened again, as if this audience might actually drown me.

"He's been sitting with us here tonight!" Sonia said, continuing the beat with her hands. "Chalkman, Chalkman, Chalkman," was moving back through the auditorium, gathering pace and strength. She began to circle her arm, asking for still more sound. Someone behind me pushed my shoulder, advising me to stand.

Sonia was looking right at us again as the noise grew in the theater, and the old classroom chant became a full-throated cheer. All around me they were yelling, "Stand up! Stand up!" When the Chalkman chorus broke from the strain of its own speed and volume, the crowd worked themselves into a transporting applause, waiting for a gesture from me, unrelenting in their enthusiasm because Sonia was pointing right at us, reaching Mississippi, Indiana, Oregon, with the support of a thousand voices.

At last we stood, Lauranette and I, to be pummeled happily as we pushed our way down the row and up the center aisle, carried back through the whistling, shouting auditorium.

We got the rest of her program on the car radio driving home from Winchester. No more about Mr. Chalk. She turned back to some of her old material about Rock Falls dogs and their masters, gave time to a string band that came up with fast and tricky lyrics to some Irish instrumentals, and then closed with her familiar theme, the old, folk love lament "Early One Morning," singing in her wistful, artless vibrato, a sweet resonance she was never going to offer again.

Lauranette, surprised at how quickly my elation in the theater had left me, was rubbing my back, reassuring me, "Don't you understand? You're a new man." And the best half of me was melting under this lovely and forgiving woman's arm (she was, after all these years, my spiritual wife, capable of arousing in me all intimacies, the purest and most obscene) while the tormented part of me went on fishing for reassurance.

"A new man in Rock Falls?"

"No," she insisted. "A new man in real time."

It came to me that she could have been responsible for this late, heroic resurrection of Mr. Chalk. She would have shamed Sonia into it. I remembered my interruption of their argument in the parking lot after the strained session between them on "Tumbleweed." All her hesitation about going to the theater, and once there, her suggestion that we leave, just Lauranette playing her expected part. For my benefit. So that I might live proud again.

"Well," she asked me, "did Sonia lie about anything?" No, I couldn't think of any particular lie.

I heard once more from Sonia before she left the country, a letter to me alone. Lauranette's name nowhere on the envelope or in the greeting:

Dear Mr. Sykes,

I was very pleased you could make it. I've felt badly for a long time about Mr. Chalk's treatment in Rock Falls. Whatever confusion existed between him and the real man, I hope our accounts are now in balance.

But I can't leave it at that. I suppose it was odd for you,

with all the cheering. Now you must know what I mean by the myth behind the applause. The lie in excessive adulation. After all, there was nothing heroic in your obsession with me. I've come to think of that as an unaccountable accident, let's say, the result of some lesion in your rather remarkable brain.

No, it wasn't your preoccupation with me that made you the mythic figure in the school. It was your persistence with the chalk, and with our minds. Your insistence that an artist could be writing our history on the roof of the mall. That bulldozers were coming to erase the past. That so much would have to be committed to memory.

Your celebrated failure,

Sonia Pless

The next week a guest host was introduced for "Shenandoah Journal." Sonia was on vacation. Then we heard she'd left the program for good. Without her there was no program worth listening to. She'd left the country.

Of all my images of Norentez, the one that comes most vividly to mind is one I never even saw, one he only described for us. He's coloring the sidewalk, making the picture of himself coloring the same sidewalk. And within the drawing is the smaller representation of the same scene. There is the suggestion of an endless progression, the artist retreating into his work. Where he most wants to be. Though someone is about to make water on the effort. And now Sonia is retreating, following after him over the border.

"She could have had anything," Lauranette said. "A silver tray and tea things. An evening at the White House." But not her artist. I knew that's what she'd really wanted. After weeks of waiting, Sarah brought me a letter Sonia had mailed from Mexico. Norentez, she wrote, had let her do his laundry for the first time. She was pleased with that much progress. He had spoken kindly to her.

There was no return address. "Don't try to find me by the postmark. I'm nowhere near there." I could only imagine what the artist was thinking: this slut of suburban America coming back to dog my days. The marvelous pinch-faced little man, probably distracted from his creations. How could he be pleased to have his peace disrupted? "He was very surprised to see me this time. He's letting me live in the small hut next to his house."

At the end of her page she wrote, "The hill people beyond here have their mysterious ritual next month. Roberto says it's none of our business. Probably no more dangerous than Halloween. He likes to mystify things. I'll find out what it's all about, even if I have to sneak off by myself."

Working at getting herself killed again? I was forced to reveries of Sonia's end. A jungle. A wasting disease. No one who cared enough to find a legitimate doctor. The venom of a tiny snake with a red ring behind its head. A boozy shaman's scalpel made of a torn American beer can. Norentez might try to steer her away from these dangers, but Sonia would resist that kind of influence. Which would just be her way of making him pay closer attention.

After the troubling letter, Sarah lost control for a while. She came to our house uninvited, still without regard for how it might affect Lauranette and me. Walked in the kitchen door and started asking questions. Her hair tangled, her face badly made up with patches of bright rouge on her cheeks.

"How can we find her? What are we going to do? Isn't there any ice in this refrigerator?"

"Sonia always lands on her feet," I said.

We were alone in the room and Sarah began to weep. "I don't think she'll ever come home."

Lauranette called from the hall that she was leaving for the station. The front door closed, and Sarah's composure returned.

"What are we going to do?" she whispered.

"About Sonia?"

"Not necessarily. You probably haven't heard. Richard and I are getting divorced." She smiled and wiggled her shoulders. I turned away, disgusted. She began to cry again.

"I'm going for a walk into town," I told her.

"I'll come with you."

"If you like." She followed me out of the house.

Actually we were already in town. The area around us had been annexed several years earlier. A lot of earth had been moved since then. And several dozen houses had gone up on the scarified land between us and the town center. The half-mile walk from our cottage to the post office and supermarket was no longer a country stroll but a trip on an incongruous sidewalk, a narrow ribbon of concrete set down in the exposed red clay, and around which no vegetation had had time, or a chance, to grow.

"Thank God, they give you something to walk on," Sarah said. She was having trouble with one of her heels. "If I was going to live this far out," she told me, "I'd buy that one." She was pointing to a Colonial. But we were also passing Georgians and Tudors, placed along the route in a repeating cycle. Sarah stopped and looked back, taking stock of the real estate. "You live in a curious house, don't you?"

Alongside all the neo styles the squat stone cottage did look quaint and very out of place, not long for this world if it lost its current guardians.

Sarah was stumbling forward again. Not much later, she told me she couldn't go another step like this. The heel was coming off. I agreed to turn around. She took both her shoes off and walked with me back to the house in her stockings.

I was parting my hair a little too close to the middle, she thought. "Still the same boots?" My over-the-ankle brogans with metal catches at the top for the laces. When we got back to the cottage she stood leaning against her car door, maybe to let me know I wasn't obliged to ask her into the house. And for a while we were able to talk at ease.

"Rita has a man now," she said. "He's studying air-conditioning and refrigeration." With no response from me, she came back to Sonia. "Richard really believes you had a hand in driving her away. You must know she'll never be able to trust you—not unless she knows who you are."

Turning away from Sarah, I walked slowly into the house. I stood for a moment at the stairway, then bent over and kissed the round top of the newel post.

Sarah came to me again, with another letter from Mexico, and it was like news from the next world. But old news. "He still doesn't know how much he likes me. The woman who stays in the main house with him makes faces. If there are spots on the plates she curses me with words she thinks I can't understand. Tomorrow when she goes to market I'll be going with Roberto on his morning walk in the hills. He still does his beautiful paintings on glass, and gives them away to anyone who admires them."

Sonia, a sooty house drudge, submissive to a shrew? Why would she send her mother details of such a degrading life? I didn't believe them. I couldn't give the words credence. Later, she wrote to Sarah, "Up there in Virginia, between the cave and the cathedral, I still wouldn't know which way to turn. I suppose that's one reason I'm here."

She's so much my daughter, even her letters reek of me, and Sarah knows it. She says, "You're the only one who can explain what she's talking about."

Sonia is going to bring the artist back across the border as her husband. It's clear as the white space in the generous margins of her letters.

Richard is gone, Sarah the solitary one, her house at peace, though she toys with peril as if we were still children. Too late, much too late. Even so, now that Sarah has Sonia's mailing address, she wants to write and tell her daughter how much her eyes look like mine.

I tell her, no, it wouldn't be smart. Still, I'm ready for the questions, thick and accusing. "If you're my father, what was I like when I was seven, nine, eleven?" All she has to do is ask and I'll tell her about perfect cartwheels and the defiant grace that set them spinning.

A NOTE ON THE TYPE

This book was set in Fournier, a type face named for Pierre Simon Fournier, a celebrated type designer in eighteenth-century France. Fournier's type is considered transitional in that it drew its inspiration from the old style yet was ingeniously innovational, providing for an elegant yet legible appearance. For some time after his death in 1768, Fournier was remembered primarily as the author of a famous manual of typography and as a pioneer of the point system. However, in 1925, his reputation was enhanced when the Monotype Corporation of London revived Fournier's roman and italic.

Composed by Adroit Graphic Composition Inc.,
New York, New York
Printed and bound by The Haddon Craftsmen, Inc.,
Scranton, Pennsylvania

Designed by Marysarah Quinn